DARK
PRINCE

BLUEBLOOD VAMPIRES BOOK ONE

1

LUCCA

Havoc. That's the name of this club. Appropriate. It's dark, loud, and brimming with humans more than ready to satiate my hunger. It took me a while to get used to the noise. Night entertainment sure as shit has changed since the last time I was awake.

My latest snack is passed out on the VIP couch, utterly spent. Feeding and fucking go hand in hand, but unlike the human currently snoring next to me, I'm far from satisfied. My strength has returned, and thanks to all the blood I've drunk already, I'm almost caught up on what I missed in the past ninety-five years. Blood remembers.

Opposite me, Saxon is busy getting it on with some random girl. Ronan and Manu have disappeared to I-don't-know-where. So much for my reawakening party. That's my inner circle in a nutshell—a bunch of assholes. Not that I'm any better.

I catch the attention of the nearest bouncer, signaling him to get rid of the passed out human. I'm ready for the next one.

Not a minute later, I find my new target. A pretty little thing in black leather is walking over, carrying one single shot on her tray. Slender yet curvy in all the right places, blonde hair cascading down her back, and full lips begging to be tasted, she's exactly what I need.

Immediately, my fangs descend, and my cock hardens. I watch her approach, not hiding the hunger that's surely shining in my eyes now. When she stops in front of me, I can hear how fast her heart is beating; I can smell her fear.

Interesting.

Most humans who come to these places aren't afraid of us. They know exactly what we want, and they give it willingly in the hopes of being turned. Little do they know we no longer have that power.

"What's your name, sugar?" I ask, not hiding the craving in my voice.

"Re-Rebecca." She clutches the tray harder while tremors run through her body.

A lie. That's not her name. I'm not surprised she wasn't truthful. She's not afraid; she's gripped by terror, which makes her even more alluring to me. I'm a predator after all.

Not taking my eyes off her face, I run my fingers up her naked legs. "What do you have for me, Rebecca?"

She doesn't answer for a couple of beats. In fact, she's not even breathing. I suspect she might bolt out of here at any second.

"A special shot. On the house," she finally replies.

My lips curl into a grin. I was wondering when Derek Blackwater, the owner of Havoc, would send me a welcome gift. He was the last human to be turned into a vampire, and thus, he's almost as old as me. But that's as far as my knowledge of his dark

2

past goes. The guy is a mystery.

"Is that so?" My hand disappears underneath her skirt, and when I squeeze her ass, she gasps.

"Yes," she breathes out.

My pulse skyrockets. *Damn it.* It's normal to be thirstier soon after an awakening, but my reaction to this human is stronger than I anticipated.

With shaking hands, she gives me the shot glass. I don't know what kind of drink this is, but I'm past the point of caring. I throw my head back and drink it in one single gulp. Immediately, my head becomes fuzzy.

With a frown, I stare at the empty glass, seeing double. "What the hell?"

I sense someone yank on my necklace, a piece of jewelry I never take off. The fucking human is trying to steal from me. My movements are sluggish now, which means she laced my drink with vampire's bane.

Motherfucker.

The necklace chain snaps at the same time that I manage to get over the poison's effect. I'm fully recharged, thanks to my ninety-five-year nap, and thus, I'm less susceptible to vampire's bane's effects. The thief is about to take off, but I grab her wrist, digging my nails into her soft skin, drawing blood. A single whiff of her scent changes everything. My vision turns crimson, my eyes zero in on her neck, and my ears only hear the sound of her blood pumping in her veins.

The desire to sink my fangs into her soft skin is no longer about retribution. This is pure and raw bloodlust.

I jump from the couch, trapping the girl between my arms. She struggles, she screams, but no one will come to her aid.

Sudden pain shoots up the back of my head, clearing my vision for a second. The human is pulled from me by Saxon, and then Manu is blocking my way.

"What the hell, Lucca! I leave you alone for a moment, and that's what you do?" Her golden eyes are glowing in the dark, showing how angry she is with me.

"She poisoned me with vampire's bane," I grit out, trying to control the feral instinct that's demanding I rip the human's throat to shreds.

"Let me go!" She fights Saxon's hold.

"Take it easy, sweet cheeks. You're not going anywhere."

I don't dare to move. I'm not over the bloodlust yet. I haven't succumbed to it since the worst evening of my life centuries ago. *Why now?*

"What's this?" Saxon pulls an object from the girl's grasp.

"My necklace," I say. "Bitch came here to steal from me."

Saxon lobs it in my direction, and then Manu whirls around, displaying her talon-like nails. *Fuck.* Now she wants a piece of the human too.

No. She's mine.

"Who sent you here?" my sister asks the girl.

The thief doesn't have a chance to reply. Ronan comes running, his face twisted in the deepest frown and his entire body exuding anger. He spares a fleeting glance at the puny human in Saxon's grasp and then turns to me.

"We've got company," he says. "Tatiana's sycophants are here."

Damn everything to hell. They had to show up now. I could simply kill the human with a single blow and be done with retaliation.

But my body immediately rejects that idea. I can't do it.

With regret, I turn to Saxon. "Forget her."

His eyebrows furrow while he watches me as if I'd lost my mind. I'm not sure I haven't. Releasing someone who poisoned me and tried to steal from me is not my MO, but my revenge will have to wait. I have an older debt to settle and a message to send.

2

VIVIENNE

Fifteen Hours Earlier

I give an overall glance at the small living room to make sure I didn't forget anything. The '70s trailer might be old, noisy, and smell funny, but it's home. Not seeing any item that I forgot to pack, I scribble a quick note for my brother and attach it to the fridge. I haven't heard from the dumbass in more than twenty-four hours, and I need to give him precise instructions for when I'm gone. Rikkon is five years older than me, but I'm the parental figure in our dysfunctional family.

With a sigh, I check my phone again. Nothing from him. I can't help the tightness in my chest. Rikkon is a trouble magnet, and if I have premature expression lines at eighteen, it's thanks to him.

Where the hell is he?

A knock on the door brings my thoughts back to the here and

now.

"Vivi, are you ready?" Karl, one of my bandmates, asks.

"Yeah, I'm coming."

I hoist the duffel bag over my shoulder, grab my purse, and then head out. Karl's ginger hair looks fierier under the morning sun, and the freckles on his face seem to have multiplied. We never meet this early in the day. He looks younger despite the scruff on his jaw.

Our other bandmates, Cheryl and Vaughn, are in the van, probably asleep already. We did practice until two in the morning.

"Got everything?" Karl reaches for my bag.

"I hope so."

Halfway to the van, I spare a glance at the trailer. Karl doesn't miss the action.

"Is something wrong?"

I shake my head. "No. Everything is fine."

There's no point in telling him about Rikkon. None of my bandmates understand why I put up with my brother's shit. They think he's a selfish junkie who doesn't appreciate me. That's true most of the time. But they don't know he risked his life to save mine. I can't turn my back on him, no matter how much I wish I could.

As I suspected, Cheryl and Vaughn are napping in the back already. I take the shotgun seat, sinking against the familiar, worn-out upholstery. A yawn sneaks up on me, which I try to cover with my hand.

"Here." Karl offers me a cup of steaming coffee. "Drink this. I can't have you falling asleep on me like those two idiots in the back. I need someone to keep *me* awake."

"Thanks. I'm tired, but I don't think I can sleep right now."

"It's exciting, isn't it? I can't believe we actually got a spot in the Battle of the Bands in New York City."

"Me neither. It all feels like a dream." I take a tentative sip of the coffee, burning my tongue in the process.

"It's not a dream, Vivi. Good things are going to happen to us."

His smile is so open and genuine that I begin to believe him. Life has never been easy for me, so dreaming isn't something I allow myself to do. Born to an absent father and a bipolar mother, my brother and I had to grow up fast. There were never unicorns and rainbows in our world. It has always been pain, struggle, and blood.

A shiver goes down my spine when dark memories begin to crawl out from their hiding spot. I shove them back as far as I can.

Karl turns on the radio, dialing the volume to the max.

Not a second later, his sister, Cheryl, tosses a shoe at him. "Cut it out, jackass. I need my beauty sleep."

Vaughn doesn't even groan. I've never met anyone who could simply fall asleep where he stood. He could sleep through a hurricane.

To keep the peace, I turn the volume down.

"You're too nice." Karl laughs.

"Keep thinking that." I smirk and then drink my coffee to hide my amusement.

I love singing in the band, but it's Karl who makes everything better. I'm not sure what it is about him that helps me forget my problems for a little while. When I joined Nocturnal, I crushed on him hard. I was only fifteen at the time and Karl nineteen. Cheryl used to call me jailbait. For obvious reasons, the feelings were one-sided. Karl treated me like a little sister, and with time, I got over my crush and started to see him as the older brother I should have had.

Guilt sneaks into my heart every time I wish Karl were my real brother. Rikkon cares about me in his demented way. He wouldn't have done what he did otherwise. We were both dealt a horrible fate in life, and while I found music as a coping mechanism, Rikkon got lost in parties and drugs.

"A penny for your thoughts," Karl pipes up.

"It's nothing."

"You had a frown, so I'm betting you were thinking about your brother. What did he do now?"

"Surprisingly, nothing."

No sooner do I speak than my phone starts to ring. It's Rikkon's ringtone. *Finally!*

"About time. Where have you been?" I ask.

"Vivi, I need your help," he replies, short of breath as if he had been running.

The tightness in my chest returns. I knew something bad was coming.

"What happened?" I ask. There's the sound of a scuffle, followed by a yelp. "Rikkon! Talk to me."

"Rikkon can't come to the phone right now," a different male voice replies. Cold. Rough.

"Who is this?"

"I'm the one your brother crossed. If you want to see him alive, come to Ember Emporium. *Alone.*"

The call goes silent.

I let my phone drop to my lap, seeing nothing in front of me.

"Vivi, what happened?" Karl asks.

"It's Rikkon. He's in trouble. I have to help him."

"What did your douche-canoe brother do now?" Cheryl sticks

her face between us.

"I-I don't know. But I have to go to Ember Emporium now, alone, to try to help him."

"That's dragon-shifter's territory," Cheryl replies. "What is your brother doing there?"

"I don't know." My voice is tight, and the only reason I'm not crying right now is because I don't want my friends to know how scared I am.

"You can't go there by yourself," Karl rebuffs. "Ember Emporium is Larsson's domain. He's the most ruthless dragon kingpin to ever set foot in Salem."

"I know that," I snap. "But if I don't go, I might never see Rikkon again."

"Good riddance," Cheryl mumbles under her breath.

"Cheryl! Come on," Karl retorts.

Balling my hands into fists, I look out the window. "I'm not asking you to understand or support my decision. But I have to help Rikkon. He's my brother."

"Then we'll all go," Karl declares.

"No!" I whip my face to him. "I was told to go alone. I don't want to piss off my brother's captor."

"Dude, that's a very bad idea," Vaughn chimes in. It seems my turmoil woke Sleeping Beauty up.

"We can't compete in the Battle of the Bands without a lead singer," Cheryl reminds us.

If possible, the guilt in my heart overflows. *Stupid, stupid Rikkon.* I can't believe he's putting me in this situation again. I hate him right now.

"I'm sorry," I whisper.

"Save it, Vivienne. We all know that the only reason you stick to your loser brother is because you're afraid to take chances," Cheryl retorts.

"That's not true. You don't know anything," I grit out.

She returns to her seat in the back, hiding her face from me. "I think it's high time we look for another singer."

"You want me to choose between saving my brother's life and the band?" My voice rises to a shrill.

"Yes," she replies.

Her answer feels like a punch to my chest. My eyes prickle, and when I stare at Karl's profile, it's hard to keep the tears at bay. His jaw is clenched, and his brows are furrowed together.

"Do you feel the same way as Cheryl?" I ask.

"I would never ask you to choose between saving a life and the band, but … I don't disagree with her. You always drop everything when it comes to Rikkon. Today, he pissed off a dragon kingpin. What is he going to do tomorrow? Kill a Blueblood?"

The wince is involuntary. I look the other way fast, hoping Karl missed my reaction. He has no idea how close he came to the truth.

With a shudder, I say, "Can you please just stop the car, so I can get out?"

"Wait, are you really going there alone?" Vaughn asks. "That's crazy, Vivi."

"It doesn't matter. I have to do this."

Karl lets out a resigned sigh. "I'll drop you off there. You're not walking all the way to downtown." His tone is kind and understanding, but there's also a finality to it.

I've let the band down too many times before, and this is probably the last straw. Cheryl could be right. Maybe I do use my brother as an excuse to not change the status quo. Not trying means I can't fail.

Karl doesn't even look at me before he peels off the curb, leaving me in front of Ember Emporium. At this hour, the bar is closed, and the street is deserted. Dragons are known to only start the day past noon, and it's not even nine in the morning yet.

Despite the Closed sign on the window, I try the door. It's unlocked. I push it open slowly, dreading what I'm going to find inside. I've never been crazy enough to venture into supe territory before. We coexist somewhat in peace, but there's no denying we're prey to most of them.

Salem is the only city in the world where the secret of supernatural existence is out. If we had gone to New York City today, my bandmates wouldn't remember about supernaturals at all. There's a spell around town that prevents anyone from blabbering once they leave the city's borders. Well, almost everyone.

Rikkon and I seem to be the only humans unaffected by the spell. Maybe we're immune, thanks to whatever drug our mother took when she was pregnant with us. Rikkon takes after her when it comes to his many addictions.

A strong combination of smells fills my nose once I'm inside. Stale beer and sweat don't make the most welcoming scent.

"Hello?" I call out. "I'm here for my brother."

My voice echoes in the empty, dim room. Shivers begin to multiply, and my heart is beating now at a staccato, like a clock.

Tick tock. Tick tock.

A door at the end of the room opens with a bang, and three large males make their grand entrance. They're built like mountains, tall and wide. Their arms are as thick as tree trunks, which stretch the fabric of their suit jackets. It's hard to tell which one of the trio is Larsson. They all exude power.

"Where's my brother?" I ask, trying to keep my voice from trembling.

"Your brother is detained," the tall blond in the middle replies.

With his sharp facial features that would cut like a knife and the cold stare of someone without a soul, it's no surprise that my heart feels as if it had been frozen.

"I want to see him," I say.

"You're in no position to demand anything from me. Your brother was caught dealing crack in my domain. He's lucky my associates didn't kill him on the spot."

So, that's Larsson.

"You said that if I wanted to see him alive, I'd have to come here," I retort angrily, forgetting for a moment who I'm dealing with.

"Yes. I have a proposition for you. I'll let your brother go free if you do something for me."

Vises of dread wrap around my chest, squeezing me like a boa constrictor.

"Do what?" I ask in a small voice.

"I want you to steal something for me." Larsson stares me down with his intense yellow eyes.

This can't be good.

"Steal what and most importantly from whom?"

"There's a precious necklace, an antique that I covet. It's worn by a vampire, and he never takes it off."

Vampire. The word I dread the most.

Immediately, my pulse skyrockets. It's thundering in my ears now. Getting air in my lungs becomes harder.

Oblivious to my growing panic, Larsson continues, "His name is Lucca Della Morte."

Della Morte. I know that last name. *Fuck.* It couldn't have been just any random vampire.

"You want me to steal from a Blueblood?" I squeak.

"My sources tell me he just woke up from hibernation. Knowing how those pompous bloodsuckers operate, he'll be celebrating his awakening in style tonight."

I don't know anything about hibernation, but it doesn't take a genius to figure out he'll be starving. I can't be anywhere near him.

"I can't do it," I say.

Larsson raises an eyebrow. "So, was your brother lying when he swore you would do anything for him?"

Shuddering, I close my eyes for a second. "No, he wasn't lying."

"Don't worry. It's not going to be that hard. You're a pretty little thing, exactly what Lucca likes. All you have to do is make sure he drinks this." Larsson sets a small glass bottle on the table in front of him. "And then he'll be putty in your hands."

With baby steps, I approach the table. My hands are shaking when I grab the vial. "What's this?"

"Vampire's bane."

My eyebrows shoot to the heavens. "I thought vampire's bane was a myth."

A slow, wicked smile blossoms on the dragon's face. "Oh, no, dear. It's real but rare and expensive." His eyes narrow dangerously.

14

"So, don't waste it."

I curl my fingers tighter around the bottle. "Where am I going to find him?"

"He'll be at Havoc tonight."

"That's an upscale club. I'll never get in."

Plus, it caters exclusively to vampires. I'm not sure I'll be able to be surrounded by them without panicking.

"Wear a tight black dress and high heels. I'll make sure your name is on the list."

I don't have any more excuses. It seems I'm really doing this.

I couldn't foresee there would come a day when I told my brother I'd had enough. But if I survive tonight, I never want to see his face again.

3

LUCCA

Hunger. That's the first sense that returns after a period of hibernation. Too bad the rest of my body doesn't want to get on with the program as quickly. While I lie in bed, waiting to recover the feeling of my arms and legs, I suffer the hollow pain that makes me want to tear everything in my path. Bloodlust is real and dangerous as fuck.

My fangs are fully extended, my mouth is parched, and yet none of the fuckers around me are willing to give me a break. I hear them talk, words and sentences that don't mean a thing to me. Manu, my younger sister, is arguing with my best friends, Ronan and Saxon, about something that happened in King's Landing, wherever that place is.

With an effort, I manage to peel my eyes open. It takes a couple of seconds for my vision to clear from the fogginess. Despite the dimness in the room, it feels like I'm staring straight at the sun—

something vampires rarely do since we're not daywalkers. My eyes begin to water, but I refuse to shut them again.

"Hey, Sleeping Beauty is finally awake." Ronan approaches the bed.

"Shit. About time," Manu replies, joining him. "How are you feeling, brother?"

My nostrils flare when I can't get my tongue to cooperate.

"Can't talk yet, huh?" Saxon chuckles. "Well, not that that's any different than your normal self."

I glare at him, and finally, I'm able to croak some words out. "Fuck... you."

He laughs. "Now we're talking."

Manu reaches for the button on the side of the bed, raising the mattress to a sitting position. "Are you hungry?"

My response is a growl.

With a shake of her head, she removes the lid of a warm blood pouch and sticks it in my mouth. The hunger only subsides to a minor discomfort after I drink at least twenty of these. Only drinking straight from the source will abate it completely.

I toss the last empty bag to the tray on my nightstand. "How long did it take to wake me up this time?"

Manu trades a meaningful glance with Ronan, which is telling enough.

"The High Witch came five days ago," Saxon answers.

"Fuck." I glance at the far wall, seeing nothing.

"We're going to break the curse this time around, Lucca. I know we will." Manu squeezes my hand, but I pull away, not wanting her touch or comfort.

Her painfully white face morphs into an expression of ache, and her golden eyes shine with emotion, but those changes only last a few seconds before the cold mask goes back in place.

"Did my uncle come to see me?" I ask.

"Yeah, King Raphael has been here every day," Ronan replies.

"What did he say?"

"What kind of question is that?" Saxon interjects. "Have you met your uncle? He suffers from the same syndrome you do—brooding in silence."

I'd flip him off if I had the will to do it. I've lived with this damn curse for almost five hundred years. Since the Nightingales left this world, taking their magic with them, all vampires—except first-generation—must hibernate to restore their powers. If I hadn't been cursed by the Nightingale queen, I'd need to sleep twenty-five years every hundred years. The last time I went in hibernation, I slept for fifty years.

"How long was I gone this time?" I ask.

"Ninety-five." Manu doesn't look at me.

"What the fuck! Why the hell did you let me sleep for so long?"

She whips her face in my direction to glower. "We didn't let you. You simply didn't wake up. We've been trying to bring you back for the past half-century!"

Shit. No wonder she looked so distraught when talking about my curse. If it took me that long to wake up this time around, it's possible I won't rise again the next time I hibernate.

"Hell to the fucking no. We're not going to dwell in self-pity and doom right now. Lucca is back, and we need to celebrate," Saxon cuts in with over-the-top enthusiasm. He hasn't changed much in the last century. He has always been ever the optimist.

"Where are we going?" I ask.

"Havoc. It's a new club owned by Derek Blackwater. You remember him, right?"

I groan. "Yeah, I remember him."

"How is your head?" Ronan asks.

"Overloaded with new information. It will take me a while to process everything. But damn, a lot has changed."

"Oh, yeah. Lots." Saxon laughs. "You've gotta appreciate the ladies' new fashion." He wiggles his eyebrows up and down, earning a disgusted sigh from Manu.

"You're a pig, Sax."

"What about Tatiana?" I ask, and immediately, the mirth disappears from my friend's face.

"Still a major bitch," Saxon retorts.

I run a hand through my long hair. It's past my shoulders now.

"It would have been nice to wake up and find out my uncle had finally offed with her head."

"Not likely to happen anytime soon," Ronan grumbles. "King Raphael and that snake reached an agreement."

"What kind of an agreement?" My eyes turn to slits.

"A truce."

"You can't be serious. After everything she's done?"

"I hate her with every fiber of my being, Luc. But our race is weakening. If we don't convince the Nightingales to return and restore our full powers, we'll be nothing but legends," he says.

"What makes you think they'll return?"

"It was the war that made them leave in the first place." Saxon shrugs. "Seems like a logical approach."

"There's nothing logical about any of this." I throw my legs to the side of the bed and stand. Fury is coursing through my veins, and I can't stay confined to my room any longer. "What does this fucking truce mean to us?"

I catch the grimace in Ronan's face. "The institutes have been integrated."

My stomach twists in knots. *This is bad.* "And the Red Guard?"

When the war between the two Blueblood royal houses started back in the thirteenth century, my uncle created a program to train non-Blueblood vampires—regulars—to become warriors. We needed the numbers. He called them the Red Guard. Bluebloods are stronger by nature, but regulars can be trained to fight as well as we do.

"It's not called the Red Guard anymore. Regulars are being trained to become Keepers, which is nothing more than glorified watchdogs." Ronan crosses his arms, scrunching his nose as if the idea nauseates him.

"Let me guess. The program includes members from both sides."

"Yep," Manu replies. "It's a disgrace."

I touch my shoulder, reliving the moment when Boone, Tatiana's son, slashed me with a blade forged with vampire's bane. The stuff will weaken vampires when ingested, but when it enters the bloodstream, it will render even Bluebloods paralyzed. The motherfucker almost killed me that night. If it wasn't for Ronan and Saxon, I'd be dead.

I can't believe we must now coexist with those filthy bastards. You can't erase seven hundred years of bad blood.

"But the Red Guard is not dead though," Saxon adds, smiling mischievously.

"What do you mean?"

"It means when Tatiana tries to steal the crown from the rightful king, we'll be ready to take the bitch down," Manu replies with a manic glint in her eyes.

"Good. How many hours until sundown?"

"You have the whole day, brother," Manu replies. I glare at her, and she continues, "Don't look at me like that. I can't control the planet's orbitational schedule. But you need that time to get ready."

"I feel fine."

"Yeah, but you look like crap. Have you seen yourself in the mirror lately?" Saxon laughs.

"God, a hundred years later, and you're still not funny."

He opens his eyes wider in indignation. "What do you mean, I'm not funny? I'm hilarious."

Ignoring the pain in the ass, I walk over to the mirror on the far wall. *Shit.* He wasn't kidding. I look like a corpse who just came back to life.

Manu stands next to me and watches my reflection. "You're so pale now; we almost look alike."

She manages to say that with a straight face, but I know how much her appearance pains her. She used to have the same coloring as me. Tanned skin, dark hair, brown eyes. But thanks to Maewe's curse, her face and her hair washed out of color. Her irises would have turned white too if my uncle hadn't stopped the Nightingale queen.

"I suppose I need a haircut," I say.

"Fo sho, bro." Saxon comes closer, sucking on something.

"What the hell do you have in your mouth?"

He pulls a dark red heart-shaped candy out. "This? It's a blood sucker. Get it? Because it's made out of blood?"

"That sounds horrible," I reply.

"Not worse than those bags of blood you just chowed down." He shrugs.

My stomach growls in response. I'm no longer at the risk of entering bloodlust, but it doesn't mean I'm not hungry. I need to feed from a live source—badly.

Ignoring him, I turn to Manu. "How much time do you need to make me look like I belong to this century?"

She smiles from ear to ear, showing a hint of her fangs. "Four, maybe five hours tops."

Ronan snorts. "You have an hour. Lucca hasn't held a blade in almost a hundred years. He needs to practice."

I lock gazes with my best friend through the mirror's reflection, reading what's in his mind loud and clear. There might be a truce in place, but the war is far from over.

4

LUCCA

Present Time

"**Y**ou sure you want to do this?" Ronan glances at me sideways as we leave the VIP area.

"The vampire's bane is already out of my system."

"I'm not talking about that. You got hurt badly the last time you faced Tatiana's minions. I can smell your thirst for revenge."

My nostrils flare. "I wasn't trying to hide it."

"No shit, but you can't challenge those bastards in the middle of Havoc," Saxon interjects. "Even if we don't agree with the truce, we can't break it. Those who do are severely punished."

I snarl in response. That's something I'll never get used to. What was my uncle thinking? How could he make peace with the monster responsible for taking so many innocent lives? My father died while fighting Tatiana's forces, and I've lost count of how many times that bitch has tried to kill every single last member of our family.

When I reach the club's main area, the crowd of humans, familiars, and vampires part to let me pass. I've been gone for a long time but not forgotten. They call me the Dark Prince with reason. I'm known to be ruthless in battle, to kill my enemies without mercy. I'm not only second-generation Blueblood; I'm also the next in line to be king.

I spot the sons of bitches right away, hanging close to the bar. There are four of them—third-generation Bluebloods—acting like they belong here. In an instant, I'm on edge again. I still haven't gotten over the incident with the human thief, and now, watching those assholes laughing like they own the place makes my blood boil. Maybe they were the ones who sent the human.

Ronan puts a hand on my shoulder, holding me in place. "Lucca, what are you doing?"

"What?" I glower at him.

"Your eyes are glowing red, and your fangs are exposed. You were going for the kill."

At that precise moment, the vermin quartet turns to me. Their first reaction is of surprise, followed by wariness.

Good. Fear me, scum.

Using all my willpower to suppress the anger, I walk over. "You're in my way. Move," I say, dangerously calm.

"Wow, someone is cranky after such a long nap." One of them chuckles.

Automatically, I peel my lips back to reveal my fangs.

Saxon jumps in front of me, blocking my path. "Why don't you just run along? No one has time for your lame repertoire."

"Last time I checked, you don't own the place, jackass," the male closest to Saxon retorts.

Fuck. I don't know if I can control the fury raging in the pit of my stomach. If I had my blade with me, none of those assholes would still have their heads attached to their necks. No wonder Ronan forbade me to come armed. But I can still turn them into pulp with my bare hands.

"They don't. But I do." Derek Blackwater appears out of nowhere.

Hell, I should have been able to sense his approach.

"And if you can't behave in a civil manner, then you're out of here."

Tatiana's puppets cower in his presence. Derek is tall and packing muscles; no one could tell at one glance that this male was made, not born. When Bluebloods had the ability to turn humans into vampires, they did so aleatorily. But whoever sired Derek knew exactly what they were doing.

"He started it." The scrawniest of the bunch points at me.

Are you fucking kidding me?

Derek tries to level me with a glare but fails. Unlike the jackasses running away with their tails in between their legs, I'm not afraid of him.

"Lucca Della Morte. Back for less than twenty-four hours and already looking for trouble."

"It will take me more than a day to get used to this new reality," I reply through clenched teeth.

"I guess you haven't spoken to the king yet." Derek reaches for the glass of whiskey his bartender set for him on the counter.

"No."

"I don't think you should be socializing with your peers until you have had time to adjust." He takes a sip of his drink.

"Those assholes are not my peers," I grit out.

"They are now." Derek switches his attention to my right shoulder. "Including the one who sent you to early hibernation."

Boone. The vampire's bane wound I sustained weakened me to the point that I had to hibernate before I was due. *Fuck.* If I cross paths with him, there's no truce or punishment that can keep me from ripping his heart out.

"We'll see about that." I begin to turn, but Derek grabs my arm.

"Lucca, I'm not kidding. You can't put your need for revenge above everything else. You've been sleeping for too long. You don't know what's at stake."

A low growl comes from deep in my throat. In an instant, Derek lets go of me and takes a step back.

"The next time you touch me, you'll lose a limb," I warn.

Seething, I whirl around. Derek doesn't know how close he was to tasting my wrath.

A barely clad human, drunk out of her mind, throws herself in my arms. Without a thought, I wrap my arm around her waist and sink my teeth hard into the soft skin of her neck. She whimpers as I feed without finesse or care. She'll have a massive bruise tomorrow. When I hear her heartbeat slow to alarming levels, I pull back and toss her aside.

She staggers on her high heels, but I don't wait to see if she remains standing or not. I'm too angry to care about the fate of blood whores.

"Lucca, where are you going?" Saxon keeps in stride with me.

"I don't know. I can't be here."

Then, I hear it—the sound of *her* scream. The little thief. My prey. She didn't run away as fast as she should have, and now, someone else has gotten her.

Not for long.

5

VIVIENNE

Oh my God. Oh my God.

I can't run out of that VIP room fast enough. My heart is racing at breakneck speed, and my pulse is pounding in my ears. I should have never trusted that damn dragon-shifter. He said vampire's bane would work on a Blueblood. He clearly lied. The poison's effect didn't even last a minute.

My vision is blurry, thanks to the tears forming in my eyes, so I can't see shit besides the shapes of moving bodies. I push people out of my way while I fight the panic attack that's just around the corner. I can't have one here, surrounded by the enemy.

Thanks to a miracle, Lucca let me go, but he might change his mind.

My breathing is coming out in bursts by the time I finally spot the exit. I make a beeline for it, but strong hands grab my arms and

"There, there, little lamb. Where are you going in such a hurry?" a vampire reeking of decay whispers close to my face.

What the hell? Lucca didn't smell like this guy. His scent was surprisingly intoxicating. Not this male. He stinks of death.

"Let me go!" I try to break free from his grasp.

He laughs. "Oh, are you going to put up a fight? Even better. I like when my snack struggles. It makes their blood taste so much sweeter."

His nails dig into my arms, drawing blood. I scream from the top of my lungs, hoping someone here will care to intervene. Roughly, he turns me around, pushing me against the wall, and then he covers my mouth as he presses his body against mine. I scream and fight while terror grips my insides. This is just like the horrible night six years ago.

I hear nothing now besides the monster's evil laughter as he cups my breast. The vampire my mother sold me to also wanted more than to drink my blood. Bile pools in my mouth, but I don't think puking all over this vampire will deter him.

His fangs graze my neck while his hand is now under my skirt. I'm dizzy, and I can't feel my legs anymore. If I pass out, it will make things easier for him. I can't go down without a fight. I stop trying to push him away; instead, I try to find something in my vicinity that I can use. When my fingers brush an empty glass on top of a table, I summon all the strength I have left to crash the object against the bloodsucker's skull.

He releases me at once, clutching the side of his head. When he pulls his hand from the wound, it reveals blood coming out of a gash. He stares at his bloody fingers for a second before he turns his red eyes at me. "You filthy blood whore. You'll pay for this."

He raises his clawed hand, ready to strike, when someone shoves him to the side. It takes me a moment to recognize my savior. It's Lucca.

He's standing not too far from me, menacing, glorious, deadly. I should flee, but my legs won't obey the command. His eyes are also glowing red, but he's not aiming his fury at me this time. He's staring at the awful vampire who is now staggering back to his feet.

"Boone," Lucca says, his tone dripping with hatred.

"Lucca. Long time no see." He straightens his jacket as if he were talking with someone of no consequence.

"If you're smart, you'll leave right this second," the female Blueblood with Lucca says.

Boone laughs. "Leave? Why? I just got here, and you interrupted my fun." He glances in my direction, licking his lips.

Lucca takes a step forward, aggression rolling out in waves from him. His intention is clear. Two Bluebloods are about to come to blows, and I'm standing here, like an idiot. Another vampire joins Lucca; it's the friend who prevented my escape earlier.

"It's four against one, Boone. Don't be fucking stupid. Get out of here. We can't kill you, but we can kick your ass."

Finally, I snap out of my paralysis. When Lucca gets rid of Boone, he's going to come after me. There's no way he has forgotten what I did to him. I take a step to the side, slowly slinking away from the scene even though I want to see Boone pay for what he tried to do to me. But not at the cost of my life.

My heart is still drumming away in my chest, and even when I finally make it outside the club, it doesn't calm down. There's a line of people waiting to get in, mostly stupid humans who are more than happy to be vampire snack.

Dumbasses.

I stride away from the place, hoping to find a cab. It's not until a block later that I sense someone is following me. *Fuck.* I increase my pace but don't look back. I wish I had brought my phone, so I could call an Uber. But I was too terrified to bring a purse or anything that could be traced back to me. I didn't even bring my ID.

Suddenly, I can't hear my stalker anymore. I finally dare to look over my shoulder, finding no one behind me. *What the hell? Did I imagine being followed?* Still confused, I turn a corner, colliding with a massive body made of steel.

I open my mouth to yell, but the stranger waves his hand in front of my face, and the fear disappears.

"It's okay. I'm not going to hurt you."

He's tall, way over six feet, and broad-shouldered. His hair and close-cropped beard are gray, but his eyes are dark red, almost black.

Shit, another vampire. Why are they all over me when there are dozens of willing humans back in the club?

"What do you want?"

"A word."

"Okay," I reply calmly.

He must have put me in a trance of some sort. I never knew vampires could thrall humans. The knowledge should make me more terrified, but I'm still as cool as a cucumber.

"Did you get the necklace?"

Ah fuck. This guy works for Larsson.

"No. The vampire's bane didn't work. It wasn't my fault. Please don't hurt my brother."

Vivi, you almost died, you're standing in front of a vampire who's messing with your head, and you're begging for Rikkon's life?

31

How stupid are you?

"I'm here to give you another chance to get close to Lucca Della Morte. Now that he's awake, he must enroll at Bloodstone Institute. You'll also join."

A bubble of panic breaks through the vampire's spell. "That's a training school for vampires. I can't go there."

"No, you can't go as a human. That's obvious. Lucca will tear you to shreds if he sees you again."

I swallow the Texas-sized lump in my throat. "You're not going to turn me, are you? I don't want to become a bloodsucker." My voice rises to a shrill, echoing in the empty street.

"I'm not going to turn you. You're going to pretend to be one of us."

"How?"

"Drink this." He hands over a glass vial with a dark liquid inside.

"What is it?" I shake the container, sloshing the substance that looks a lot like blood.

"A witch's potion that will make you look and smell like a vampire."

My eyes widen. "Will I get fangs?"

"Yes. But it will be all an illusion. You won't need to drink blood, and you can still walk in the sun."

I curl my fingers tighter around the small container. "How long does it last?"

"I was told a month, but that can vary. I'd err on the side of caution and not take more than three weeks to complete your task."

Staring at the witch's potion, I can't believe I'm seriously considering this.

"What if I refuse?" I ask. "Will Larsson really kill my brother?"

"Can't say, but he's definitely coming after you."

"Whatever for? I didn't do anything to him."

"You did. You failed to steal Lucca's necklace tonight. And dragons never forget."

"So, my only two options are death by dragon or death by vampire. Great."

"Don't be so pessimistic. If you do everything right, no one has to die."

I open my mouth to offer a retort, but he goes up in black smoke and vanishes into the night.

6

VIVIENNE

I'm still on edge when I finally make it back to the trailer park. Therefore, when I see a shadowy figure sitting on my front steps, my first instinct is to flee.

"Vivi?" Karl calls my name.

Pressing a hand over my chest, I walk over. "Damn it, Karl. You scared me to death. What are you doing here?"

"I came to check on you. I felt like a douche for letting you go into Ember Emporium alone. I was worried."

"As you can see, I'm in one piece." I lift a potted plant next to the steps and fish out my keys.

"You know that's not a very smart hiding place, right?" He stands up, letting me get to the door.

"I know."

"Where's your brother?"

"Still detained by Larsson."

"And?" Karl presses.

"And nothing. Larsson wanted money to let Rikkon go free. I told him I didn't have any. Now, Rikkon has to work for the dragon kingpin until his debt is paid."

Wow, I can't believe I lied like that without blinking. But Karl is watching me through slits. I'm not sure if he bought my story. I look away first, unable to withstand his probing stare.

Once inside, I turn around. Karl has his hands in his pockets, but he doesn't make a motion to follow me in. There's obvious tension between us now, and I put it there.

"Is Cheryl still mad at me?" I ask to change the subject. I don't want Karl to keep asking me about Rikkon.

"Yes, but she'll get over it."

"And you?"

He doesn't answer for a couple of beats, and his silence says it all. There's a new tightness in my chest that has nothing to do with fear of what I must do. Karl, Cheryl, and Vaughn are like family, and the idea that I'm going to lose them because of one of my brother's mistakes kills me.

"I'm not mad at you, Vivi. I'm disappointed."

I laugh without humor. "That's almost worse."

"Not at you," he amends. "At life in general."

"I see. Well, I'm disappointed too. I was looking forward to the Battle of the Bands despite what Cheryl said about me using my brother as an excuse."

"I know you were." He takes a deep breath, glancing at the sky for a second. "I didn't only come here to check on you."

"Oh?"

He meets my stare again with pained eyes. "We've decided to

take a break from Nocturnal."

And just like that, my only glimmer of hope is crushed under the moonlight. "Because of me?"

Shaking his head, he stares at the yellowed grass on the ground. "No. Not because of you. Something unexpected came up, and I won't have time to practice or perform for a while."

It's clear that Karl doesn't want to share what that something is. I don't push. He's entitled to his secrets, just like I'm entitled to mine.

"Will I still see you?" I ask in a small voice. I don't even know if I'll survive my sting at Bloodstone Institute.

"Honestly, I don't know. Maybe not for a while."

I nod once, swallowing hard. As sad as I am to lose his company, this couldn't have happened at a better time. Now, I don't have to explain my absence.

"I'd better get going. It's late," he says.

He turns to leave, but I can't let him go like that. I run to him, jumping into his arms. He crushes me into a bear hug while I press my face against his chest.

"I'll miss you," I say.

He kisses the top of my head. "I'll miss you too, Vivi." We pull away after a moment, and then he pushes a strand of my hair to the side. "Take care, little sis."

My eyes fill with tears. Karl has always been my brother of the heart, but I didn't know he felt the same way about me. When he walks away and disappears into the night, my tears fall freely down my cheeks.

"Take care, big brother."

A thick black envelope is waiting for me on my steps the next morning. There's no sender's address, only my name written with silver ink and in cursive. Apprehension drips down my spine as the feeling of doom hangs over my head. I close the door quickly, forgetting already where I was going to go a minute ago.

Like a coward, I set the envelope on my kitchen counter and stare at it, almost afraid it's going to turn into some nightmarish creature. After a minute of being paralyzed by fear, I finally dare to open the damn thing. Inside is a brochure featuring an imposing gothic building on the front. The name Bloodstone Institute is written in silver lettering just underneath the school's insignia.

I begin to hyperventilate in an instant. This is really happening. I didn't imagine going to Havoc last night and almost getting chowed by two Blueblood vampires. Shaking, I pull up a chair and practically collapse on the seat. I need a good minute to be able to breathe right again.

The envelope contains more than just the brochure. There's also a welcome letter inside. *Shit.* I'm not only enrolled as a student, but I'm also going in using my own name. Not that Salem is a big city, but using an alias would have been preferable. Nocturnal isn't a popular band by any stretch of the imagination, but we've played in several local bars. I'm sure vampires were in attendance.

This is bad. This is really bad.

My phone rings, loud and obnoxious. It's Rikkon's ringtone again. I pull my hair back, yanking at the strands. *Does the dragon kingpin know already about my epic fail? Duh, of course he does.* If I had succeeded in stealing from Lucca, I'd be banging on his door, demanding my brother's release.

"Oh, for fuck's sake." I reach for the damn phone. "Hello?"

"Where's my necklace?" Larsson barks.

"I didn't get it."

There's a long pause before he replies, "I hope you understand what your failure means to your brother."

My brother. It's thanks to him that I'm in this colossal mess. Guilt and anger wrestle for dominance inside of my chest. I think anger is winning now.

"I do. But you said vampire's bane would work on Lucca, and it didn't. I almost got killed."

"Not my problem. You have twenty-four hours to get me what I want, or I'll start to chop off little bits of your brother and feed it to the dogs."

I close my eyes, pinching my nose to avoid getting all teared up again. *Rikkon, you stupid son of a bitch. If I manage to get you out of this mess, I'm going to kill you myself.*

"I'm going to need more than that," I reply.

"You seem to be under the mis—"

"Do you want your goddamn prize or not!" I snap, not caring that I'm yelling at a dangerous supernatural criminal.

There's no immediate reply, and for a second, I believe Larsson is giving orders to his lackeys to come kill me.

"You're lucky that I want that necklace," he replies in a voice that's cold and tight. "How much time do you need?"

"Three weeks."

"That's a long time, and I'm not a very patient dragon."

"Lucca already knows I'm after his jewelry. I have to be stealthy now."

"Fine. And how do you plan on getting close to him since you fucked up so royally?"

I grind my teeth. If I fucked up, it was thanks to his half-baked plan. I keep the angry retort to myself though.

"Let me worry about that. Just please don't hurt my brother in the meantime. I'll get your damn necklace."

"You'd better deliver this time, girlie. I don't usually hand out second chances. Don't squander it."

7

LUCCA

Ronan comes at me with the rage of a thousand soldiers. I barely have time to block his attacks as he pushes me off the tatami. My body is covered in sweat, and my arms and legs ache from the intense workout. I'm out of breath and out of shape. *Damn it.*

Lying on the bench, Saxon laughs. "And you thought you could take Boone the other night."

"Fuck off." I wipe the sweat from my forehead with the back of my arm and step inside the tatami again.

"Let's take a break." Ronan drops his blade.

"I don't want a fucking break. Let's keep going."

"I've come close to removing your pretty head from your body twice. We're taking a break." His tone is final.

Clenching my jaw, I follow him to the bench not occupied by Saxon. Ronan sits down and wipes his face with a white towel, not that he really needs it. He barely broke a sweat.

I do the same, but instead of drying off, I lean forward and let my head drop between my shoulders. I'm dizzy, which means I need to feed soon. But the prospect of drinking blood from one of the humans employed by my uncle isn't appealing. I'm still thinking about the sweet scent of that little thief. She awakened the deepest hunger in me. She gave me bloodlust, and now, I can't stop obsessing about her. This is demented.

The door to the gym opens with a loud bang. I don't need to look up to know my sister is the one marching across the room with the determination of a female vampire on a mission.

Fuck. What now?

"Who stole your Barbie doll, Manu?" Saxon asks.

"Bite me, asshole." She stops in front of me with her hands on her hips.

"What?" I look up.

"You have to speak to Uncle."

"Uh, in case you haven't noticed, I haven't seen the guy since I woke up from almost a hundred years of hibernation."

"What? He hasn't come to see you yet?" Her eyebrows arch, almost meeting her hairline.

"That's what I just said. What's the problem?"

Manu spares a fleeting glance in Ronan's direction. My friend pretends he doesn't see it, keeping his gaze forward.

Did something happen between them while I was sleeping?

"He wants my familiar to join the institute."

Ronan grinds his teeth so hard that we all can hear it.

"You haven't seen him in how long? Almost five hundred years? Is he even alive?"

"Yeah, he's alive all right," Saxon scoffs.

"He moved to Salem sixty years ago." Manu crosses her arms and looks away.

"Okay. So, what's the problem?"

"What's the problem? *What's the problem?*" she screams, gesturing widely with her arms. "There's a reason I haven't seen him all this time. I don't know why Uncle is forcing him down my throat now."

Ronan stands up abruptly. "You should have thought about that before you decided to acquire a familiar."

He strides out of the room with tense shoulders, almost pulling the door off its hinges.

"What has gotten into him?" Saxon asks.

When Manu doesn't answer, I continue, "If Uncle wants your familiar to join Bloodstone, there's nothing you can do about it. He's the king after all. His word is law." The words are bitter in my mouth. I haven't accepted his decision to coexist peacefully with Tatiana yet. I never will.

With a groan, Manu throws her hands up in the air. "This is so unfair."

"Why are you whining about it?" Saxon interjects. "Familiars are great. They're like your own personal assistant. I wish I had one."

"You can have mine." She pouts.

"You're acting like a child," I say. "Familiars are handy."

She glowers. "Then why don't you have one?"

Saxon replies before I can, "Because Lucca is such a beast that the Nightingales couldn't find a single animal that liked him."

When the Nightingales created us, they also bestowed upon us familiars, which were animals magically turned into human shifters.

Once a familiar was linked to a vampire, their life forces were combined, allowing familiars to live as long as their vampire masters did. Like us, familiars bred and multiplied, and with time, the newer generations lost the ability to shift between forms, remaining stuck in their two-legged versions.

"Pot, meet kettle." I get up.

The dizziness hasn't passed, and this conversation is not helping. I sway on the spot, almost falling on my ass.

"Whoa, are you all right, buddy?" Saxon is by my side in the next second, holding me by the elbow.

Irritated, I step aside. "I'm fine."

Manu narrows her eyes. "When was the last time you fed?"

"I had a few bags before training."

"I'm talking fed from a human?"

"Can't remember." I veer for the exit.

"You haven't fed since Havoc." She follows me. "You need to eat, Lucca. Packed blood is not a replacement for the real deal."

"I'll eat after I shower." I head for the stairs out of the basement.

The four of us live in a gothic mansion hidden deep in the woods near the town's border. But that will change once we head to Bloodstone Institute, which is a much larger building nearby and not concealed from the rest of town.

Manu and my friends have already gone through their required rehabilitation training after they woke from hibernation, but we made a deal a long time ago to always stick together. That means they will endure the absurd program again for me.

Institutes were put in place when hibernation became a necessity. They have existed for almost five hundred years. Back in the old days, only Bluebloods attended, but with our dwindling numbers and the incorporation of the training of the Red Guard into the program, they're no longer as elitist.

I expect to find the house empty and shrouded in darkness when I reach the ground floor, but there's a fire going in the living room, bathing the area in orange light. On the grandfather chair near the fireplace, a lonely figure sits. My uncle, King Raphael.

Manu and Saxon stop next to me, but neither says a word. That's the effect my uncle has on everyone.

"Lucca." It's all he says.

I glance briefly at Saxon and then at Manu, who has her gaze fixed on him. With a nod of his head, Saxon steers Manu up the grand staircase before she has the chance to ruin my first meeting with the king post-awakening. She can complain about her familiar later.

I walk over to the fireplace, bowing to my uncle before I take a seat on the couch facing the warm fire. It's not even winter yet, but my uncle seems to be eternally cold.

"It's good to see you awake, son."

"It's good to be back."

We don't speak for several beats, and during the loaded silence, I maintain my uncle's stare. Few are able to do it.

"You aren't happy about the truce," he finally says.

"No."

"You've been gone for a long time. A lot has changed."

"It's what I keep hearing, but so far, I haven't seen enough evidence to justify a truce. I bumped into Boone last night. He's still the same scum he used to be."

"I know. I didn't agree to peace because I believed Tatiana and her followers had changed. I did it to save our race from extinction."

"You really believe the Nightingales will return if they think the war is over?" I snort.

"No."

"What the hell? Then why are you doing this?"

He clamps his jaw tight and narrows his gaze. "I can't tell you yet."

I jump from the couch, propelled by the fury I've been trying to suppress since I found out about this idiotic truce. "That's bullshit! I have the right to know why I can't rip Boone's heart out without facing execution."

"Sit down," he commands.

Flaring my nostrils, I stare him down for a couple of seconds before obeying. I don't know why I thought I could get a straight answer from him. The male wrote the book on evasion.

"Instead of wasting your time with demanding explanations, you should be focusing on breaking the curse."

And just like that, he punctures my lungs with a steely knife. I never want to think about that. *Ever.*

"Why bother? It can't be broken. The Nightingale queen made sure of that."

"I didn't raise you to be a whiny bitch."

I wince at the remark. He only resorts to name-calling when he's mad as hell.

"Even if I could control my hunger and not kill, I don't see a plethora of Nightingales flying around. They're gone, Uncle."

"Not all of them, Lucca. You're forgetting that the Nightingales liked to mingle with mortals before they left."

"You're talking about a descendant?"

He nods.

"Impossible. Even if I found one by chance, their blood would be too diluted. It wouldn't work."

Plus, I'd most likely drink the human dry, damning me forever.

"You'd rather not try then? I never pegged you for a coward."

My hands ball into fists while I fight to keep the angry retort stuck in my throat.

"This is your last chance, Luc," he continues in a softer tone. "If you go into hibernation again, you won't wake up."

Fuck. And don't I know that.

8

VIVIENNE

⟜══✦══⟞

I've been standing outside of Bloodstone Institute for over an hour, hiding under the shadows of an ancient oak tree across the dark road leading to its towering gates. There's nothing here besides the school. Tall walls keep unwanted visitors out, and surrounding the property, a thick forest adds another level of spookiness to the place.

The merciless vise of dread wraps around me, sending chills down my back. This will be my home for the next three weeks—that is, if I'm not found out and killed beforehand.

Secured in my hand is the potion that will transform me into a vampire. I wanted to wait until the last minute to drink it. Now, I'm just wasting time. The howl of a wolf sounding in the distance tells me my time is up. The sun has set, and it's getting late. I can't forget there are other monsters roaming freely in this town.

I unscrew the bottle cap and drink the potion in one single gulp.

It's bitter as fuck, and it almost makes me gag. My stomach revolts, but I keep my mouth clamped shut. Throwing up is not an option. Bracing against the tree, I wait for the nausea to pass.

It takes a few minutes, but then a tingling sensation spreads through my body, freaking me out. *Is this the spell at work?* Frantically, I reach inside my bag and pull my cell phone out. *What do I look like now?*

I put on the camera and stare at a face that's exactly the same as it was five minutes ago. I don't know what I was expecting. Vampires look human until their eyes begin to glow and they reveal their fangs. I inspect my teeth, noticing the tips of sharper canines. It doesn't matter; this won't keep Lucca from recognizing me.

"What are you waiting for?" a male voice asks from behind me.

I yelp, dropping my phone. It's the same gray-haired vampire who gave me the potion last night.

"What the hell!"

"Sorry. I didn't mean to startle you."

"Then quit sneaking up on me." I bend over to retrieve the device.

Once again, I don't feel the terror that usually takes over me when I'm in the presence of a bloodsucker. This Blueblood is using his mojo on me again. Without fear, all that's left is irritation.

"Answer me. What are you waiting for?"

"You said this potion would make me look like a vampire. Well, I still look like myself, so it obviously didn't work."

"It *did* work. You don't feel human to me."

"So you say. It doesn't matter. Lucca will see right through the deception. He got a good look at me last night."

"He won't recognize you. Trust me."

"Trust you? I don't even know you."

His eyes narrow. "What did Larsson say he was going to do to your brother if he didn't get what he wanted?"

He had to remind me of that conversation. I had been doing an okay job, not thinking about Rikkon and the possibility of his imminent death. I have a bunch of conflicted emotions when it comes to the dumbass, but I obviously don't want him to die.

This vampire, however, seems to know too much about my dealings with the dragon kingpin. *What's his game?*

"I don't want to repeat it." I look at the dark building again.

"Time is ticking, Vivienne."

There's a gust of wind, and when I glance in his direction, he's gone.

"Stupid-ass bloodsucker," I mutter under my breath.

I fix the strap of my duffel bag, and with a steadying breath, I stride across the street. Suddenly, headlights illuminate my face, followed by the screeching of tires and a loud horn. I jump back, clutching at my chest as I stare at the black SUV that almost ran me over. I can't see who is behind the wheel, thanks to the blinding lights, until the driver rolls his window down and sticks his head out.

"What the hell are you doing? Get the fuck out of the way."

Oh my God. It's Lucca. He's the one driving, and now, he's just glaring at me without an ounce of recognition on his face. I scramble to the curb and stare dumbly at his car as he drives past me and through the now-open gates of the institute.

I'll be damned. The spell *did* work.

The gates begin to shut once more, so I run toward them, managing to slip through just before they close. I'm still breathing hard when two security guards wearing black suits materialize in front of me in a split second. *Crap.* They can move fast.

"This is private property." One of them reaches for my shoulder. I jump back. "Hey, I'm a student here."

They trade a glance before the one who spoke first looks at me. "Name?"

"Vivienne Gale."

Cold light illuminates his gaunt face when he glances down at his phone. "She's on the list."

His coworker pierces me with a stern stare. "Head to the administration office. And next time, don't try to sneak in."

"I won't. Thanks."

I hurry to the front of the building, hoping they can't hear the sound of my heart beating like a drum. Unlike in fiction, vampires do have heartbeats, but does it go out of control like that whenever they're nervous?

Trying to get out of the guards' sight as fast as possible, I almost burst through the heavy front doors. But once I'm inside the building, I freeze. The high vaulted ceiling is well lit, and the interior isn't dark or gloomy, but the place is already crawling with vampires. I can't help the terror that grips me in a strong hold. I'm already feeling light-headed, and dark spots appear in my line of vision. I'm going to make a spectacle out of myself within seconds.

"Are you new too?" a female voice asks next to me.

"What?" I squeak, glancing at her.

She's a petite brunette with big, round doe eyes and corkscrew curly hair reaching her shoulders. She also looks twelve.

"I'm new too. Don't worry. We'll be fine." She smiles at me, showing a hint of fangs. "I'm Cassandra, by the way, but everyone calls me Cassie. What's your name?"

"Vivienne."

She extends her hand, but instead of shaking it, I simply stare at it. Cassie's friendly smile begins to wilt, making me feel bad for my inadequacy. I finally reach over.

"Nice to meet you," I say.

A wash of relief shows on her face, and nothing bad happens to me after the handshake. Maybe I can do this after all.

We walk together to the administration office. It's nearby, but in that short time span, she manages to tell me her entire life story. Her parents are from Boston and not Bluebloods. Like the vast majority of vampires living outside of Salem, they have to work for humans and hope no one will discover their secret.

Cassie has been on the waitlist to attend Bloodstone for over fifty years. She hopes to become a Keeper and be employed by a Blueblood family. I have no idea what a Keeper is, but I can't ask.

The positive side of her conversation monopoly is that I don't have to answer any questions about myself. Things happened so fast that I didn't have the chance to concoct a background story.

We wait in the administration office with five other students. They're all regular vampires who have been waiting a long time to come here. The mysterious vampire helping me managed to get me a spot in less than twenty-four hours. He must be someone very important, which makes me leery of his motives.

"Vivienne Gale?" the vamp behind the counter calls.

I jump out of my chair and say, "Present," like a dimwit, causing a ripple of giggles to spread in the waiting room. With my face in flames, I walk over to the counter, avoiding making eye contact with anyone on the way.

"I'm Vivienne Gale," I say.

Without looking at me, she types away on her keyboard and then frowns at the computer screen. "That's odd."

"What is?"

She gives me a scrutinizing glance.

Shit. Does she suspect I'm not a vampire?

"You're not a Blueblood, but you've been assigned a room in the Blueblood wing."

Fuuuuck. The coin has finally dropped. Despite packing a bag with clothes and some personal items, I forgot I'd be boarding with vampires. Or maybe I was still in shock when I got ready to come here.

"Am I sharing that room?"

"Not the room, dear. The apartment. Bluebloods don't share rooms."

I exhale loudly, partially relieved. Sharing an apartment is definitely better than sharing a room. "Okay then."

Furrowing her eyebrows, she says, "Don't get too comfortable. This was most likely a mistake, and you *will* be reassigned once registration is closed."

Crap on toast.

She slides a skeleton key across the counter. "You're in apartment 46B. Keepers training orientation starts in fifteen minutes. Hanson doesn't tolerate tardiness, so you'd better head to that first before you settle in."

"Huh? Keepers training? I didn't sign up for that."

The female gives me a droll stare. "If you didn't sign up for that, then you have no business being here. Scribers training is officially closed until further notice."

Don't know what that is either. I'm way over my head, so I should really keep my mouth shut and go with the flow.

"Did I say I didn't sign up for Keepers training?" I laugh nervously. "I meant, Scribers training."

Before she can call me on my bullshit, I take the key and walk out of the office. Cassie is waiting for me, which strangely makes me glad. I never thought the day would come when I'd be happy to be in the company of a vampire.

"Which room did you get?" she asks.

"I'm in apartment 46B."

"Wait, you got an apartment?" Her eyebrows shoot to the heavens. "I thought only Bluebloods stayed in those."

I shrug. "It was a mistake. They'll sort it out once registration is closed."

Unlikely. I'm in the Blueblood wing by design. I just hope I'm not sharing the apartment with someone awful like that Boone vampire.

Cassie and I head to the auditorium for orientation, and I begin to relax. But of course, I don't get to stay in the comfort zone for long. There's a sudden change in the air. Conversations drop to murmurs, and everyone seems to freeze and stare at the end of the hallway. I follow their gazes and then understand the commotion. Lucca is coming over, followed by his entourage. Goose bumps spread down my arms while my stomach twists into knots. I take a step back, trying to blend with the background. I should drop my eyes to the floor too, but I can't look away. I'm drawn to Lucca's dark allure like a moth to a flame.

He doesn't seem to care about all the stares as he moves like he owns the place. That is, until he passes by where I stand and turns to me. Our gazes lock for a second, and in that fleeting moment, I catch the hint of crimson in his brown eyes.

Did I imagine that, or even as a vampire, am I still prey to him?

9

LUCCA

———⚔———

Relief. That's what I feel as I stride down the hallway of Bloodstone Institute. I was away for a long time, and there have been drastic changes in our society. I didn't know what kind of reception I'd get. It was easy for worry to take hold. But vampires—regulars and Bluebloods alike—still stare at me in awe and fear. I haven't lost my touch.

I don't make eye contact with anyone until a strange force makes me glance to my right. And there I find her, the idiotic regular who ran in front of my car earlier. I had already forgotten about the incident but seeing her properly now stirs something in my memory.

Have I met her before tonight?

She's a regular, pretty but ordinary. I'd fuck her once and move on without a second thought. *Why is she beguiling me like this?*

I force my eyes away from her face. I can't get distracted by fresh meat. Exerting dominance has to be my main focus. No one can suspect that my days are numbered. My uncle's words return to aggravate me. He's wrong. I'm not a coward. I'm hopeless.

When I veer toward the auditorium, Saxon asks, "Why are we here? This is Keepers training orientation."

"I want to see what this nonsense is all about."

I head straight to the front row. I don't want the moron in charge to miss my presence. Ronan briefly explained to me what's in the curriculum, and it's appalling. When these new recruits graduate, they won't stand a chance fighting in a real war.

Slowly, the place begins to fill. I don't think the majority of the audience cares about Keepers training, but I'm here, so the flock follows. The division between classes is clear though. Bluebloods and regulars don't usually mingle. It's an elitist custom that goes back generations. It's not something I support, but I don't care to change it either.

From the corner of my eye, I catch the approach of Therese Schutz, a second-generation vampire like us. Tall and slender and with striking facial features, she could be a supermodel nowadays. She wears her long ebony hair straight now, parted down the middle, and her clothes reveal much more skin than they used to. Not that I haven't seen what she has to offer many times before. I think the new term for what we had is *fuck buddy*.

Manu groans next to me. "Please, don't start this again. I can't stand that bitch."

I'm ready to tell my sister to suck it, but watching Therese sashay in my direction, oozing sex appeal, is doing nothing for me today.

"Lucca," she purrs when she stops in front of me. "It's good to see you."

"Likewise," I lie, not wanting to deal with the drama of turning Therese down on my first day back.

"I've missed you." She bites her lower lip while puffing out her chest.

My eyes drop to her cleavage and remain there for a moment. I'm a male after all, and I have a lot of catching up to do in the sack, but hell, there isn't even a stir in my pants.

Hanson, the male responsible for training the new Keepers, jumps onto the stage and grabs the mic.

"Stop throwing yourself at my brother and sit down, Therese. Lucca is not going to bang you right this second," Manu chimes in.

She narrows her eyes to slits. "At least I have males forming a line for the chance to fuck me. Who is going after you, darling?"

Manu makes a motion to stand, but Ronan grabs her wrist and keeps her in place. She breaks free from his hold with a brusque movement and then glowers at Therese's back as she walks away.

"I take it you still don't like her." I chuckle.

"What's to like? She has the personality of a blow-up doll."

"You would think differently if you had a dick." Saxon laughs.

"Gross. Save your crass comments for your blood whores."

Hanson begins to speak, interrupting Manu and Saxon's banter. He first welcomes the new students, and then, as if it were an afterthought, he acknowledges my presence. *Fucker.* He's a Blueblood but third-generation. It's easy to understand why he got the job. He never picked a side in the war, preferring to remain neutral. The thing is, there isn't such a thing in our world. Neutral truly means *I'll pick the winning side when this is over.* It's cowardly and revolting.

The sneer that unfurls on my lips stays there for the duration of his speech.

"Now, I'd like to ask the newcomers to join me on the stage," he says.

I look over my shoulder to locate the regular who caught my eye earlier. She looks paler than before as she follows a petite brunette to the stage. I zero in on her, stretching my predatorial instincts to the max. Her heartbeat is accelerated, which matches the panicked expression she has now. It can be challenging for newbies to stand in front of an audience made out of Bluebloods, but her fear seems to go beyond stage fright. It's also familiar as hell.

"Oh, this should be fun," Manu says under her breath.

"Hell, the blonde one is shaking like a leaf. What kind of parameters are they using to recruit those noobs?" Saxon scoffs.

Hanson proceeds to bore the crowd with endless talking of how important the job of the Keepers is. They're supposed to protect our kind from external threats, such as vampire hunters and other supernaturals. What a load of crap. We haven't had an issue with hunters since the last Van Helsing descendant died, taking his obsession and hatred to the grave.

"Let's see how skilled you already are with the blade." Hanson hands over a small dagger to each of the five recruits.

To regular vampires, becoming a Keeper is an honor and a way to have a more meaningful life. They all take the weapon with eagerness and even awe. The blonde girl doesn't. She hesitates, and when she finally accepts the dagger, she doesn't seem to know what to do with it.

Suddenly, she winces and brings her thumb to her mouth.

My nostrils flare, and my fangs descend fully. In a head rush, everything comes back to me, and I know who she is. A single drop of her spilled blood broke the spell concealing her true nature. She's the thief from Havoc.

A growl escapes my lips as my vision becomes tinged in red. I grip the arms of the chair, digging my nails in the leather.

"Lucca, are you okay?" Manu asks.

"Can't you see who that is?"

"No. Should I know her?"

It's a struggle to peel my eyes off the human and stare at my sister. "You don't recognize her?"

"Never seen her before in my life."

"Holy shit, Luc. Your eyes are glowing red." Saxon stares with concern.

I'm beginning to lose the grip on my free will. The bloodlust is taking over, and if I don't leave now, I'm going to bleed that girl dry. She more than deserves it, but I can't kill a human like that in front of everyone.

"I … need … to go," I grit out.

"No. If you run off like that, people will talk." Manu glances at the stage again. "If the blonde regular is the problem, I'll deal with her."

"And how do you plan to whisk her off the stage without a commotion?" Ronan asks.

Manu stretches her neck and looks over the crowd. "Aha! I got it."

She pulls her cell phone out and begins texting with supernatural speed. A second later, there's a reply.

"Stupid witch. Can't she just do something without asking a thousand questions?" she mutters as she types again.

"Whatever you plan to do, you'd better do it fast. Lucca is

turning purple," Saxon pipes up.

Only because I'm fighting with everything that I have to control the urge to feed.

"Who are you texting?" Ronan tries to look over her shoulder, but Manu pushes him off.

"Aurora."

A second later, the lights in the auditorium begin to flicker until they go out completely. A gust of wind brushes my arm. That was Manu rushing off from her seat. I hear a clear gasp up on the stage. She's got the human. Vampires can see in the dark, but it takes a few seconds for our eyes to adjust. However, the lights turn back on a moment later. Manu and the human are gone.

My bloodlust begins to dissipate but not my rage. If the human came here disguised as a vampire, it means she's still after my necklace. I gave her a free pass once. This time, I won't let her escape without retribution.

10

VIVIENNE

One moment, I make the stupid mistake of cutting my thumb with the dagger, and in the next, the lights are out, and a hand is covering my mouth. I'm being whisked away without having any chance of calling for help. My kidnapper only stops moving at breakneck speed when we're in a different part of the institute, a place I haven't been before.

They release me with a hard shove, and I end up sprawled on the floor.

"Who the fuck are you?" the white-haired Blueblood asks.

I scramble back to my feet as fast as I can and then shuffle back until my spine meets the wall. "I'm a nobody. Just a regular vampire."

"Bullshit." She takes a step forward, trembling with barely contained rage. "You did something to my brother. He almost went berserk a moment ago thanks to you."

She doesn't remember me, so my best option is to keep lying.

"I didn't do anything to your brother. I've never met him until today."

"What's going on here?" another female voice asks.

The deranged Blueblood turns around and hisses at the newcomer. "This doesn't concern you, Aurora."

Calmly, the brunette meets the vampire's demented gaze without flinching. "You asked for my help. Now, I'm involved. Just spill the beans already. I don't have time for Blueblood theatrics."

I look closely at her, trying to pinpoint what's different about her demeanor. She has tanned skin, straight light-brown hair, and almond-shaped whiskey-colored eyes. She's beautiful but not in an otherworldly way. Then, it finally hits me. She's not a vampire. She's human. *How come she can go head-to-head with a Blueblood without fear?* And the vampire girl doesn't seem inclined to attack her either.

Suddenly, my blood runs cold, and the hairs on the back of my neck stand on end. A new tightness forms in my chest, and it has nothing to do with this current standoff. I feel his presence nearby, watching me. Slowly, I look to the right. There he is, standing at the end of the hallway with eyes glowing red. Even in the distance, I can see the white tips of his fangs peeking from his partially open lips. I swallow hard. As scary as his predatorial stance is, I can't look away.

"Hey. Are you okay?" Aurora steps in front of me, blocking my view of Lucca.

"Yes."

I notice then that the white-haired Blueblood is gone. The sense of doom recedes slowly, and I'm not surprised to realize Lucca has also disappeared.

I brush a rogue strand of hair off my face. "I don't know what just happened."

She raises an eyebrow. "Really?"

"Yeah, *really*."

She grabs my left hand and runs her finger over the cut on my thumb. "You need to be more careful with blades. Blood has power. It can break the strongest spells."

My eyes widen of their own accord. I pull my hand free and step away from her. "You know what I am?"

She grins. "I didn't at first. But you had to go and cut yourself in a room filled with bloodsuckers."

I glance at the spot where Lucca was standing a minute ago. "Does that mean my cover is blown?"

"No. Manu had no idea you weren't a vampire. I know you're human because I'm a witch."

I cover my face with my hands. "I knew this was a terrible idea. I can't do it."

"Can't do what?"

Fuck. I've said too much already. "Never mind. I need to find my apartment and get my thoughts in order."

"Apartment? Where are you staying?"

"In the Bluebloods wing. Apartment 46B."

Aurora stares at me without blinking for a moment before she bursts out laughing. "Oh my God. I don't know why you're here, pretending to be a vampire, but whoever set you up, they didn't have the best intentions."

"What do you mean? Do you know who my roommate is?"

"Oh, yeah. You just met her."

"Fuck. That deranged Blueblood is my roommate?"

"Yep. I'd sleep with one eye open if I were you. Manu can be savage, especially if she perceives someone as a threat to her family."

I close my eyes for a moment, fighting the urge to simply forget the deal and get out. But I can't give up on Rikkon even if I say I won't put up with his shit anymore. He's my brother, and I love him.

"I don't want to harm anyone," I reply in a small voice.

"You'd better make sure she knows that. Anyway, I hope to see you tomorrow. Take care, new girl."

I want to grill the witch further, but we're no longer alone. The orientation must be over, and the hallway is slowly filling up with vamps. She vanishes in the crowd before I have the chance to get her phone number. I don't know yet how I feel about Aurora knowing my secret. She didn't rat me out to Manu now, but it doesn't mean she won't.

Still rattled by the witch's revelation, I return to the auditorium to collect my stuff, finding Cassie waiting for me at the door. She has my duffel bag. *Thank goodness.*

"There you are. I was beginning to worry."

"I'm sorry."

"Where did you go?"

"I had to use the restroom."

She doesn't watch me with suspicion, which is something I expected her to do. I'm a bad liar, and I know it. One more reason to add to the list of why I'm going to fail this mission. No way I can pretend I'm a vampire while sharing an apartment with that crazy Blueblood. And she has to be Lucca's sister to boot.

Maybe my mysterious friend did it on purpose, thinking that it would help me get closer to my target. He obviously doesn't know how disaster prone I am. I almost blew the entire thing in less than an hour.

Cassie is talking about something as we walk together to our quarters, but I'm barely listening. My internal monologue is louder. She stops suddenly in front of a set of stairs, bringing me back down to earth.

"Well, this is where we part. My dorm room is that way." She points with her head to the left.

I finally pay attention to my surroundings and see the sign with directions. The apartments are up the stairs.

"Okay. See you later," I say.

"Wait, what's your phone number? I'll text you once I'm settled."

I recite my digits to her, and then she texts me, so I can save her info.

I'm a ball of dread by the time I stop in front of my new home for the next three or four weeks. Taking a steadying breath, I unlock the door and walk in slowly. A surprisingly cozy living room greets me. It's lively and modern, featuring a comfortable-looking sectional couch covered by colorful pillows and a couple blankets. Abstract art hangs from the light-gray walls, and the metal shutters on the windows are semi-hidden by thick white curtains.

"Hello?" I call out.

Complete silence. *Phew.* Manu is not back yet. Maybe I won't have to see her at all tonight. I check out the open kitchen, which looks like something out of a home decor magazine with its brand-new stainless steel appliances and white granite countertops. I bet that the regular dorms are not this nice.

I open the fridge, cringing at the sight of several blood bags and nothing else. *Shit. Why would there be food here when vampires don't eat anything but blood?* That's going to be a major problem. I can't eat human food without giving away my identity. I could maybe store dry snacks in my room, but that would be risky. I wouldn't put it past Manu to raid my bedroom.

Maybe you can go three weeks without eating, Vivi.

"Yeah, right."

I continue the apartment exploration. The first bedroom I check is definitely occupied, and it's an explosion of loud colors. It looks like someone had a crayon party in there. There's not a single white surface or object in sight. I wonder if Manu's tastes have anything to do with her own lack of coloring.

I try to locate the bathroom, finding none. So, that means each bedroom is a suite. *Let's hope so.* I'm about to inspect the second room when Manu walks in. We both freeze at the same time, and then she's holding me by the throat.

"What are you doing in my apartment, bitch?" She squeezes my neck so hard I'm afraid she'll break it.

I kick my legs as I try to break free from her death grip. "Let … me … go. I live … here … psycho."

Surprisingly, she drops me to the floor. "What did you say?"

Clutching my neck, I gasp for air. "I said, I live here."

"You can't be my roommate. You're a regular vampire. You should be staying in the dorms."

Slowly, I get back on my feet, glowering at the Blueblood. "I'm sure it was a mistake, but administration won't fix it until registration is closed."

Her golden eyes become nothing but slits. "Hmm, maybe you

should stay. You're hiding something, and I have every intention of finding out what it is. I'll call them and say everything is fine."

It's hard to keep my expression neutral under her hard stare, but I don't look away. Only when her cell phone rings does she break the connection.

I win. Ha!

"Hi, Sax. What's up?" She walks over to the couch with the phone glued to her ear. Then, she looks over her shoulder with the hint of a smirk curling the corners of her lips. "Yeah, I've met my new roomie."

Ignoring her malicious smile, I collect my duffel bag from the floor and head for my bedroom.

"Party? Sure. I can make an appearance," she says. "Yeah, I'll bring her."

I'm almost home free when she calls out, "Hey, roomie. Don't get too comfortable. We're going to a party. And don't even think about refusing. Attendance is mandatory."

11

LUCCA

———⊰⊱———

I'm pacing in my apartment, burning a hole through the carpet, while Ronan and Saxon sit leisurely on the leather couch in the living room, playing a video game.

When we got back to the apartment, they wanted to know what the deal was in the auditorium. I was close to telling them the new Keeper prospect was the human thief from Havoc. But if I tell any of my friends or my sister, they'll meddle. That will spoil my plan of slowly torturing the little human.

A human pretending to be a vampire in Bloodstone Institute. She's either fucking stupid or she's hiding a trump card under her sleeve. Either way, she'll regret ever crossing paths with me.

I head for the wet bar and pour myself a glass of whiskey. We don't need to drink anything else but blood to live, and it's what we crave the most, but sometimes, I like the taste of fine spirits. It doesn't do jack to Bluebloods though. You won't ever see us drunk

Regulars stay away from the stuff; they're too weak to handle it. They usually get incredibly ill.

While I sip my drink, I begin to imagine the cruel ways I can make the little thief suffer. Vivienne is her real name—it was information easy to find, which boggles my mind. *Why risk so much, only to steal something from me?*

"Motherfucker." Saxon tosses the game controller aside while Ronan laughs.

"Don't be such a sore loser."

"Bite me, asshole." He gets up with his cell phone in hand.

Ronan glances at me. "How about you give it a try, Luc?"

A scoff is the reply he gets from me. Saxon tried to explain the appeal of video games, but he lost me after a minute. Sitting idle in front of a screen, killing animated characters, is not my idea of fun. I'd much rather spend time on the tatami, acquiring real skills that I can use against the likes of Boone.

I finish my drink while Saxon talks on the phone with Manu. Something about a party. He has always been the social butterfly in our group, which works because Ronan is a reclusive by nature and I couldn't give a fuck about mingling with ass-kissers.

Done with the call, Saxon turns to me. "Party in an hour in the catacombs. Everyone is invited; that means your regular friend should be there too."

Hunger mixes with an odd excitement. It's the thrill of the hunt, something I haven't felt in a long time.

I curve my lips into a grin. "Excellent."

Saxon squints, crossing his arms. "You really not gonna tell us what you see in that female, are you?"

"There's nothing to tell."

"Bullshit. But whatever. I'd rather hook up with a human anytime. They taste better, and I don't have to deal with the aftermath."

"You know that if everyone was invited, Tatiana's followers will be there too," Ronan pipes up, killing my good mood in an instant.

"If they're dumb enough to show up, no one can blame us if they get roughed up." Saxon smiles impishly.

Ronan pierces me with a stern stare. "Boone is at Bloodstone. Are you going to be able to control yourself this time?"

The whiskey glass shatters in my hand. "Of course."

With an air of resignation, Ronan shakes his head. "Just please stay away from any of his blades. He got you once; he's gonna try again."

My nostrils flare. "Let him. Isn't self-defense killing allowed in the Accords?"

"Allegedly," Saxon replies. "But if you kill Boone, Tatiana will demand your head on a spike."

"She already wants my head on a spike—along with every single member of my family," I reply, letting the bitterness fester in my chest.

I reach inside my shirt and clutch my mother's necklace. It's the only thing I have left of her. Tatiana might not have delivered the killing blow, but my mother is dead in part because of her. Revenge belongs to my uncle, but considering the things he's allowed to happen in the last century, he doesn't seem inclined to end that bitch anytime soon. He claims he wants to save our race from extinction. How noble of him. If I have the chance to kill Tatiana, I'll do it in a heartbeat even if that condemns us all.

VIVIENNE

Manu wasn't kidding when she said I had no choice about attending this party. She's practically dragging me there, pinching her talon-like nails on my skin. If I wasn't wearing a jacket, she would draw blood. I really can't allow that to happen anymore even though it feels like an impossible task when I'm surrounded by sharp teeth and claws.

"You can let me go now. I'm not going to run," I say.

"Of course you aren't. A regular vampire is no match for a Blueblood in everything that counts."

Wow, I had no idea there was such a division between the bloodsuckers. To me, they're all equally bad. The vampire who drank from me when I was younger was a regular, and he was freakishly strong.

Despite her comment, Manu doesn't let go until we reach the bowels of the institute. We're underground, and this place matches the spooky exterior of the building. Now, it feels like I'm living in a haunted mansion. The stone walls are dark and mossy, and the stagnant air smells of mildew. It's also chilly here, and I'm glad that I had the foresight to grab a leather jacket.

"Who is throwing this party anyway?" I ask.

"Who cares?"

"What's this place?"

"The catacombs."

"The catacombs? Could this party be more cliché?"

Surprisingly, Manu laughs. "Our existence is cliché, thanks to all the horrendous fiction out there."

I bite my tongue. I have to remember that I'm pretending to be a vampire, and I can't make comments only a human would. There's a lull in the conversation, and all I hear now is the noise of our steps echoing in the damp corridor.

Then, the muffled sound of techno music reaches us.

Manu lets go of my arm and turns to me. "Wait here."

"Why?"

"There's no way in hell I'm arriving at this party with a regular." She zaps ahead, turning into a blur before she disappears around the bend.

Fucking great. I hug myself when a chilly wind comes blowing in the corridor. A new sense of dread takes hold of me, but it's different than when Lucca was watching me earlier today.

Release me, the chilly breeze seems to say.

That's crazy. My brain tells me I should get going, get out of this dark tunnel at once. But I'm pulled in a different direction from the party, and like an idiot, I follow the invisible force. I hear the same command again. *Am I imagining things or is this place truly haunted?*

I don't know where I'm going, but I can no longer hear the music. I'm shaking nonstop, terrified of what I might find at the end of this narrow corridor, and yet I keep putting one foot in front of the other.

Maybe there's another vampire down here who can compel me. *Shit. Shit. Shit.* If that's the case, I have to break free from the thrall. I only stop when I can't go on any longer. There's a wrought iron gate blocking my path. Curling my fingers around the bars, I try to open it, but it's locked. There's barely any illumination here. The only source of light is coming from a dangling lamp a couple of feet behind me.

I pull my cell phone out to use the Flashlight app. It's stupid that I didn't think to do it until now. The bright beam shows me a small chamber where five stone tombs are laid out in a circular pattern.

I hear it again. The creepy, whispered words. Then, my cell phone light goes out, and someone touches my shoulder. My scream pierces the silence, but it's cut short when my mouth is covered by a hand.

"Chill. It's me, Aurora."

She releases me at once, and I lean against the stone wall, trying to catch my breath. "What the hell? You scared the crap out of me."

"How did you get here?"

"I don't know. I got lost."

There's no chance in hell I'm telling her I was hearing voices.

"Come on. Let's go. We can't be here."

"Why not? Is it because of those five tombs in the chamber?"

She glances at the gate and doesn't answer for a couple of beats. I wish the corridor weren't so dim and I could see her face better.

"Do you know who is inside them?" I press.

"No. All I know is that there's a powerful spell concealing this chamber. No one is supposed to know it's here or even find the way to this spot. How did you do it?"

"I have no idea. How come *you* got here?"

"I'm a witch. I already told you that."

"How many witches are attending Bloodstone?"

"You ask way too many questions. Come on." She grabs my hand and steers me back to the place Manu abandoned me.

I press my feet against the ground, halting our progress. "Wait."

With eyebrows pinched together, Aurora turns to me. "What now?"

"Who am I going to find at this party?"

Sighing loudly, she drops my hand and fixes the sleeves of her kimono-style jacket. "The invite was sent to everyone, so expect to see Bluebloods, regulars, humans, and familiars."

"What about witches?"

She narrows her gaze. "I'm the only witch in residence."

"Oh. Why?"

"It's an old tradition. My mother is the High Witch. She serves King Raphael, and when she passes, I'll inherit the title. Therefore, I must train at Bloodstone."

"I didn't know that."

"I think we should start with what you *do* know about vampires and go from there. If you don't want to be discovered, you can't ask questions that are common knowledge around here."

"Can you help me?"

She squints. "What do you think I'm doing now?" Animated voices echo in the tunnel behind us. "Let's get going. It would have been smarter if you hadn't come, but the sooner you make an appearance, the sooner you can leave."

I couldn't agree with her more, but I came to Bloodstone to get closer to Lucca and steal his necklace. Staying locked in my room will not get me anywhere.

The party is being held in a large room with a high ceiling that makes it look like a cave. Several little alcoves in the wall have candles in them, giving a truly spooky vibe to the place. There are tombs everywhere, which are now being used as makeshift tables and seating areas. A DJ has his stuff set up at the end of the chamber, and large speakers, strategically placed throughout, spew out loud techno music.

Some couples are dancing provocatively in the middle of the room. One in particular seems to be going all the way in front of everyone. Then, the male sinks his teeth in the neck of his human partner. She lets out a loud moan, melting against his body.

Aurora yanks me to the side. "Stop gawking as if you've never seen shit like that. You're a vampire for crying out loud."

"He's screwing her in front of everyone while he feeds," I whisper-shout, not hiding the disgust in my tone.

"Vampires don't suffer from fake modesty syndrome."

"Do they always need to fuck when they drink blood?"

"No, but I've been told the experience is very erotic for both parties."

Chills run through my body again. All I felt was terror and repugnance when a vampire fed on me. He might have done more than drink my blood if Rikkon hadn't shown up. The worst part of my story is that my mother had put me in that situation. I avoid thinking about her most of the time, but when I do, all I feel is anger. *How can a mother sell her own daughter like that, to be ravished in more ways than one?*

I avert my gaze from the dance floor and inspect the rest of the party. Small clusters of individuals have formed, and mostly, the attendees are keeping to their own species. It's easy to distinguish between vampires and humans. At first glance, they all seem human, but vampires do have an otherworldly quality to them. Also, the humans are staring at the bloodsuckers as if they were some kind of gods. *Gag me.*

Continuing my perusal, I find a group of people, not human or vampire.

"Who are they?" I ask.

"Familiars. You know that many Bluebloods have them, right?"

"Yeah, I just don't know what they are."

"They were animals certain vampires had more affinity to, changed magically by the Nightingales into human form to serve the Bluebloods. Back when they were first created, familiars could change between animal and human forms at will. But their magic weakened with time, and now, very few familiars can return to their original animal forms."

"I'm sorry. You lost me. Who are the Nightingales?"

Aurora glances at me with a look of pure astonishment. "Oh my God. You're truly clueless, aren't you? The Nightingales created the vampires, and please don't ask me to get into the details about that. It's too long of a story, and we don't want anyone overhearing me explaining Vampire History 101 to you. It'd be suspicious."

"Fine. What about the familiars? Are they immortals too?"

"Yep. Their life force is linked to their vampire's. If the vampire dies, their familiar dies too."

Anger develops in my chest, bubbling up my throat. "So, they're basically slaves then."

"In a way, yeah. But many familiars don't see it that way. They're glad to serve."

I glance at her. "How about you? Are you glad to serve them too?"

Aurora's eyebrows furrow together, and her lips turn into a slash. "The witches' relationship to vampires is different."

"You didn't answer my question."

Her posture becomes tenser, but I don't think it has anything to do with me. She's staring over my shoulder now. Curious, I whirl around, and now, I'm the one turning into stone.

Lucca is here.

12

VIVIENNE

I can't breathe, and my thoughts become vapor as my eyes lock with Lucca's. The hint of a wicked smile unfurls on his cruelly beautiful face, and I swear, I feel the weight of that stare deep in my loins. Our connection is broken when a Blueblood female enters his orbit, curling a possessive arm around his waist. Some horrible new sensation develops in my chest, a stiffness that's filled with anger and pain.

"Who is that?" I ask.

"Therese Schutz, Lucca's main squeeze."

"His girlfriend?" The word leaves a bad taste in my mouth.

Am I jealous of that vampire? If that's true, then I need to be sent to a psych ward.

Aurora scoffs. "She wishes. No, Lucca has never really cared about anyone to commit to a serious relationship."

"He seems tight with his friends."

"Yeah, but that's different. They're like family."

I can't take my eyes off them. Lucca glances in my direction again before pushing Therese away. She follows his line of vision, and almost immediately, her eyes turn to slits.

Shit.

"Oh crap. I think Therese has noticed Lucca's interest in you. You'll have to watch your back with that one."

"Hey, Vivi." Cassie comes over to say hello. "Cool party, huh?"

"Yeah."

Cassie turns her attention to Aurora. "Hi, I'm Cassandra, but everyone calls me Cassie."

"Then why not introduce yourself as Cassie from the get-go?" Aurora replies a little too harshly.

The vampire girl shrinks into herself. "Uh, I don't know."

"Hi, I'm Damon." The lanky guy next to Cassie extends his hand to Aurora.

I think he's another regular. I don't sense a lot of power coming from him.

Aurora drops her gaze to his offered hand, and for a moment, I fear she's going to ignore it. But to my surprise, she shakes hands with the male. She doesn't seem to care much about bloodsuckers. It seems we're in the same boat, forced into an unpleasant situation thanks to family obligations.

"Making new friends, Aurora?" a seductive male voice asks from behind us.

Tension takes hold of me when one of Lucca's friends, the blond vampire who looks like a rock star, stops next to the witch. By the glower she's aiming in his direction, I don't think she's happy to see him.

"Piss off, Saxon."

"Ooh, I love when you talk dirty." He laughs, unfazed by her angry reply. He turns to me, giving me a once-over. "Who do we have here?"

"My name is Vivienne." I cross my arms, hella uncomfortable by his proximity.

He was the one who stopped me from escaping Lucca back at the night in Havoc.

The music changes to a mellow song, and Saxon peers across the room. "What fresh hell is this?"

He speed-walks toward the DJ booth and pushes the guy off his station. In an instant, the music changes back to techno.

"Oh my God. Saxon is so hot. I'd do anything for him to notice me," Cassie says, watching the Blueblood with open admiration.

"Please don't talk about hot Blueblood vampires in front of regular males," Damon pipes up. "We already suffer from an inferiority complex as it is."

I can't tell if he's joking or not.

"Saxon is a narcissist ass. I'd stay away from him," Aurora adds before walking away.

Uh, bad blood between her and the blond vampire?

Cassie and Damon engage in a conversation about where they're from, and since I'd rather not participate, my attention is free to search for Lucca again in the crowd. My mission is to get closer to him, but I should be reluctant to do so, not feel this insane pull toward him. The first time I laid my eyes on him at Havoc, I was terrified beyond my wits. I know I came close to dying that night by his hands, so logically and considering my past, I should be a hundred times more afraid than before. He must have put a spell on me. That's the only explanation.

I don't find him right away. It's so dark in here. It's probably perfect for vampires since they can see better at night than humans. After a minute or so, I see him dancing with a human. She's all over him, writhing her body against his as if she were trying to become one with him. My hands curl into fists without me willing them so. Lucca turns the human around, so her back is now pressed against his chest. Still mimicking a sex act as they dance, Lucca brushes her hair aside and licks her neck. She lets out a content moan, arching her back like a fucking whore. I hate her immediately.

He glances at me and then takes a bite, keeping our stares locked as he feeds. I refuse to look away first even though the sight sickens me. A small, demented part of me wants to be the human in his arms, and that's what bothers me the most.

Someone touches my arm, making me jump.

"Hey, Vivi. Damon and I are going to get something to eat. Do you want to come?"

The mention of food makes my stomach rumble loudly. I can't remember the last time I ate.

Damon laughs. "I guess that answers it."

"Where are you going?" I ask.

"To the feeding room. The humans here are for the Bluebloods only."

Fuck. I can't go with them. I need to find real food.

"Uh, actually, I'm going to pass. There are blood bags in my apartment. I'll eat later."

"Gross." Cassie twists her nose. "Why would you eat that when you could have fresh blood?"

Shit. Think fast, Vivi. Think fast.

"I'm a shy eater. I don't like to feed in front of others."

Cassie and Damon trade a glance.

"Your family must have been well-to-do then. Remember the time when we had to hunt for our meals, Cassie?" Damon asks.

"Oh my God. Those were the worst times. Sometimes, we had to wait days without a single human to get by."

"Wait, did you used to feed from unwilling humans before?" I ask before I can stop myself.

Cassie and Damon are staring at me like I've grown a second head.

"Duh, of course. Back in the old days, our kind was perceived as monsters, demons even. Very few humans offered their blood to us of their own free will," she replies.

"And the few who did wanted to be turned."

"But only Bluebloods have the power to do so," she adds.

I'm shocked about all this even though I shouldn't be. I can't believe how quickly I forgot that Cassie is a vampire, and to me, they're all monsters.

"Well, we're going now. Are you sure you don't want to come?" Cassie asks again.

"Yeah, I'm good. I might just head back to my apartment soon."

"Okay. We'll be back in thirty minutes or so. If you're not here, we'll see you tomorrow."

I watch Cassie and Damon walk away until they disappear into the darkness. Then, I search for Aurora again. Witches eat real food; maybe she can hook me up. I definitely don't want to go on an exploration mission through the institute, looking for food. If I get caught munching on a cracker, it will be hard to explain.

I catch a flash of white hair in the crowd. It's Manu, so I steer in the opposite direction. There's a catacomb being used as a table with refreshments, and upon closer inspection, I see that there's actual booze here. Tequila, whiskey, and even Baileys. Hmm, that has a milk quality to it. Maybe if I drink some, it will hold me over. I just have to be careful not to drink too much.

"Hey," says one regular next to me. "How can you drink that stuff and not get sick?"

"Huh?"

Lucca drank what I gave him at the club without a second thought. The red Solo cup gets knocked out of my hand before I have the chance to ask about his remark.

"What the hell!" I glare at the person responsible, who turns out to be Therese, Lucca's fuck buddy.

She invades my personal space, pointing a manicured finger at my face. "I don't know what hole you crawled from, but let me make myself very clear: stay away from Lucca."

I step back, hating that I can't say what's stuck in my throat out of fear I'll be discovered. One single strike from this bitch, and I'll bleed, revealing my secret. I also don't think I could win a fight against her. She's a Blueblood, and I'm only a puny human.

"Like I want to get close to that jackass."

Her lips curl into a cruel smile. "Oh, darling. Everyone wants to get close to him. You've been warned."

When she walks away, I find Aurora looking at me from across the room. She seems worried, but I can't tell in the gloom. *Fuck.* I think I've had enough of this party.

"Here." Someone offers me a napkin.

Mad as I am, I accept the offer without looking up. "Thanks."

"So, you really don't want to get close to me, huh?"

I freeze and then slowly turn around. Standing next to me with a shit-eating grin is none other than Lucca.

13

LUCCA

~━══╡❯───

I saw the exact moment Therese set her eyes on Vivienne. She was alone and distracted, and like I had predicted, Therese didn't waste any time in marking her territory. I moved closer, keeping myself concealed until Therese walked away.

Now, Vivienne is staring at me like a deer caught in headlights. It's an adorable look on her, if I'm being honest with myself. It makes me want to do bad things to her, like fuck her against the wall while I drink from her sweet neck.

"Where the hell did you come from?" she asks.

"What do you mean? I was standing right here." I smile, showing my fangs.

"You were obviously hidden since your girlfriend had no idea you were here either."

"What makes you think she didn't know?"

Her eyebrows arch ever so slightly before they furrow together.

"Fine. She's as sick as you are."

She makes a motion to walk around me, but I grab her arm.

"Where are you going? I'm not done with you yet."

I read the fight gathering in her stormy eyes. She's afraid, but I think the hatred she feels for me is winning. Many theories run through my head in the blink of an eye. Here, I have a terrified, feisty human, risking her life to steal from me. I missed a lot of things during my long hibernation, but no one has mentioned anything about the resurrection of the Van Helsing movement. The man and his followers had a sick obsession with hunting us down. *Could she be part of their cult?*

"What do you want from me?" She lifts her chin in a defiant manner, trying to show a brave face.

I know that's not what she truly wanted to say though.

"Dance with me."

Her bee-stung lips make a perfect O, and my cock responds immediately. I'm lusting for this thief like I've never done for any human before in all my five hundred and twenty-one years of existence.

"But … I'm all sticky."

I ignore her weak excuse, grabbing her by the hips and bringing her flush against my body. Tense and shaking nonstop, she rests her hands on my biceps and maintains her gaze fixed on the hollow of my throat. Maybe she's trying to see if I'm wearing the necklace she covets.

The reminder of why she's here renews my anger. For a moment, I let my attraction to her distract me from my end goal. I sink my fingers harder into her hips, bringing her closer. I'm rocking a major boner now, and I'm sure she can't miss that. Her breathing changes;

it becomes shallow. Finally, her fear is the winning emotion now. *Good.* I was beginning to think I'd lost my touch.

"Relax, honey. I'm not going to bite," I whisper in her ear, but it's not the smart thing to do.

Her blood is calling to me. I hear it pumping in her veins loud and clear. It's like a luring symphony designed to make me lose control. The urge to feed hits me hard, and I'm salivating already. Before I know it, I'm licking her neck. She gasps and then shivers even more. Her fingers curl around the fabric of my jacket, and I don't know if she's trying to push me away or melt into me.

"You said you weren't going to bite." Her voice is feeble, almost a whisper.

I snap away from her neck, noticing the little marks my teeth left behind. Fuck, I didn't realize how close I was to puncturing her skin. As much as I want to punish Vivienne, I don't want to expose her secret right away. And feeding from her will surely reveal she's not a vampire.

"I'm not. I prefer human blood. It tastes that much sweeter, don't you think?" I watch her closely, catching the wince.

"Uh-huh." She glances away.

"So, Vivienne, where are you from?"

"Born and raised in Salem," she answers without pause.

"Really? You were here for the witch trials then?"

It's a known fact that regular vampires haven't been able to procreate in generations. If Vivienne was truly one of us, she'd have been born at least three hundred years ago.

She glances at me with a look of pure anguish in her eyes. *Does she even know that regular vampires aren't popping babies left and right anymore? Who sent her here with so little information about our kind?* There's no way she was able to acquire such a powerful spell of disguise on her own.

"Yeah, I was."

"Tell me then, how was it?"

"What do you mean, how was it? Awful, obviously." Her indignation is cute. It shows how human she is.

She doesn't know that the trials were simply the outcome of a war between two powerful covens and that the witches who perished were part of the Van Helsing army. They deserved to die.

"I'll take your word for it." I chuckle. "Why do you want to become a Keeper?"

"I'm a regular. It's the only chance to have a better existence. Bluebloods have no idea how difficult life for us regulars is."

I'm taken aback by her answer. Immediately, I know those aren't her words. She heard it from another regular. In the back of my mind, I knew regulars had a harder time with getting by. Many migrated to Salem because it's the only place in the world where humans are aware of our existence and mostly okay with it. But in other cities, vampires have to hide and scavenge for human blood. There are blood brothels everywhere, but they aren't cheap.

"You decided to pledge your life to defend one of us?"

She blinks a couple of times, almost as if that's the first time she's heard any of this. *Fuck, didn't Hanson cover the basics of his program with prospects before they were accepted?* That male needs to go. But that's a problem for another time.

"I guess I did," she replies.

Unable to resist, I caress her cheek. Her skin is so soft and warm; it makes it really hard for me to resist taking a bite. The hunger is still present, swirling in my chest, begging to be set free. But right now, I'm able to fight it. As long as she doesn't bleed, I'll be fine.

"What do you want from me?" she asks, not taking her eyes from mine.

I run my hand up and down the side of her torso, purposely brushing my fingers near her breast. "Many things, Vivienne."

Her eyelids drop, and a hint of desire shines in her blue eyes. "Make your girlfriend jealous?"

I rub my thumb over her lower lip, dying for a taste, while the corners of my lips twitch up. "I don't have a girlfriend."

I'm an inch away from her mouth, ready to claim her lips, when the back of my neck prickles. I stand up straight at once, curling my lips into a sneer when I spot Boone and his followers at the entrance of the party.

Motherfucker.

14

VIVIENNE

———◆———

Lucca pushes me away like I'm nothing but a toy he's done playing with and faces the white-blond vampire who attacked me at Havoc. A rough hand grabs my arm and pulls me back. It's Saxon of all people.

"You'd better stay out of range, sweetheart," he says before stepping nearer his friend.

My body is still on fire from the close proximity to Lucca, but quickly, the lust vanishes as I get blasted by the stark reality. Lucca's posture is tense, ready to strike. It seems to me that everyone here is sitting at the edge of their seats, waiting for the worst to happen.

"You really have some nerve, showing up here," Lucca says through clenched teeth.

The evil Blueblood smiles. "I was invited, buddy. Times have changed, and you're no longer the prince around here."

"This pathetic truce means nothing to me. If you want to keep your head attached to your body, I suggest you leave now." Lucca's hands turn into sharp claws.

I can't see his face, but I'm sure he looks like the monster he truly is. And I almost kissed that monster.

Aurora stands next to me. "I don't think you should stay, Vivi. Things can get lethal pretty fast."

"What's going on? Why does Lucca want to shred that vampire to pieces?"

Not that I'd care one bit. He's the foulest creature that has ever come near me, worse even than the vampire I was sold to. I don't know why he felt that wrong, that depraved.

"Boone is Tatiana's son. He tried to kill Lucca before, and he almost succeeded."

"Am I supposed to know who Tatiana is?" I whisper back.

"Girl, you're truly clueless."

Boone throws his head back and laughs, a gesture that his companions follow. "Lucca, you're fucking hilarious. You can't touch me. If you hurt me—which I doubt you could—your uncle will pay the ultimate price."

"What the hell are you talking about?" Lucca growls.

Boone switches his attention to Manu, who is standing by her brother's side, also as tense as a coiled spring. Next to her, a massive Blueblood is watching Boone like a hawk. He's part of Lucca's inner circle. He has a don't-mess-with-me attitude, which, paired with his Viking warrior physique, can really put the fear in the heart of any creature—I bet even the dragon kingpin Larsson.

But Boone doesn't seem to care when he switches his attention to him. "You didn't tell Luc boy here about the details of the Accords?"

"King Raphael never agreed with those terms, so there's nothing to tell," he replies.

"Oh, is that the lie he told you lot? He did agree, signed in blood. The witch's spawn there can testify to it. Her mother was there."

Everyone turns to stare at Aurora. Her jaw clenches hard, and when Lucca focuses on her, she answers the question displayed in his gaze. "It's true. If any of King Raphael's followers hurt Tatiana's sympathizers unprovoked, he loses the crown."

Lucca's face contorts into an expression of pure fury. Even though he's not aiming the aggression at me, I feel it deep in my bones.

Boone smiles smugly. "You can't touch me, asshole."

"Maybe I didn't make myself clear, bonehead." Aurora speaks loudly. "*Unprovoked.* If you step out of line, anyone here can put you back in your place, which is at the bottom of a sewage lake."

"You little bitch." He advances in her direction, faster than a bullet. But before he can strike Aurora, he bounces off an invisible barrier, falling on his ass.

Half the room snickers; the other half doesn't know what to do.

"Go now," Aurora urges me in a whisper. "This will get ugly."

Despite my curiosity about vampire history, it's not worth risking my life. I slide to the side, trying to disappear into the shadows. But there are people in my way, so sneaking out easily and unseen doesn't seem to be in the cards for me.

Boone is back on his feet, staring daggers in Aurora's direction. Lucca hasn't changed his stance yet. I don't think he will relax until the jackass Blueblood is gone. I finally manage to break through the wall of bodies in my way toward the exit when Boone grabs my arm.

"Where do you think you're going in such a hurry, darling? The party has ju—" His tirade is cut short when Lucca tosses him across the room.

"Don't touch her," he snarls, stalking in his direction.

Boone is already standing, baring his teeth and dark claws at Lucca. "You just sealed your fate, motherfucker. I can end you now without fear of prosecution."

"End me? Aren't you delusional," Lucca taunts.

They clash in the middle of the room, a blur of blows and swings. I can only see them when one or the other gets shoved against a wall. Boone gets pushed more often than Lucca, and every time he gets knocked down, his fury increases. But it's Lucca who gets my attention the most. He's not holding back, displaying his savagery for everyone to see. The scene should repel me, make me run for the hills, but instead, I'm drawn to his bloodlust. I want him to tear Boone to pieces and bathe in his blood.

Fuck. What am I turning into? A vampire groupie? A blood whore?

Lucca has Boone pinned to the floor, holding his enemy by the neck while his other clawed hand is ready to deliver the final blow—to pierce his chest and rip his heart out.

"Enough!" A stern woman appears in the room.

All the lights from the candles glow brighter, allowing me to see her features more clearly. She looks familiar, but it's not until Aurora steps closer to her that I see the connection. That must be her mother.

But Lucca doesn't move, nor does he show any inclination that he wants to let Boone go. His friends have to drag him off the vampire, who doesn't get up. I can only see a few scratches on his face, nothing to warrant his immobility. When he starts to moan and bitch about his nonexistent wounds, I see what he's doing. He's milking it to get Lucca in trouble.

Aurora's mother approaches him. "Oh, come on already. You're not hurt."

"He attacked me, unprovoked," Boone whines, earning a snort from both Aurora and Saxon.

"You went after Lucca's date. I wouldn't call that unprovoked," Manu retorts.

Boone sits up and glares at me. "That's his date? A regular? Yeah, no one believes that excuse."

"I don't care about the reason for this ridiculous fight. If you can't behave your age, pack your shit and leave." The witch stares at Boone and Lucca. "Both of you."

She turns to the exit and glances at her daughter. "You, come with me."

Aurora sighs loudly and then spares a fleeting glance in Saxon's direction. He gives her two thumbs-up and a silly-ass grin. I'm not sure what their exchange means. But there are more pressing problems to worry about. Manu just declared Lucca fought because of me, which puts a target on my back. I'm way too visible now, and that's very bad news for me. One false move, one wrong answer, and the truth will be exposed.

That should be the height of my concerns, but there's something else competing for space in my head—the idea that Lucca might crave me. And I don't mind that one bit.

15

VIVIENNE

———◆———

When I finally got back to my apartment in the early hours of the morning, I was exhausted but also light-headed, thanks to the lack of food. To my surprise, I found a couple of Snickers hidden under my pillow. Starving, I inhaled them without stopping to consider their source. Lucky for me, it wasn't a prank. I suspected Aurora had left the gift for me. How she'd gotten in, I didn't know, but I wasn't going to complain to her about privacy when she was feeding me.

Despite everything, I slept like the dead, only waking up because of Manu's loud banging in the kitchen. Pissed off with the noise, I jump out of bed. Still half-asleep, I march to the common area, ready to kick up a storm.

"What's with the ruckus …" I trail off when I see the scene I've walked in on.

Manu is not alone. She's currently latched on to an attractive guy's neck while he fucks her on the counter. Heat spreads up my neck and cheeks. I retreat slowly, trying not to make a sound.

I don't leave my room until I'm positive I'm alone in the apartment.

Tiptoeing, I head for the front door. My hand is around the doorknob when I sense Manu's presence behind me.

"Did you enjoy the show, *roomie?*"

I don't turn around, or she will notice my red face. Do vampires even blush? Maybe she won't see my reaction, thanks to the spell.

"I'm sorry. I didn't know you had company."

"You're not embarrassed, are you?"

I laugh to hide exactly that. "No. Why would I be?"

"Prove it. Turn around, so I can look at your face."

Sighing, I do as she said, trying to school my expression into a neutral zone. "There. Satisfied?"

"Yeah, you're totally embarrassed. Don't tell me you're one of those prude regulars who doesn't screw your humans while you feed."

Shit. I don't know how to answer that. If I say I do, will she be able to tell the lie? God, the furthest I've gone with a guy was giving a blow job to my sophomore-year boyfriend. We broke up soon after because I didn't want to go all the way.

"Sometimes, but I like to feed in private."

"This is my apartment. It doesn't get any more private than that."

I want to say, *Your room is more private*, but I keep the comment to myself. She seems to be in a good mood, and there's no reason to change that.

"Okay then. I'll try to not walk in on you while you feed."

She shrugs. "I don't care either way."

I don't breathe easily until I put a good distance between myself and my apartment. I meet up with Cassie and Damon at the bottom of the stairs, and we head together to our first Keepers class. I'm nervous about it. I don't want to mess up and hurt myself in front of everyone. But those worrisome thoughts get pushed aside when all Cassie and Damon want to know about is the fight between Lucca and Boone.

"Is it true that Lucca fought him because of you?" Cassie asks.

"I don't think so."

"That's what everyone is talking about," Damon interjects.

"Manu had to say that, so Lucca wouldn't get in trouble. You know he can't fight Boone unprovoked."

"Yeah, that's thanks to the Accords." Damon looks left and right in a cagey manner. "Between us, I think the Accords are totally BS. Tatiana waged war against the rightful king for centuries, and now, they're at peace? Many of the king's supporters are livid, and there've been talks of rebellion."

"Really?" I say.

"Oh, come on, Damon. Those rumors are crazy nonsense. Everyone loves King Raphael."

"No, *half* the vampire population loves him. The other half loves his former betrothed."

"Wait, former betrothed?" I ask.

Cassie and Damon stop to stare at me in a funny way.

"Please tell me you know Tatiana was once promised to marry King Raphael," Cassie replies.

Oh shit. I should have known that. Ugh. Big, stupid mouth.

"Oh, yeah. Of course. Duh. I thought you were talking about

someone else."

"Who else? King Raphael hasn't been linked to anyone romantically after that fiasco engagement," Damon supplies.

"Oh, that's not true," Cassie retorts. "There were rumors that he actually fell in love with a Van Helsing."

"Shut up." Damon shakes his head and laughs. "That's a total lie, fabricated by humans."

We continue our trek to the classroom, but I keep my mouth shut while I absorb as much information as I can from Cassie and Damon's argument.

"No, it wasn't. I'm telling you, he did fall in love with a Van Helsing; that's why he broke off the engagement with Tatiana. She then killed the girl, and thus began Abraham Van Helsing's obsession with killing all of us."

"You're crazy. Why must females be such hopeless romantics?" Damon asks me.

"Who says I'm a romantic?"

"Riiight." He stops in front of the classroom and swings his arm toward it. "Ladies first."

There are fifteen students in total in this class. Five are novices, including Cassie and me. Damon has been here for over a year. No one gives a fig about my companions, but they sure are interested in me. *Damn. So much for wishing vampires had a short memory.*

Hanson, the class's instructor, joins us in the middle of the gym. He walks over to the table where five new shiny blades are displayed. "These are the blades each of the novices will practice with. By the end of this program, they'll become an extension of your bodies."

"Do we get to practice with them now?" Cassie asks eagerly.

"No. Today, we'll practice with the bo staff. It's an ancient form of battle that relies heavily on dexterity, agility, and flexibility."

Each student in the circle collects a staff from next to the table. I follow Cassie, grabbing my weapon, mega happy that I won't have to handle sharp objects today.

For the next five minutes, Hanson explains some basic moves to the newbies while the seasoned students practice on their own. It's hard not to look. They move fast, like ninjas, and they aren't Bluebloods.

How in the world am I going to pretend I possess vampire reflexes and speed? God, this will be a fucking disaster.

Hanson then pairs us up, so we can practice. We're an odd number, so I'm the unlucky one to get stuck with him.

"All right, we're doing the first advance movement. Let's see what you've got. Attack me." He positions his staff in a defensive stance.

I do as he said, but my hit does nothing to him. I don't even make him step backward. It's like I just hit a marble statue.

"What the hell was that, Vivienne? Attack me like you mean it. Remember, you'll be defending a Blueblood. You can't half-ass your way through it."

I have no idea why vampires think Bluebloods need protection—much less protection provided by regulars. Bluebloods are ten times stronger and faster than regulars. So, what's the deal? By a miracle, I keep all these comments bottled up inside.

"I'm not trying to half-ass my way through anything. I've never handled a staff before."

"You're not even holding it right." He drops his weapon to the floor and circles around me.

He guides my hands to the proper position, but all I can think about is that he's too close, and my panic is rising. It doesn't help that he smells like the vampire who attacked me, who had a preference for a sickly-sweet perfume.

"I-I think I've got it," I say.

The gym door opens with a loud bang, prompting Hanson to step away from me. I breathe out loudly in relief, but it's short-lived. Lucca and his friends are the newcomers. My heart continues to beat at a faster pace, but it's not because I'm panicking. It's excitement that's screwing with my pulse.

When did I make the switch in relation to Lucca? It has been only a few days since he threatened to kill me. He's not treating me with animosity now because he thinks I'm one of them. *What's going to happen if he discovers my deception?*

Stupid is as stupid does. That's for sure. I've turned into a walking cliché, yearning for the bad boy. *Fuck me.*

I can't let lust cloud my judgment, distract me from my end goal. My brother needs me. God knows what Larsson is doing to him.

"Lucca, to what do I owe the honor of your presence here?" Hanson asks, not hiding the contempt in his voice.

With an arrogant smirk, he replies, "I came to see firsthand what your Keepers training program is all about."

"I suppose since you've missed so much, you could benefit from a refresher."

Lucca trades a quick glance with his Viking-looking friend, and then he watches Hanson with eyes that are filled with mirth. "Sure."

No. No. No. If I was nervous before, making a fool out of myself in front of Lucca will turn my jitters into a seizure. My palms are sweating, and I can't hold the damn staff steady. I rest the end on the floor, so it's not obvious that I'm shaking.

"It seems you're a fighter short," Saxon chimes in. "I'll spar with Vivienne."

Lucca sends him a glower, but the male is already walking over, smiling from ear to ear. *Crap.*

"I'm not very good," I say.

"Don't fret, darling. I'll be gentle."

A rogue staff comes flying, hitting him on the back of his head. "Ouch!" He massages the sore spot, glaring over his shoulder in Lucca's direction.

"That's enough," Hanson retorts. "If you came here only to disrupt my lesson, you'd better leave."

"Sorry," Lucca replies. "Ronan and I will just watch for now."

They walk off the tatami, and Hanson resumes his lesson. Saxon assumes a defensive stance while I'm supposed to attack. Not wanting to be the obvious human here, I give my all, remembering the last time we were up and close—aka when he thwarted my escape at Havoc. My arms strain from the blows, and it's sad for me to realize that Saxon is not even trying to block my attacks. But at least he doesn't make any cynical remarks about my lack of skills.

"All right, switch positions," Hanson commands.

Ah hell. Saxon is going to make pâté out of me.

Maybe reading the fear in my eyes, he whispers, "Don't worry. I'll go easy on you."

I raise my staff and brace for his attack. True to his words, he barely makes contact with my weapon. It's like we're rehearsing a fake battle scene for a movie. After a minute or so of this, Hanson notices that Saxon is not really trying and stops our exercise.

"What the hell do you think you're doing?" He glares at my sparring partner.

"You don't seriously expect me to fight an inexperienced regular, do you?" he rebuffs angrily.

"She's never going to improve if she's not challenged."

Lucca snorts. "She's never going to improve, period. None of your students will."

Hanson whirls around. His spine is rigid, and his animosity is clear. "Let me guess. You don't approve of my methods. Why am I not surprised? How about you show the class *your* skills?"

The mischievous smile that blossoms on Lucca's face tells me that's exactly what he was hoping to achieve. I watch him push off the wall and walk over with all the confidence and swagger only a powerful Blueblood vampire can muster.

"Are you challenging me, Hanson?" he asks.

"Yes, I'm challenging you."

He raises his staff, assuming an aggressive stance, but Lucca simply shakes his head and approaches the table where the five daggers meant for us are on display.

"Oh no. If we're putting up a show for your students, we're doing it right."

Lucca picks up a blade and twirls it around his dexterous fingers without even looking at it. If I tried to do that, I'd probably lose one. I have never been quick on my feet. My only true talent is singing, which I'm beginning to miss terribly. I wonder what Karl, Cheryl, and Vaughn are doing right now.

Hanson drops his staff and grabs a dagger as well. Saxon steers me off the tatami, and the other students follow suit. Lucca and Hanson begin to circle each other, and once again, I become enthralled by Lucca's movements. His eyes are narrowed, and his body is ready, but there's no tension around his mouth. He seems amused.

Hanson makes the first move, going on the offensive. Lucca easily evades the attack, circling around his opponent with the grace of a dancer. No, that's not the right way to describe him. Lucca is a predator, nimble as a panther.

This dance continues for another minute until Lucca, instead of sliding away from Hanson's attack, blocks his blow. What happens next is too fast for me to follow with my human eyes. There seems to be a lot of slashing though, but the fight is over after less than a minute when Hanson's dagger flies out of his hand and Lucca's blade presses against his neck.

"It seems to me you're the one in need of a refresher," Lucca says, cold and hard, before stepping away.

He glances at me then, and holy baby llamas, a surge of heat comes from deep in my belly, spreading like wildfire through my veins. His eyes have a hint of red, and when he smiles, the tips of his fangs show. Once again, I don't understand why I'm not repulsed or afraid of him.

Before I combust on the spot, I switch my attention to Hanson. My fire is doused when I read the pure hatred shining in his eyes as he glowers in Lucca's direction.

Shit. He just made an enemy.

I can't believe this. I'm actually worried now about the dark prince. *Did this damn concealing spell mess up my brain?*

16

VIVIENNE

Lucca and his entourage left soon after he humiliated Hanson. During the rest of the class, the male vampire took out his frustrations on us. He had special words to describe how useless we all were, and by the end of the lesson, not only was my self-esteem down in the sewers, but Cassie's and Damon's were as well.

"Damn, that was rough," Damon says. "Could you please tell your boyfriend to not show up anymore in our class?"

"My boyfriend?" I squeak. "Don't be ludicrous."

"Boyfriend or not, there was clearly a pissing contest back there," Cassie adds.

"It's not my fault Bluebloods feel the need to compete about the sizes of their dicks all the time."

Cassie snorts while Damon laughs out loud.

"So, you're thinking about dicks, huh?" he says.

Heat creeps up my neck, spreading through my cheeks. I *am*

thinking about Lucca's dick now, and the thought is making me hot and bothered. *Shit.*

A commotion ahead rescues my mind from the gutter. There's a circle of students shouting and waving their arms in a manic manner.

"Uh-oh, let's find another way to Etiquette class," Damon says.

"Why? What's going—"

Someone grabs my arm hard and steers me toward the crowd.

"Hey! Let go of me."

"Shut up, fresh meat. It's time for you to pay your dues," a wiry Blueblood male retorts.

"What?" I look over my shoulder, seeing that both Damon and Cassie are also being dragged by other Bluebloods.

Before I can make eye contact with Damon and ask what the hell is going on, I'm shoved forward, landing inside the circle next to another regular. She's crying already.

When Damon and Cassie join us, I ask, "What's this?"

"The welcome committee has found us," Damon replies with a grimace. "Every year, a group of Bluebloods makes it their mission to prank newcomers."

"But you're not a newcomer," Cassie argues.

"Apparently, it doesn't matter. I'm hanging out with you guys, so I'm fair game."

"Prank us? What does that mean?" I ask through my growing panic.

"I don't know. Each year, the prank is different."

A tanned male with black-blue hair jumps in the circle, and at once, the crowd quiets down. "Welcome, everyone, to this year's fresh-meat party. It has been a while since we had new regulars join our prestigious school. And thanks to that, we've been deprived of some good old fun."

Shouts of agreement echo all around us.

Fucking great. I hope their idea of fun is not cutting us to bits.

I'm sandwiched now between Cassie and Damon, which helps me a little with the shakes but not by much.

"What are you going to do to us?" a brave male across from us asks.

"Do? I'm not going to hurt you. Sadly, that's not allowed anymore." He does look upset about that part. *Fucker.*

He signals at someone in the crowd, who hands over a large black plastic bag to the male in charge.

"Since we're so close to All Hallows' Eve, I thought it would be fun to find out why humans go nuts over Halloween candy." He turns over the bag, dumping hundreds of delicious treats on the floor.

My stomach rumbles, and my mouth begins to salivate in an instant. The Snickers bars Aurora left in my room didn't even make a dent in my hunger.

"You can't be serious," Damon complains.

The ringleader turns to us with a wicked smile on his face. "Oh, I'm dead serious. I hope you're hungry, fresh meat. Feast."

"What if we don't?" another courageous male asks.

The Blueblood's demeanor changes in the blink of an eye. His green eyes become darker, almost black with a hint of crimson. "Oh, you don't want to find out. We might not be allowed to hurt you, but there are places in the institute where no one can hear you scream."

Goose bumps break out on my arms. I don't think he's bluffing. And neither do any of my companions. They reach for a candy bar with shaking hands. I do the same, but I suspect the tremors running through my body are of hunger, not fear. I grab the biggest chocolate bar I can find and take a large bite without hesitation. It's a struggle not to moan out loud. *God, this tastes good.*

I sense Cassie's and Damon's stares. They haven't eaten their treats yet.

With my mouth still half-full, I ask, "What?"

"I can't believe you just took a huge bite of that disgusting thing without flinching," Cassie says.

Ah damn. I don't know what eating human food does to vampires. My guess is, they find it pretty repugnant, just like I think drinking blood is gross.

"Oh, it seems we have a tough one here, folks." The annoying Blueblood moves closer. He glowers at Cassie and Damon and shouts, "What are you waiting for? Eat!"

I try to make a sickened expression while I swallow a piece of heaven. I'm dying for another bite, but I want to see what the chocolate will do to Cassie and Damon first. Cassie slowly turns green as she chews on a piece of a Snickers bar. By her scrunched-up face, it looks like she's eating poop instead.

"Come on. Don't stop now. Keep eating, fresh meat," the Blueblood yells in my face.

You don't need to ask twice, buddy.

I take another big bite, trying to portray an appearance of defiance and revulsion. So far, the nimrod hasn't realized I'm eating the chocolate with gusto. Damon makes a gagging sound next to me before he spews his guts out.

Gross. Now I want to puke.

Cassie takes another bite. Then, she covers her mouth with her hands and takes off, pushing anyone in her way.

Ah damn. It's my cue. With regret, I toss the unfinished candy bar to the side and follow her into the restroom while the audience behind us hollers and laughs. *Fuckers. All of them.*

I take the stall next to Cassie's, becoming nauseated for real as I listen to her throw up. Sadly, I have to make gagging sounds myself to pretend I'm as sick as her, which ends up forcing the little bit of chocolate I ate to come out.

Kill me now. Vomiting is the worst, and the fact that I didn't even need to be doing this is just the cherry on top. My eyes are watering by the time I'm done.

I flush the toilet and sit down on the tiled floor, wondering when my next meal will be. I begin to imagine the most delicious dishes. Succulent burger with all the works and chili fries, pepperoni pizza, tacos. Ugh! That's it. I have to go in search of human food, even at the risk of being found out. I have to eat.

The toilet next door flushes, and then Cassie's raspy voice calls my name.

"Are you okay?" She knocks on my door.

"Yeah, I'm fine." I jump to my feet and walk out.

Cassie looks positively ill. Her white complexion is even paler, and there are dark circles under her eyes that were most definitely not there before.

What the hell? How bad is human food to vampires? A lot of the vampires at Havoc were drinking alcohol without a problem.

"You look better than me. I can't believe you took such big chunks of that disgusting brown thing." She stares at her reflection in the mirror, and then she splashes cold water on her face.

"That wasn't the first time I had been forced to eat human food."

"Oh? How many times before?" She arches her eyebrows.

I make a noncommittal gesture with my hand. "I don't know. A few times. It was brutal in the beginning."

"I bet. God, it was the first time for me, and not only did it make me ill the moment it touched my tongue, but I felt light-headed too. Human food is poison to us."

"Yeah. Isn't it strange though that we can drink alcohol?"

Her eyebrows furrow. "I can't. Can you?"

Ah shit. Did I say something wrong again?

"Eh, yeah, kind of."

"Damn, Vivi. You're hardcore. Only Bluebloods seem to handle the stuff without getting sick." She narrows her eyes. "Are you sure you're not a Blueblood?"

I snort. *What a ridiculous idea.* "Pfft. Did you not see me in Keepers class?"

"Honestly, I wasn't paying much attention to anybody. I was too busy trying not to screw up."

I shove my hands into my pockets. "Well, I sucked harder than a starving vampire."

Shaking her head, she laughs. "You say the strangest things."

"Yes, I'm a weirdo. Let's see if Damon survived."

I'm also hoping there's some candy left that I can sneak into my pocket.

But the moment I step foot outside the restroom, my brilliant plan to scavenge for food is forgotten. Lucca is waiting for me.

"There you are." He walks over. "Got rid of all that nasty shit already?"

"How do you know I was forced to eat candy?" I ask.

"You don't know? It was my idea." He smiles like the devil that he is. "Gordon couldn't come up with anything grand, so I gave him the suggestion."

From the corner of my eye, I catch Cassie slinking away. I'd stop her, but I don't want to end my current staring contest with Lucca.

"That was mean," I say.

"Nah, that was tame compared to the good old days."

"You mean, before your grandpa nap?" I raise an eyebrow, not knowing where the sassy remarks are coming from.

This is Lucca, the most powerful Blueblood in the entire institute. Even staying as far away from the bloodsuckers as I could, I've heard stories about him.

He pinches his lips, narrowing his eyes. "I think I've had enough of smart-talking from you. Come on. I'm here to take you to a proper feeding. I could hear your stomach growling from the other side of the institute."

He grabs my hand, and I freeze. "Feeding?"

The corners of his lips turn upward. "Yep. Let's take care of that hunger of yours."

17

LUCCA

＊

I'm enjoying the feeling of Vivienne's hand in mine too much. She's a human, a thief. I can't allow myself to relish anything besides torturing her. When Gordon came to me to whine about the new rules at the institute, I couldn't have thought of a better prank. Vivienne is starving, and since vampires become physically ill if we eat an ounce of human food, she's in a tight spot. If she's caught eating anything, she'll be exposed for the fraud that she is. There's human food around—familiars and our snacks must eat—but getting to it is the issue.

She didn't notice my presence, but I was there, watching her squirm as she tried to appear revulsed by what she was eating when in fact she wanted to gobble it all down. I can't wait to see how she'll get out of this new situation I'm forcing

The feeding room is mostly used by regulars. Many humans come here to serve as nourishment for our kind. We pay them, but there's a selection process. The younger, more attractive humans are reserved for Bluebloods. What's left is shared by the rest. Since Blueblood money pays for the snacks, it's more than fair that we take the best.

But not even the most beautiful humans are giving me what I need. All I can think about when I feed is Vivienne. I haven't even fucked any of the girls who begged to feed me, and I've felt unfulfilled after each meal.

I steal a glance in her direction. Her stubborn chin is raised high, but her mouth is tense, and her brows are furrowed. Her hand is sweating in mine, which would be a major turnoff in any other circumstance. She's terrified of what might happen in the feeding room. I wonder if she'll actually try to drink from another human.

This is going to be very entertaining.

We turn a corner, almost at our destination, when Therese decides to show up and sour my mood. She blocks my path, spares a scathing glance in Vivienne's direction, and then turns her displeased gaze on me.

"Lucca, I was wondering where you were. Aren't you going to the Living in a Digital World class?"

"No."

My simple answer doesn't sit well with her. Tough shit. We had good times together; I won't deny it. But I don't care for her enough to make an eternal commitment like some vampires do. Mating was a thing back in the old days, but it has become less and less important now that we can't procreate anymore.

"Where are you going with her?"

"I don't see why I have to tell you that."

Vivienne's hand tenses in mine. I'm sure she wants to run away now that Therese is wasting my time. But I tighten my hold and then do one better as I rub my thumb over her wrist. Her pulse accelerates with the touch, and her breathing becomes shallow.

"Fine. Have your fun with this filthy whore. You'll get tired of her eventually and come running back to me, like you always do."

I open my mouth to reply, but Vivienne beats me to it.

"I'm not a whore," she says through clenched teeth.

"Who says you can speak to me, bitch?" Therese turns to the human, body poised to strike.

She would have, too, if I hadn't stepped in front of Vivienne. She's my toy, my prey, and no one else can touch her.

"Get lost already, Therese. Desperation is a very unattractive trait."

"Fuck off, Lucca. You're not the only royal in town."

She strides away, but her comment gets to me. *Who the fuck is she referring to?* She'd better not be speaking about Boone, that rat who deserves nothing but a slow death.

"Ow!" Vivienne complains.

"What?" I snap, still riding on the anger triggered by Therese's comment.

"My hand. You're going to crush all the bones."

Hell. I didn't realize what I had been doing. I release the pressure but don't apologize. She doesn't deserve any kindness from me.

"Let's go already."

"Oh, like it's my fault we stopped."

Where is this feistiness coming from? She was a meek, trembling human when we first met. It seems that by pretending to be one of us, she's gained some courage. I like this new version. It will be much more fun to punish her when she's putting up a fight. I've never cared for cowards.

Since classes are in session at this hour, the feeding room is almost empty. The few regulars waiting in line do pay attention to us though. All thanks to Manu's lie that I fought Boone to defend Vivienne. And now, I'm escorting her. To the rumor mill, we're an item now. Relationship gossip is not something I care for. I only pay attention to whispers when it's related to politics.

The coordinator, a regular vampire who stopped aging when he turned around fifty, walks over with his clipboard in hand. "May I help you, sir?"

"Yes. My friend needs to feed." I shove Vivienne forward. "Please pick a fresh one. She hasn't eaten in a while."

He gives her a stern look. "Not feeding regularly is not smart, young lady. It can trigger bloodlust, and no one wants to deal with the aftermath of that. Come on; follow me."

He turns around, making a tsk sound. Vivienne doesn't move though.

"What's the matter, sugar?" I ask in my most seductive voice.

"I don't like to feed in public," she replies without meeting my stare.

"Nonsense. All vampires do. It's in our nature. Unless there's a reason you're being picky about who sees you chomping down on some delectable human." I smile, knowing very well what my comment will trigger.

She whips her face to mine with eyes as round as saucers. "No reason."

The coordinator, finally noticing that Vivienne didn't follow him, calls her name.

I place my hand on her lower back and push her forward. "Come on. It won't be that hard. As a matter of fact, I'm going to watch it, so you can practice feeding with an audience."

She's shaking more violently than before, but she doesn't try to convince me to leave. We reach the booth where a plump, middle-aged woman is waiting. She glances at Vivienne with an air of bored resignation, but when she turns to me, her dull eyes sparkle.

"Oh, I didn't know I was feeding a Blueblood," she says.

"You're not. She's the one in need of some nourishment." I give Vivienne a nudge toward the human, and then I pull up a chair to enjoy the show more comfortably.

"Hi," she says shyly.

The older woman sighs loudly, cocking her head to the side to expose her neck. Vivienne is at a complete loss of what to do. She doesn't even know how to position herself. Finally, she settles for standing behind the woman, who is shorter than her. She opens her mouth, revealing sharp fangs that I know are fake. I've looked up the type of spell she's using. Everything we see is an illusion. Vivienne's teeth are blunt, like always.

Before she takes a bite, she lifts her eyes to mine. Something indiscernible flashes in them, and I hate that it came and went too fast for me to comprehend. She closes her eyes and bites the woman's neck like she means business. But since she doesn't have sharp teeth, nor does she produce the special pheromone that makes humans relax when we puncture their skins, the woman lets out a scream.

Vivienne jumps back while the human turns around, pressing her hand to her neck.

"What did you do to me?" she asks.

"I'm sorry."

There's a hint of blood on her lips. She was actually going to drink from a fellow human.

Why does she want my necklace so badly that she would go through all the obstacles and dangers to accomplish her goal? Who is she really?

The coordinator comes rushing by, clipboard in hand. He stares at Vivienne first and then at the blubbering woman. "What happened?"

"I don't know. Her bite, it hurt too much. This has never happened before," the woman replies.

"I think Vivienne has forgotten how to feed properly. You know how it is with regulars; they have no manners," I say.

"Ugh, I'm so sorry," she says again before she takes off.

She's covering her face, but I smell her tears anyway.

That's right. Cry, little thief, and get used to it.

18

VIVIENNE

———◆———

I tried to be strong. I thought that if I drank only a little bit, Lucca would leave me alone. But he stayed, and I messed up. Of course my bite would hurt that poor human. It's not like I have real sharp fangs or the venom in them that makes humans pliable.

I still remember my first bite. It hurt like a mother, but I think it was only because the regular enjoyed making his victims suffer. A lot of bloodsuckers thrive on human pain, and I bet Lucca is one of them. If he can find humor in torturing one of his own—fake-vampire me—then he will do much worse when he finds out I'm the human who poisoned him.

I'm crying, which sucks, but it doesn't suck harder than bumping into a brick wall as I try to escape to my apartment. I don't need to look up to guess who I collided with. Immediately, the putrid smell wafting off him makes me gag.

"Where are you going in such a hurry, fresh meat?" He holds

me by the arms, digging his nails into my jacket.

"Let go." I try to break free, but it only makes him dig his nails in further.

If he keeps applying pressure, he's going to make me bleed. I can't have that, so I stop struggling at once.

"Ah, that's much better. Now, let's see what Lucca finds so fascinating about you."

With a flick of his hand, he rips the first three buttons off my shirt, exposing my bra. My pulse skyrockets, and I think I might be sick for real. This is déjà vu, and when Boone fixates his hungry gaze on my neck, I wince, dreading what's sure to come. He's going to bite me and then probably rip my throat open once he tastes my human blood.

"Leave me alone," I beg, hating how I can barely utter those words.

"I don't think so. Lucca likes you, so I must make you suffer."

A great force collides with Boone, sending him flying backward. He lands on the floor with a loud thud and continues to slide down the hallway until he hits the far wall. Lucca is suddenly in front of me but only for a second.

He breaks into a run, not bothering to use his super-speed this time. It's almost like he wants Boone to see him approach. The other vampire jumps back to his feet and bares his fangs. He tries to catch Lucca with a swipe of his arm, but he twists out of range, jumping at an almost-horizontal angle to land behind Boone. In the next moment, Lucca lashes Boone's face with his nails, leaving four angry, bloody gashes.

Boone cries out, enraged, turning to retaliate. Lucca is already out of reach but far from done. A shiny blade drops from his sleeve, similar to the daggers we used in class today.

Oh no. Is he going to kill Boone?

As much as I want the other vampire gone, Lucca can't hurt him. He'll be punished, and I can't let him get in trouble on my account, no matter how awful he is.

I hear running footsteps behind me. I hope whoever is coming is not one of Boone's friends. I look over my shoulder, relieved to see a vampire wearing a jacket with the institute's emblem. He must work here. The male steps in between Lucca and Boone, but he glares only at Lucca.

"What do you think you're doing?" he shouts.

"Fuck off. This doesn't concern you." Lucca shoves the male to the side, making him stagger.

Shit, I don't think that vampire can hold his own against Lucca even though he's also a Blueblood.

Suddenly, Ronan and Saxon are there. The pressure on my chest eases off a fraction. But this is not over yet. Lucca is still watching Boone with murderous intentions.

"Lucca, put the blade down." Ronan gets in front of him.

"No," he growls. "He needs to pay for what he's done."

"I know. But you can't do this now. Think about your uncle."

It seems mentioning Lucca's relative works. The dagger retracts, disappearing from view. I can't help but to admire the trick and wish I could do something like that.

The institute employee approaches Boone and asks if he's okay. The jackass lashes out with a tirade of curses and how Lucca will pay for what he's done. Saxon flips him off, a gesture the hallway monitor catches and frowns upon.

He turns his disapproving stare to Lucca. "You're in a heap of trouble, Lucca Della Morte."

"The attack wasn't unprovoked. He assaulted Vivienne." He whirls around and points at my open shirt.

Mortification makes my face hot. I was so consumed by the fight that I forgot my bra was exposed. Hastily, I cover myself and glance down.

"That didn't warrant the use of a weapon. You should have called for help," the male retorts.

"Help? Are you fucking kidding me? I don't need help to deal with Boone."

"Clearly. But it doesn't matter. You're suspended from attending any classes until further notice. Return to your quarters at once."

"With pleasure," he sneers.

The hallway monitor walks over. "Did Boone attack you?"

"Yes."

"Why?"

"Why?" I repeat his question like I'm a moron.

"Yes, why? Did you provoke him?"

My jaw drops to the floor. "You're joking, right? He attacked me because he's a perverted psycho."

Lucca comes over and drapes his arm over my shoulders, sending a shock wave through my body. "Come, Vivi. Don't waste your time answering these asinine questions. It's obvious Mr. Ross is under Tatiana's payroll."

The male twists his face in anger. "How dare you. I'm a loyal subject of King Raphael."

"You sure don't act like it," Saxon butts in.

"If I'm being extra careful, it's because I know what's at stake. Lucca has attacked Boone twice now. This won't go unchecked."

"I'm trembling in fear," Lucca scoffs.

"You should be. Boone has many allies here, even undeclared ones. He almost killed you once; don't forget that." The male walks away with squared shoulders and heavy steps.

Meanwhile, my mind is whirling. It's hard to imagine Boone almost killed Lucca. There's no doubt Lucca is much stronger and the better fighter. *So, what happened?*

"Vivienne looks like she's going to pass out." Saxon squints at me.

"She hasn't fed in a while," Lucca replies.

"Why not?" the cocky blond asks.

"Because she's shy." He laughs.

Ugh, what an infuriating Blueblood.

I elbow him in the abs—which are rock solid—and step away from his embrace. "I'm fine. You don't need to escort me."

Lucca watches me through slits. "I insist. It's evident you can't go anywhere alone."

I shouldn't be sending him away. The whole point of me coming here was to get close to him and steal his damn necklace. But I'm afraid of what his constant proximity is doing to me. I shouldn't be craving his touch when I know how bad he can be.

Ignoring his comment, I head to my apartment. I hope Manu is not there. Despite my protest, Lucca and his friends follow me. *Great, now I have a whole security detail.* The doors lining the hallway open almost at the same time, and vampires begin to pour out. An audience. That's what we were missing before. I keep my eyes straight ahead, pretending I don't notice the stares.

But my step falters when I spot a familiar face coming down the corridor in my direction. I can't believe it. When his eyes connect with mine, I know I'm not seeing things.

"Karl?" I say.

"How do you know Karl?" Saxon asks.

I blink rapidly, trying to understand what's going on here. *Why is Karl at Bloodstone? Did he somehow follow me here? Is he going to expose my secret?* I'm so busy freaking out that I don't notice until a few seconds later that Manu is with him and that he looks just as shocked as I am about this encounter.

"Vivi, uh, what are you doing here?" he asks.

"I could ask you the same question."

"How do you know my roommate, Karl?" Manu watches us both with suspicion.

"Wait, Vivi is your roommate?" He stares at the vampire with wide eyes.

I'm so confused. Someone had better explain things soon before I say something I shouldn't.

"How do you know my sister's familiar, Vivienne?" Lucca steps closer.

Familiar? No, that's impossible. I thought Karl was human. Oh my God. This is a nightmare.

Now, his words on the night we said good-bye are beginning to make sense. He mentioned he had to go away for a while.

"We have a friend in common," Karl replies.

All this time, I thought I knew Karl. But it turns out, he was lying all along. He made me believe that he hated vampires as much as I did, but he was a fucking familiar to one. I've never felt more betrayed than now.

"Right. That's how we know each other," I say. I don't think anyone is buying this lie, but I don't care. "I have to go. I don't feel well."

I walk around Manu and run as fast as I can, hoping Lucca doesn't follow me. I'm on the verge of crying again. I hate how this place makes me feel weaker than I already did. When I'm finally in my room, I let the tears fall. It was foolish of me to consider Karl family. I only have one person in this world who's truly my flesh and blood, and he needs me.

Without any hope that anyone will pick up the phone, I call Rikkon's number. It rings several times until, finally, Larsson's gruff voice answers.

"I hope you're calling me with good news."

"Not yet. I just want to check on how my brother is doing."

"He's fine. Don't call again unless it's to tell me you've got the necklace."

"Can I speak to him? Please?"

There's a pause, and then Larsson replies, "He can't come to the phone."

"Why not?" My heart squeezes in anguish.

"Can't you guess? Your brother is a junkie, and he doesn't have access to his drugs right now."

Understanding finally dawns on me. Rikkon is going through a forced detox.

"Yeah, I can guess. Thank you."

"Whatever for?" The dragon seems genuinely surprised.

"For keeping him out of trouble. And don't worry. I'll get your necklace."

19

LUCCA

I don't need to interrogate Karl to know where he knows Vivienne from. They play in the same band, Nocturnal. A simple internet search of her name showed me. It's amusing that she didn't know he was a familiar. I don't follow her, because now Manu is looking at Karl like she wants to destroy him, and I need to run interference.

"What friend do you have in common with that regular, Karl?" Manu is up in his face.

"He's human; you don't know him," he replies calmly.

I've never really understood their deal. Karl is not a common familiar. He wasn't an animal that the Nightingales turned into human and bound to one of us. He was a wolf-shifter, the son of an alpha, and he chose to become Manu's familiar, turning his back on his pack and family.

"Can you please stop arguing like an old married couple? People are staring," Saxon pipes up.

Manu hisses at him, "Fuck them. I don't care."

"This is pathetic," Ronan grumbles. "You sent him away, and now, you're pissed that he's sniffing up someone else's skirt."

A primal instinct of possession hits me, and I want to rip Karl's throat open. *What the fuck? Was that just because Ronan insinuated a romantic connection between the wolf and the human?*

"Shut up, jackass. No one asked your opinion," Manu retorts.

"Shit. If Manu were human, I'd ask if it was her time of the month," Saxon jokes.

In the blink of an eye, she shoves Saxon so hard that he flies backward, almost landing on his ass. A less dexterous vampire would have.

"Manu, cut it out," I say.

Someone clears their throat behind me. I turn, finding Isadora Leal, the High Witch, standing in the hallway, watching us as if she finds our lot abhorrent. Her hands are clasped together, semi-hidden by the wide sleeves of her jacket.

"Can I help you?" I ask.

"Yes. You can follow me."

"Follow you where?"

"Where do you think, Lucca?" She raises an eyebrow.

Manu steps closer to me. "What's going on?"

"Lucca got into an altercation with Boone again," Ronan replies.

"What the hell? Why are you so damn stupid?" she screams in my ear.

"Oh, you're one to talk." I glare at her, annoyed that she's chastising me for doing what's right.

Isadora pinches the bridge of her nose. "God, it doesn't really matter how long you live, does it? You'll never grow up."

"Nope. Perks of being second-generation." Saxon smiles like an idiot.

Now, everyone in the hallway is looking at us, which is pissing me off even more.

"Let's get this over with." I follow the High Witch to another part of the institute where the decor is darker and more severe. I guess this is an older block of the building that they haven't gotten around to renovating yet.

Far away from prying eyes and out of earshot, I ask, "Where are we going?"

"To the headmaster's office."

"Who is the headmaster now?"

"Same individual as it was a hundred years ago."

"No shit. Solomon Corvicus still holds that position? I'm shocked."

"Why? You don't think he's qualified?"

As the oldest familiar in the history of familiars and the only one not associated to any vampire, I'd say he's overqualified to babysit a bunch of insolent Bluebloods. But I keep my thoughts to myself.

"I do. I'm just surprised that hasn't changed when so many other things have."

"You're not happy about those changes. I get that. But you should know, there's more at stake here than what meets the eye."

"Right. The fate of our entire race. The king already gave me that speech."

"You don't agree with his decision."

"Nope."

"That's why he's the king and not you."

I snort. "Like I've ever wanted that fucking crown."

"You *are* his heir. If he dies, you will wear it."

The possibility that my uncle might cease to exist makes my chest unbearably heavy. I don't want to even consider it. I've lost too much already. We fight a lot, but I love him. He's like a father to me.

We stop in front of a heavy wooden door with an intricately carved design. It depicts Maewe, the Nightingale queen, as she blesses my uncle after the great Battle of the Moors. Years later, she cursed us. *What a bitch.* I can't help the sneer that unfurls on my lips.

The door opens by itself, meaning by witch's magic. Isadora walks in first, heading over to the long table set up at the end of the room. There are other people sitting behind that table, and soon, it becomes clear that this is not a simple meeting with the headmaster, it's an inquisition. Solomon is sitting in between Jacques Tellier, Tatiana's former advisor, and Morgan Crane, my mother's best friend. I'd say it's good to see her, but Jacques's presence here is enraging.

"I'm here. What do you want?"

"The arrogance of your bloodline doesn't change, no matter how many years pass," Jacques replies.

"Fuck off, leech. You might be sitting behind that table, but you're still vermin to me."

"Lucca, please. Let's not lose our temper." Solomon speaks calmly, watching me with his beady eyes, barely visible under his bushy eyebrows.

He used to be a possum before he was turned into a familiar and became the Nightingales' emissary. He still looks like one, even in his human form.

"There are some serious allegations against you, son," Morgan adds. "I'm sure you were told about the Accords?"

"Yes, I've heard something about it." I shrug. "What are the allegations against me?"

"You attacked Tatiana's son. That's in complete violation of the Accords. You ought to be put to death." Jacques hits the desk with a closed fist.

I roll my eyes. "Please. I want to see someone try to kill me. Have you forgotten the carnage of 1879?"

His nostrils flare while his face twists into a fit of rage. I smile broadly, remembering the occasion. Ronan, Saxon, and I alone killed fifty of Tatiana's highest-ranking officers in one bloody evening, just before Christmas. Fun times.

"Lucca, this is serious," Morgan replies sternly, erasing my smile. "Boone has filed an official complaint against you, and I hear it's the second time you've attacked him in less than twenty-four hours."

My vision becomes tinted with red, and my fangs elongate. Of course that weasel would bitch about me.

"I can't believe you're wasting my time, reprimanding me, when Boone was the one out of line."

"How was he out of line?" Jacques scoffs. "Because your girlfriend preferred his company over yours?"

I take a step forward, hissing. "Vivienne did not welcome his advances. I guarantee you that. No female in her right mind would."

Jacques opens his mouth, but Solomon speaks before he can. "Very well. We'll speak with Miss Gale about the incident. If her story matches with yours, then you'll just receive a warning."

Jacques turns to the headmaster. "That's preposterous. You saw what that beast did to Boone's face."

"What? I thought it was an improvement," I rebuff.

"Lucca, shut your piehole," Isadora commands, and then turns to Tatiana's ass-kisser. "The rules of the Accords apply to everyone, Jacques, including regulars. If Boone attacked Vivienne first, then he's in the wrong. What Lucca did was justifiable."

Finally, someone sides with me. I was beginning to think everyone had lost their fucking minds—or worse, had fallen under some kind of spell.

"Tatiana will hear of this, and she won't be pleased."

"If no rules were broken, then no punishment can be awarded," Solomon replies. "However, I'd suggest you, Lucca, stay clear of Boone and any of his associates for the remainder of your stay here."

"Fine—as long as he doesn't cross my path. Are we done here?"

Solomon glances at his companions, and when no one adds anything, he replies, "Yeah, we're done."

I switch my attention to Morgan to make sure she knows how angry I am that she didn't stand up for me. She was my mother's friend; she knows firsthand about the horrors Tatiana and her army caused us. *How can she just sit there and pretend she's Switzerland?*

Not reining in my aggression, I shove the door open. It bangs against the wall, and there's the distinct sound of wood splintering. *Good.* That damn carving is also a lie.

I'm about to blow, and the need to break things is immense, but oddly, I don't seek out Ronan or Saxon for a round in the gym. Instead, I head to Manu's apartment—to *her* apartment. I need to see Vivienne—and not to use her as a punching bag to let out my frustration. I just want her.

20

VIVIENNE

———◆———

There are still a few hours left in the night before sunrise. I'm hungry, but it's not so obvious, more like an annoyance in the background. Stress always makes me lose my appetite. I'm also too on edge to go look for food now. I'm afraid to bump into Boone or Therese—two Bluebloods who most likely want my head on a platter.

I lie down and close my eyes. Truth be told, I'm exhausted. My body is still not used to being up all night even though I had some long evenings when I played with the band. Thinking about Nocturnal makes me remember Karl and his betrayal.

Sadness takes over, but it's not as acute as before. I think speaking to Larsson worked to re-shift my focus to what's important—Lucca's necklace. I need to figure out how I'm going to steal it without him finding out. He'd have to be sleeping or something.

He probably gets tired after sex.

Ugh. I can't believe I just thought of that. I'm not sleeping with him to steal any jewelry.

No, you're just going to do it because you want to.

"Shut up, brain. You're such a whore."

A chuckle from my door makes me open my eyes and jerk to a sitting position. Lucca is standing there, all smug and damn sexy.

"What the hell are you doing in my room?" I get up.

"Technically, I'm not in your room, and this is my sister's apartment. I have the key." His gaze drops to my toes and then slowly travels up the length of my body.

Shit. I'm only wearing tight sleeping shorts and a tank top that's most definitely see-through.

I cross my arms, trying to hide my nipples, which are as hard as little pebbles. "I'm pretty sure my door was closed."

He smiles like the cat that ate the canary. "It was open when I got here. Maybe there was a draft."

Liar.

I march over, ready to bang the door in his face, but Lucca comes in and shuts it. I halt. *Fuck.* I'm trapped with him now. *What am I going to do?*

"What are you doing?" I retreat even if it's stupid to do so. There's nowhere to go.

"I think it's high time we get to know each other a little bit better, don't you think?"

"No. I think it's high time you get a clue and leave. I don't want anything to do with you."

"Really?"

He begins to unbutton his shirt, revealing the necklace around his neck. My eyes immediately focus on that, and it's like my brain gets rewired. I can't kick him out. I do need to gain his trust. But I'm afraid of what he thinks is going to happen here. As much as my body is now a pile of goo and I have butterflies wreaking havoc in my stomach, I don't think I can sleep with a vampire even if that vampire is Lucca, a veritable god.

"Fine. You got me. I'm attracted to you. So wha—"

He pounces, crushing his lips with mine. I don't even have time for a gasp of surprise before his tongue darts into my mouth, possessive and hungry. I fight him, not wanting to surrender to the desire that's quickly taking control. It must be the last vestiges of my human instinct trying to save me from a situation that will surely turn bad. But a few more sweeps of his tongue, and I'm his. His fingers are in my hair. His hand is at my waist, and then it slides across my back and under my shirt, making me melt.

He's not cold as I expected him to be. He's as hot as the sun, scorching, vital. We don't stop kissing when he pushes me back on my bed and lies next to me. But his hands wander, touching and squeezing wherever they please. When he switches his attention to my neck, licking and kissing me there, I tense.

Shit, is he going to bite me? Do vampires bite each other during sex?

His fangs do graze my skin, but he doesn't do more than that. He moves on to my chest, running his tongue over each nipple through the fabric of my shirt. I arch my back on reflex, purring like a kitten—or in my case, a sex-deprived woman.

He continues to kiss down my belly, but when he reaches the waistband of my shorts, he stops. Leaning on my elbows, I peer down. Our gazes crash, and what I see in his stare makes my breath hitch. Red eyes filled with a hunger I've only seen once in my life are staring at me. His fangs are fully extended. He's a monster, and he wants to devour me. I begin to shake uncontrollably.

"I'm not going to hurt you," he says.

"Then why are you looking at me like that?"

"Because you taste so fucking good, and I want more."

LUCCA

Vivienne has finally caught on that I'm a vampire about to lose my mind. Bloodlust can be triggered between vampires, but it's rare. In her case, I knew it was a possibility since she's human, and the smell of her blood had caused it twice before. So what made me think tasting her sweet lips wouldn't have the same effect? Her blood is pumping like a factory, calling to me, and it's taking every ounce of self-control I have to not answer it.

"Please don't bite me," she begs in a small voice.

Her eyes are round and dark with fear. Seeing her like this should make me happy, but it has the opposite effect. I don't want her to fear me. I want her to surrender to me, to the desire that has wrapped around us both.

"I'm not going to bite you. I want to make you feel good. Will you let me?"

She blinks a couple of times, probably taken aback by my asking for permission. Truthfully, I've never had to ask. All the humans and vampires I've fucked were more than willing to please me.

"I've never done this before." Heat spreads through her cheeks, making her even more enticing to me.

"Done what? Have sex?"

She bites her lower lip and nods.

Fuck. She's a virgin. I can't believe this, but at the same time, I suddenly want to be her first—and last and forever.

What the hell? What am I thinking?

This bloodlust thing is messing with my head; it's the only explanation. I want to fuck her while I drink her blood, nothing more.

"We don't have to do it tonight. But will you let me taste you?"

"Okay."

Damn. I don't know what I'm doing anymore. I must be a glutton for punishment. I'm not only denying the primal hunger that just wants me to drink until there's nothing left, but now, I'm denying my cock some fun too.

But I peel Vivienne's shorts and panties off just the same. Her pussy is all smooth, save for a little dark blonde hair over her pubic bone. It's a thing of beauty, and I just want to feast on it. I lick once, nice and slow, savoring her taste. Gasping, she jerks her hips upward.

"Easy, darling."

I open her legs wider, keeping her hips down, and lick her again and again. She's shaking under my touch; her breathing is coming out in bursts. I don't want to ever stop tasting her even if this would be much better if I could bite her a little. When I suck her clit into my mouth, that sends her over the edge. She squirms, crying out words that don't mean a thing. Her orgasm is violent and potent. It might be her first one given by a lover.

My balls are tight as hell. Losing the battle against myself, I stick my hand inside my pants to manage at least one of my pains. It doesn't take long. I'm still fucking Vivienne's pussy with my mouth when the wave of pleasure hits us both. She climaxes a second time, and that's what I call a perfect ending.

21

VIVIENNE

❬━╼◆╾━❭

I wake up alone in my room. Looking at the clock, I see that I slept through the day, and it's time to get up and get ready for class. I rub my eyes, wondering if Lucca showing up in my room and what followed was nothing but a vivid dream. But the throbbing between my legs is there, and I'm definitely naked from the waist down. He was here, and he did give me the best orgasms of my life.

Shit. Does that mean he's done playing his conquest game with me? Did I lose my chance to steal his necklace? Why did I fall asleep, damn it?

My mood doesn't improve when I'm ready to walk out the door. Manu is in the kitchen, alone this time but sucking on a blood bag. *Ugh.* I don't know what's a worse scene to witness early in my day—Manu feasting from a blood bag or a human.

"Good morning, roomie. Sleep well?" She's smirking, and there's definitely a knowing tone in her question.

Oh my God. She must have heard us last night. Fucking fantastic.

"Yeah, like the dead." I head for the door.

"Hey, aren't you going to have breakfast first? Sex does open one's appetite."

I turn to see her holding a blood bag in her hand. My stomach twists savagely, rebelling at the sight. I feel queasy now.

"I didn't have sex," I say through clenched teeth.

"No? You had fun though, right? I'm always ravenous after having a good orgasm."

"Ugh! I don't want to talk about what happened in my own room. Stay out of my business." I stride out, shutting the front door hard.

I can hear Manu's annoying laughter, even when I take the stairs down. I'm glad that it's early and Cassie is not at our meeting spot at the bottom of the stairs. I'll text her later to let her know I'll be waiting for her in the gym. I have another priority right now—find food. If I don't eat today, I'm going to pass out.

I stop in the middle of an intersection of corridors and put my hands on my hips. *Where the hell are the humans' dorms?* The signs are worthless. They just give directions to places I don't need to go. The sound of footsteps behind me has me whirling on the spot. It's Karl, which brings me relief and annoyance at the same time.

"Vivi, I'm glad I bumped into you. We need to talk."

"I have nothing to say to you." I begin to turn away, but Karl grabs my arm and stops me.

"Please, Vivi. Give me a chance to explain." His green eyes are so conflicted and sad that I end up caving.

"Fine."

He steers me to an empty room, locking the door behind us for good measure. I sit on the desk and watch my best friend pace in front of me while not saying a word.

"I thought you wanted to explain things," I say.

He stops moving and glances at me. "I do. I just don't know where to start."

"How about from the beginning?"

"Right." He runs a nervous hand over his hair. "Well, I'm a little bit older than you."

"I figured as much. When were you born?"

"In 1499."

Holy shit. I'm glad that I'm sitting because I would have dropped to the floor.

"So, not a little older."

He smirks. "No. I was once a wolf-shifter. My father was the alpha of our pack, and I was destined to eventually take his place."

"So, what happened? Did Manu kidnap you and force you to become her pet instead?"

Karl winces and looks away, rubbing his scruffy jaw. "It was my choice. Familiars are never forced to take the pledge."

"Why would you choose a life of servitude?"

He laughs without humor. "Because I was a fool."

Oh my God. Everything is so obvious now. Karl's sporadically haunted looks, his preference for gut-wrenching melodies. My friend has been nursing a broken heart for centuries, and I never knew.

"You fell in love with her, didn't you?"

He doesn't answer, nor does he look at me.

Yeah, he totally did. He wasn't a fool; he was crazy. *But how could he have fallen for such a mercurial vampire like Manu?*

"It doesn't matter anymore," he replies.

"I thought a familiar couldn't leave their master's side."

"In theory, we can't—unless the master sends us away." Karl looks at me, displaying a great deal of pain in the depths of his eyes.

"Why would she do that?"

He shakes his head, looking away again. "I don't know."

I think he does, but maybe the reason is too awful to relive.

"Is Cheryl also a familiar?"

Karl chuckles. "No."

"Then she's not your blood sister."

He pierces me with a droll stare. "Have you seen us side by side? I'm her male version."

"She's much prettier than you." I smirk.

He smiles, and it's like nothing has changed between us. But it has. He lied.

"I don't understand. Don't shifters have a similar life span as us humans? How can she be alive after all these years and look no older than eighteen?"

"Not all shifters have a short life span. Dragon-shifters, for example, can live for centuries, and when they reach maturity, they stop aging."

"That doesn't explain Cheryl's case." I squint. "Unless she's part dragon."

"Cheryl is something else. I think you need to hear her story from her."

I suppose that's fair. But God knows when I will see her again.

"You still haven't explained why you had to return to Manu's side. Did she call you back?"

The corners of his mouth tense, and his stare hardens. "No. King

Raphael asked me as a personal favor. Manu still wants nothing to do with me."

I open my mouth to ask how Karl could see through my spell, but he cuts me off. "Enough about me. You have to tell me now what you are doing here, disguised as a vampire?"

"Oh, so you know about the spell?"

"I could see the glamour for a moment, but then it broke for me. Maybe because I'm a familiar, I'm immune to it."

"Aurora was also able to see through the spell."

"I'm not surprised. She's training to become a High Witch. Now, answer my question."

Sagging my shoulders, I let out a heavy sigh. "I'm here because Larsson asked me to steal Lucca's necklace in exchange for Rikkon's freedom."

Karl doesn't move, doesn't even blink as he stares at me with wide eyes. Then, his green eyes darken and narrow.

"Are you fucking crazy?" he yells. "Lucca is one of the most vicious Bluebloods I've ever met, and he can hold a grudge like no other. You don't steal from him and hope to live much longer."

"What do you want me to do? Let Larsson kill Rikkon instead?" I jump off the desk, suddenly filled with restless energy.

"No! Of course not. You should have told me. I would have thought of something."

Shaking my head, I begin to pace. "You can't help me, Karl. Unless you have something more valuable to offer the dragon kingpin instead of Lucca's necklace, I have to see this through."

"I thought vampires terrified you."

"Some still do." I think about Boone and shudder. "But I've gotten to know a few regulars, and they aren't so bad."

"And Lucca?" Karl raises an eyebrow.

Heat spreads through my cheeks. I remember last night, and my embarrassment doubles. I look away. "He's not that bad either."

"Vivi, please tell me you're not falling for him." Karl holds me by the shoulder and turns me around to face him.

"I'm not." I bat his hand away. "That's ludicrous."

"I wasn't born yesterday, you know."

"Yeah, we covered that already." I smirk.

"I'm older and wiser, so you should listen to me." He returns the grin.

"Are you taking your cues from *The Sound of Music* soundtrack?"

He snorts. "I've never listened to that."

"Riiight."

My stomach rumbles like a damn earthquake, reminding me of what I was doing before.

"Are you hungry?" He arches an eyebrow.

"You have no idea. The last meal I had was a couple of Snickers bars, like, a day ago."

"Shit. We can't have you starving." He shoves his hand into his pocket and retrieves a piece of gum. "This is the only thing I have. But I'll make a trip to the familiars' cafeteria and grab some stuff."

I snag the gum from his hand and shove it in my mouth, almost forgetting to remove the wrapper first. This will only make me hungrier, but I'll enjoy the few seconds of sweetness it provides.

"Getting the food won't be a problem. The tricky part will be you eating without anyone finding out."

"Don't worry, Karl. I'll find a way. It's do or die now."

"You should get going. Don't you have Keepers class?"

"How do you know?"

"Bloodstone Institute only accepts regulars to join that program, and even so, the competition is fierce. How did you manage to get a spot in such a short period of time?"

"I, uh, Larsson arranged it."

Karl watches me closely. "Larsson, huh? I didn't think he had the connections."

I shrug. "I think he's very motivated. Do you have any idea why he would want Lucca's necklace? Is it some kind of magical amulet?"

"I have no clue." Suddenly, Karl's spine becomes rigid. "Shit."

"Wha—"

The door opens with a bang, and Manu enters with nostrils flaring and eyes sparkling red. I suppose locking it was pointless. I quickly swallow the gum.

Karl jumps in front of me, becoming my own human—*familiar*—shield.

"Manu—"

"What are you doing here with her, Karl?" she snarls.

"I was having a private conversation. Why were you following me?"

"You're my familiar, not hers!" She takes a step forward.

I step out from Karl's shadow. "We were just catching up, Manu. Nothing more."

"Shut up. I know exactly what you're doing. First, my brother, and now, Karl."

He tenses, sparing me a fleeting accusatory glance. Then, he shifts his attention to Manu again.

"You have no right to demand my devotion, not when you banished me from your life," Karl retorts.

His remark seems to cause Manu physical pain. She winces and loses some of her fury. "That's right. And do you want to know why? Because you were such a lame familiar, an embarrassment really."

Karl clenches his jaw so tight I can hear his teeth grinding. "I'm sorry that I wasn't up to your standards, princess."

"Don't call me that."

"Why not? It's what you are, isn't it? A pampered and rude princess."

Manu slaps Karl's face so hard that the sound echoes in the room. I flinch as if the pain were mine.

"What the hell? That was uncalled for," I yell.

Manu ignores my outburst. Her eyes are wide but at least no longer glowing red. She's breathing hard though, as if she had run a marathon. Karl touches his cheek and then rewards her with a scathing glance that would make anyone feel like the scum of the earth. I've never seen him look at someone with so much loathing.

"Karl … I'm so sorry."

"Nothing to be sorry for, princess. That's what I'm here for."

Surprising me even more, her eyes fill with tears. She whirls around and bolts out of the room before we can actually see them fall.

22

LUCCA

"Hey, Luc. We're about to head down to the humans' dorms to score some snacks. Do you want to come?" Saxon asks as soon as I step out of my room.

I could eat, but there's only one human I want to drink from.

"Nah, I think I'll just have a bag." I head for the fridge, not missing the silent exchange between him and Ronan.

"How did the meeting with the High Witch go?" Ronan asks.

"Fucking fantastic. What do you think?" I pierce the plastic bag, drinking a large gulp of cold blood. It's disgusting.

"Did they punish you for attacking Boone?" Saxon's brows make a deep V in his forehead.

"No. I got away with a warning, pending they confirm what had happened with Vivienne." I toss the empty bag in the sink. "The worst part of the meeting was standing in Jacques's presence and not being able to slash his throat."

"We've been suffering his presence for years, bro. I want to say it gets easier to pretend he's not around, but that'd be a lie," Ronan replies.

The door to our apartment opens with a loud bang, and hurricane Manu comes in, stomping her feet like a petulant child. She stops in front of me, poking my chest with her finger. "What are your plans for that regular, Lucca?"

I grab her wrist and push her away from me. "I don't know what crawled up your ass, but back off, Manu. I'm not in the mood for one of your tantrums."

"Answer me, damn it! What are you planning to do with Vivienne?"

Watching her through slits now, I ask, "Why do you care?"

"I don't, but if you plan to nail that bitch, you'd better do it soon. You have competition."

Without a second thought, I invade her personal space, holding her by the shoulders. "Who?"

"Karl," she sneers. "I just caught the two of them having a private meeting in one of the empty classrooms."

"And you can't have that, can you, sunshine?" Ronan crosses his arms and pierces Manu with a pissed-off stare.

"He's *my* familiar," she hisses, turning her body to him.

"Sounds like someone is jelly." Saxon guffaws.

I shake her, forcing her to look at me. "What makes you say he's going after Vivienne? What were they doing?"

Manu's eyes widen first and then become narrowed. She shoves me off. "What's your deal with that regular? Why are you obsessed with her?"

Fuck. I don't know how to answer that, nor do I want to waste

146

another second discussing Vivienne with them.

I push Manu aside and head out. Saxon and Ronan call my name, but their voices are muffled by the rage roaring in my ears now. No one will come between Vivienne and me. *No one.* In the back of my head, I know I'm acting like an irrational animal, but I'm not willing to control this raw instinct that's telling me to take possession of what's mine.

Once in the main hallway, all it takes is a deep breath to catch her scent in the air. She has Keepers class again today, but I know exactly which room she secretly met with Karl when I pass by it. Their scents are all over the front of that classroom. They went in opposite directions after they met, and part of me wants to follow Karl's scent instead. But if I do, I might end up killing Manu's familiar, and that would be a very bad thing.

To avoid the early evening traffic of vampires, I take an alternative route through a part of the institute that's currently not in use. I'm almost at the Keepers class when I hear Solomon's and Isadora's voices. They're whispering behind closed doors, which is never a good sign. The urge to hunt Vivienne down and stake my claim recedes. Maybe it's my survival instinct kicking in. Now, I must know what those two individuals are talking about.

They've chosen the last room in an empty hallway to hold their meeting. I don't need to press my ear against the door to hear them clearly.

"Are you sure the new student found the secret chamber on her first day here?" Solomon asks.

"That's what Aurora told me."

"You said the wards would hold, Isadora."

"That's what's strange, Solomon. The wards are still there,

strong as ever."

"That means then that Vivienne Gale is immune to their magic."

The muscles on my back become taut in an instant. *What the hell are they talking about? What is Vivienne immune to?*

"I know, but the reason is what's puzzling me. The wards are meant to keep the chamber hidden to everyone—vampires, familiars, and humans. What's so special about her that she can get through?"

"Maybe she's a lost witch?"

Isadora scoffs, "Solomon, please. We're not vampires who used to procreate like rabbits with anyone willing. We know everything about our lineages."

"You must have some theories though."

"I do."

I'm at the edge of my seat, waiting for Isadora to finally shed some light as to why I'm so drawn to Vivienne.

"Lucca. I thought I saw you come here." Therese's loud voice carries down the corridor.

Fuck me. I've never believed in Karma, but I'm beginning to change my mind.

The headmaster and High Witch's conversation ceases in an instant. I stride away from the door, not wanting to explain myself to them. Therese follows me, like the annoying pest that she is. *Hell, has she always been like this?*

"Luc, wait."

Once back in the main part of the building, I whirl on her, grabbing her by the neck and pushing her against the wall. I keep her above the floor, cutting off her ability to scream.

"What. Do. You. Want?"

She lashes my face with her nails, drawing blood, but I don't care.

"Let … me … go."

"I want to make one thing crystal clear. I do not want you following me around. Don't speak to me, don't make eye contact, and when you see me down the hall, walk the other way."

I drop her then, stepping out of her reach. She's a Blueblood; she will retaliate, but one strike at me is all she'd get.

"You asshole," she screeches.

A small crowd gathers around us, but I haven't given a fuck about the opinions of others in centuries.

I sense when Ronan and Saxon join the fray, but instead of moving toward them, I head in the opposite direction. I should be going to some idiotic class about living in this current world, but everyone knows the institutes exist only to keep Bluebloods occupied and out of trouble. We can learn quite a lot by drinking human blood since it carries their memories.

I can't be here tonight, not while I'm out of control like this. There are only two possible outcomes if I stay while riding this uncontrollable rage. I will either kill Karl or expose Vivienne as the human that she is by drinking from her in front of everyone.

Both are terrible scenarios.

23

VIVIENNE

Hanson continued to drill us like a sergeant in class, but at least I managed not to humiliate myself completely. It helped that there wasn't an audience. But I'm running on fumes now, so the first thing I do when I get out of class is go look for Aurora. Karl must be busy now, dealing with his vampire master.

I feel bad for him. I can't begin to imagine how horrible it must be to be bound for all eternity to the female you once loved when the relationship has gone sour. I never knew familiars could get involved with their masters in the first place. I've always assumed it was forbidden. Coming to Bloodstone has shown me how much I don't know about vampires and their world.

Not wanting to be caught by surprise by Boone or any other nasty vampires, I find a little nook in the hallway and pull my cell out to text Aurora. Her reply comes swiftly, and a minute later, I spot her walking down the hall in my direction.

I step out of my hiding spot and meet her halfway. "Please tell me you have something edible with you."

"How long has it been since you ate?" she whispers since we're not alone.

Shit. I have to be more careful.

"Too long."

"Come on. I have something for you in my quarters."

My stomach is grumbling loudly already, and my mouth is salivating.

"How is everything going for you?" she asks.

"Fine. Everything is going fine besides the food situation."

"I heard Boone attacked you yesterday," she says casually, but my reaction is anything but.

All my muscles become rigid, and my stomach turns into a ball of anxiety. I wish she hadn't brought it up.

"Yeah. He's a nasty piece of work. It's not the first time he's tried."

"Do you mean the party incident?"

"No. I've met him before at Havoc."

Aurora halts suddenly and grabs my arm. "Are you saying he has met you when you weren't in disguise?" Her pretty eyes are rounder and her pupils dilate.

"Yes. Why are you looking at me like that? You're freaking me out."

"You should be freaked out. That's three times now that Boone has come after you. Bluebloods can develop obsessive behaviors that never end well for their prey. Stay away from him."

"Trust me, I'm trying."

She lets go of my arm, and we resume walking. But now, my

heart wants to flee the confines of my chest. My stomach is hurting, and it's not only from hunger. *Fuck.* I hate feeling this afraid. Maybe I would be better off going somewhere else, live in a big city where I could simply disappear into the crowd.

"Can I ask you something?" I break the silence.

"Sure."

"Have you ever lived anywhere besides Salem?"

"Yes, of course."

"But you didn't forget about the vampires, did you?"

She stares at me like I'm an idiot. "I'm part of the supernatural community. The spell only works on humans. How about you? Have you ever been to another city?"

"Yeah, once. My mother took my brother and me to Boston when I was ten."

"Did you know about the supernatural stuff then?"

"I don't remember a time in my life when I didn't know." I can't help the anger that bubbles up my throat.

My mother not only loved the supernaturals, she also had a preference for the worst kind.

"Did it freak you out when you returned and your memories did too?" Aurora asks.

I snort out loud without meaning to.

"What was that?"

Shit. I really need to control my reactions better. I could lie; actually, that's what I should do, but I'm tired of deception. "I've never told anyone this, but the memory spell only worked for a few hours when I was in Boston."

Aurora grabs my arm, looking more alarmed than before. "What do you mean?" I open my mouth to reply, but she talks over me. "Hold that thought. We're almost at my place."

We walk around a corner, and then Aurora stops in front of a simple, dark wooden door. A skeleton key also opens this one. The moment I walk in, the smell of fresh-baked cookies fills my nostrils. Without any manners, I follow the delicious scent into the kitchen, finding them still in the oven.

"I think they're ready," I say with my hand already on the stove door. "May I?"

She drops her bag on the counter and waves nonchalantly. "Sure, go ahead."

They're hot, and they burn my fingers and my tongue, but they're so gooey and delicious that I don't care. I'm moaning after the first bite.

"I have more food here, you know. What do you feel like eating besides cookies?"

"Everything," I reply through a mouth half-full, dropping some cookie crumbs on the floor.

She shakes her head. "You really should have thought things through before you decided to join the institute as a vampire."

Aurora reaches over the kitchen counter and pulls out crackers, chips, and other snacks. I'll probably get a bellyache, but at the moment, all I care about is stuffing my face.

"This should hold you over. Now, explain to me what exactly happened on your trip to Boston."

I swallow a big lump of cookie and then open a bag of potato chips and stuff a few in my mouth. I have zero manners now.

"Well, the moment we crossed the border out of Salem, I sensed some fuzziness in my brain, like the feeling you have when you're forgetting something but you can't quite remember what. I ignored that since I was so excited about going on a road trip to Boston. My mother never did nice things with Rikkon and me." I reach for another cookie, taking a few bites before I continue.

"Do you want some milk with that?" Aurora heads for the fridge.

"Sure. That'd be nice."

"Anyway, we were outside a movie theater, waiting to meet with one of my mother's friends, when I saw a poster for a vampire movie. And just like that, I remembered they were real."

Aurora is watching me closely now, almost as if she were trying to read my mind. Maybe I shouldn't have told her that story.

"That shouldn't have happened," she says. "Was it only you?"

"No. Rikkon also knew. We couldn't understand why our mother didn't remember a thing. We thought she was joking in the beginning."

She walks around me and pulls an old leather-bound book from her bag. "This is very troubling, Vivienne. If there are more humans who are immune to the spell, our secret will be out to the world."

"But why would that be so bad?"

"The only reason Salem works is because of the town's history. It was founded by supernaturals."

"Really? Then what was the deal with the witch trials?"

"The nasty results of a war between rival covens."

"Were Bluebloods the real founders of Salem?"

"No, witches. Vampires flocked here because this was the last place the Nightingales had been seen."

Aurora has her face buried in her book now, rapidly turning the pages after scanning them with a single glance.

"Are you going to tell me about the Nightingales now? Why did they create the vampires?"

She sighs. "You really want to know, huh? Well, to cut a long story short, King Raphael was once human. He and his allies helped the Nightingales win a war against some nasties from their realm, and as a thank-you, the Nightingales gave them immortality."

"That's it? What a lame-ass gift."

Aurora lifts her gaze from her book, watching me in a surprised manner. "Why do you say that? They gave those humans eternal life, youth, and power."

"But they also made them allergic to the sun and only able to survive by drinking blood."

She doesn't offer a retort; instead, she keeps staring at me. After a moment, she shakes her head and then asks, "So, you didn't know about Karl?"

Whoa, what a way to change the subject. I don't know why she doesn't want to talk about the Nightingales, but by mentioning Karl, she has my full attention.

"How did you know Karl was my friend?"

"Salem is not a big city, girl."

I want to ask Aurora more questions, but there's a knock on her door. We trade a worried glance, and then she looks at the chip in my hand. I hastily drop the snack and then wipe my mouth.

"Who is it?" she asks.

"It's me, Saxon."

Fuck. That's Lucca's friend. *What is he doing here?*

24

LUCCA

⊶═══▪▸

Walking out of Bloodstone Institute grounds didn't even occur to me before. As soon as I clear the gates, I run straight to the woods. I need the solitude only nature can provide. My veins are still on fire, my throat is parched, and my fangs are fully extended. I need to calm the fuck down, or I'll be a menace to any human who crosses paths with me.

I hear dry twigs snapping nearby, a deer just running away from me. It must have sensed a predator is in the area. I draw the line at feeding from animals though. I'm not a savage, demented vampire who has to resort to feeding from furry creatures in order to control their hunger. I'm better than that.

The farther away I get from the institute, the less I feel the anger. The hunger abates even though it's still in the background, painful and easily accessible. I only stop running when I reach the main road that will lead to downtown. I do need to feed until I'm completely satiated; there's no denying that.

I should have never gone to see that little thief yesterday. I can still taste her on my tongue—the best thing I've ever had other than blood. The memory makes my cock hard, which reminds me of another ache. Now, I not only want to drink from her, but I also want to plunge my cock into her sweet pussy until she forgets her own name. I can only imagine what doing both at the same time would be like. Pure ecstasy.

Fuck, the bloodlust is coming back again. With a roar, I punch the nearest tree on the side of the road, splitting the trunk in half. I will not be controlled by anything, especially not by an urge triggered by a mere human.

My hand is throbbing from the hit, but I welcome the pain. It helps me regain focus. I head to Havoc, the only place in this town that will have what I need.

But suddenly, my body has other ideas. My nose picks up Vivienne's scent, and my feet lead me toward it. The trail is faint, maybe a week old, but it doesn't matter. Now that I'm onto it, nothing will deter me from following it.

Her scent leads me to a trailer park in the outskirts of town. It's not the worst neighborhood I've seen, but it's clearly not a place where happy childhood memories are made. It's too fucking depressing for that. The ground is either covered by overgrown grass or has brown patches that must turn into mud puddles when it rains. Broken toys are scattered in front of some trailers, and the stench of stale beer wafts from many homes I pass by.

Vivienne is poor, but that doesn't explain why she's risking her life to steal from me.

I find her trailer at the end of the row. Without pause, I yank the door open, busting the lock. Unlike vampire lore in fiction, we don't need a formal invitation to enter a human's home. At a first glance, I see nothing out of the ordinary inside. It looks kind of cozy. Definitely better than the depressing state out front.

"What are you hiding, Vivienne?" I mutter to myself.

In her bedroom, there are posters of bands on the walls and an old acoustic guitar tucked away in the corner. Among the posters, I also find a picture of Vivienne onstage, singing with her band. Karl is next to her, playing the guitar, and Cheryl is behind the drums. Another dude is in the picture, playing bass. Behind them, a cheap-looking sign says *Nocturnal*.

There's a stack of CDs next to an old stereo. I quickly peruse through them, finding a homemade one with the name of the band written on the cover. This is not the type of information I was looking to find, but I can't help sticking the CD in the stereo and listening to Vivienne's singing.

The voice that pours out of the speakers takes my breath away. If her blood ignites a destructive hunger in me, her singing calms me down. I end up listening to the entire CD, and when the final song ends, I'm not sure how I feel anymore. *How can I destroy something so beautiful?*

Get a grip on yourself, Lucca. She might sing like an angel, but she's a lying thief.

The inner dialogue doesn't help. I'm still conflicted as hell, but I resume my search, opening every single cabinet and drawer that I come across. When that doesn't yield anything important, I look under furniture, behind paintings, and any other places that could hide something worthwhile. The place is now completely ransacked, and I have nothing to show for it besides the CD that I tucked in my jacket pocket. I guess, now, I'm a thief too.

I'm staring at the mess I've made, pissed already for the wasted time, when my eyes land on a picture frame peeking from behind an ugly cat figurine. The frame is covered in dust, and the photo inside is yellowed out, but I recognize Vivienne right away. The photo is old, but Vivienne looks exactly the same. There's also an older woman who looks like a dirty junkie along with a guy in his twenties. He and Vivienne resemble each other. Same hair color and high cheekbones. It wouldn't be farfetched to assume they're siblings.

I trace my finger over her smiling face without a clue as to why I felt compelled to do so. It clears the dust in that spot, leaving an obvious path. I end up wiping the entire frame off, and that's when I notice the strange leather band she has on her wrist. Her brother also has the same band. Squinting, I look at the picture closer. There are small charms dangling from the band, and I can't be sure, but it looks like they have ancient runes written on them.

I don't know if this means anything or not, but I remove the picture from the frame and tuck it in my pocket. I bet Aurora would know what they mean.

In a hurry to head back to Bloodstone now, I burst out of Vivienne's trailer. But I don't expect to come face-to-face with an angry gray wolf growling at me. A ray of silvery moonlight catches the wolf's eyes, revealing their crimson glow.

My lips turn upward. "Hello, Cheryl. It's been a while."

The wolf's form begins to tremble and shimmer, and a moment later, Karl's sister is standing in front of me, fully dressed.

I give her an overall glance. "That's a neat trick."

"I was tired of you lot ogling me every time I shifted back, so I found a solution. What are you doing here, Lucca?"

"Research."

Cheryl glances at Vivienne's wide-open door. "What do you want with Vivienne?"

"Oh, come on. Don't play that game with me. We go way back, Cher."

She narrows her eyes. "Yes, and not a day has gone by when I don't regret ever meeting you and your besties." There's enough venom in her tone to kill an elephant.

Who knew wolf-shifters could hold grudges as long as vampires? But again, she's more than just a wolf now.

"I'll cut straight to the chase. Why is Vivienne Gale at Bloodstone, pretending to be a vampire?"

Cheryl's eyebrows arch almost to her hairline. "Wait, Vivi is at Bloodstone?"

I pay attention to her breathing and heartbeat. There's barely any change, which means she's not lying.

"Yes. And she also came to Havoc the night before and poisoned me with vampire's bane."

Cheryl's jaw drops. "No way, José. Vivi is terrified of vampires, like she will go into a full-blown panic attack if one even comes near her."

"Maybe you don't know your friend that well."

She crosses her arms, and the glower intensifies. "Larsson has her brother."

I didn't expect that revelation to come out of Cheryl's mouth. She's been prickly with me ever since I refused to grant her a favor many centuries ago.

"The dragon-shifter kingpin?"

"Do you know any other dragon by that name living in Salem?"

"Why would Larsson take her brother hostage?"

"Because Rikkon is a piece of shit who always gets into trouble and hopes Vivi will bail him out."

And I'm furious all over again, but this time, I can and will aim my aggression at someone deserving. There is nothing in the Accords that says I can't fight a dragon.

"Where are you going?" Cheryl asks.

"Where do you think?" I say before taking off faster than she can run.

Ember Emporium, Larsson's domain, is on the opposite side of town—as far away as possible from Bloodstone. Supernatural species learned to coexist a long time ago, but we all try to remain in our own turf. Invisible lines exist everywhere, even outside of Salem where humans are unaware of our existence.

I should remain in the shadows when I cross that border, but I'm too pissed to care. I don't know if the source of my anger is discovering that Larsson sent Vivienne to steal from me or the fact that he's blackmailing her to do so. *And why does he want my mother's necklace?*

Several bikers are stationed in front of Larsson's bar. All of them are dragon-shifters and the meanest-looking creatures I've ever seen. Throughout the centuries, they've always preferred to live on the wrong side of the tracks. Once a barbarian, always a barbarian.

I cross the street, determined to see Larsson even if I have to cut his soldiers into little pieces of lizard meat. But a shadow crosses my path, solidifying into the last person I'd expect to see here. My uncle.

"Lucca, where do you think you're going?"

"To have a word with Larsson. What, is that forbidden too?"

"Cheryl called me."

"Oh, I didn't realize you were best buddies now."

"Go back to the institute, son. There's nothing to be gained here by confronting the dragon."

I flare my nostrils, feeling deep in my bones the compulsion to obey. I fight it with every fiber of my being, but fuck, I can already sense my resolution waning. *Damn it.*

"Give up, Lucca. It's futile to resist."

The voice in my head isn't mine. It's his. And he's right. There's only one other vampire in the world who can resist my uncle's legendary compulsion powers—Tatiana—for reasons I don't know.

"Another thing, Lucca," he says. "Don't fight the hunger. Surrender to it."

What the hell does that mean?

25

VIVIENNE

❦

I couldn't get out of Aurora's apartment fast enough. I didn't want to give Saxon any chance to ask me what I was doing with the resident witch. But as I walk back to the main section of the institute, hoping to catch up with Cassie and Damon, I begin to wonder what the cocky vampire was doing there.

Aurora wasn't happy with his impromptu visit; that's for sure. Maybe I can ask her later. I did tell her a lot about me without much probing on her side.

Hell, why did I have to tell her about my immunity to the spell that protects the supernaturals' secret? I've never told a soul, and I decided to blabber to the person who might have an issue with it. Her mother is probably responsible for the spell.

Damn it, Vivi. Sometimes, you do act like the color of your hair.

While I'm distracted by having a conversation with myself, a rough hand comes out of nowhere, clamping my mouth shut, and a steely arm traps me in a vise hold. The first thought that runs through my mind is that Boone has found me again, but when a distinct female perfume reaches my nose, I know it's not him.

"Finally found you alone, bitch."

Ah fuck. Therese.

She's not alone. Two other Blueblood females make sure no one can see me struggling in between them. I try to scream over the hand keeping me silenced, but only muffled murmurs can be heard. There's also the problem that I don't think anyone is around.

My heartbeat rate has spiked to dangerous levels, and breathing is becoming increasingly difficult. Therese drags me down a corridor until we stop in front of a big iron door. One of her friends uses a skeleton key to unlock it. Once it's open, Therese shoves me forward so hard that I fall on the ground after a couple of staggering steps. I'm now outside of the building, and the grass softened my fall.

I stand as fast as I can, not knowing when the vicious attack will commence. But Therese just watches me from the door, her eyes gleaming with delight.

"What do you want from me?" I ask through my ragged breathing.

"I want nothing from you. I just want you to disappear. *Forever.*" She glances up at the sky. "Which should happen in a few minutes. Sunrise is just around the corner. Buh-bye." She waves her fingers and then shuts the door with a loud clank.

I stare at it for a few seconds, trying to comprehend what just happened. Then, the coin finally drops. *You're a vampire to them, Vivi, which means you'd die if caught out in the sun.*

A bubble of laughter goes up my throat, but I clamp it shut, not knowing if Therese and her minions are watching me from inside. I won't die with sunup, but if I don't get back inside beforehand, they will know I'm not a real vampire. *Crap on toast.*

I look around, having no clue what side of the building I am on. The forest is behind me, but it's not thick enough to provide cover from the sun. The only way to get out of this mess is to find another way in. I pick a random direction and run the perimeter of the building. There's nothing but smooth stone walls on this side, and the windows are too high up for me to reach them.

"Damn it!" I glance at the sky, which is already pink. Not much longer now.

Without a choice, I keep on running until I hear someone call my name from the woods. I don't recognize the voice, but I'm running out of time. Maybe if I hide under the thick foliage, I can bullshit Therese into believing that was protection enough.

As I break through the forest, I hear the voice calling my name again. Like an idiot, I follow it. It leads me to a small cemetery, which is creepy as fuck. The few tombstones are crooked or cracked, and vines cover most of them. It seems no one has been hired to take care of the place. A chilly wind comes from behind me, and as it travels past the old trees, it sounds like they're moaning. Goose bumps form on my arms. I hug myself, trying to stop the shivering.

There's only one mausoleum here, and that's where my feet take me. I can hide inside. The wrought iron door is not padded with a lock. It creaks loudly as I open it.

My heart is thumping so hard in my chest that the sound echoes in the dark room. The smell of mildew and decay is strong here. This is beginning to feel like a horror movie. I should get out, but some strange force is keeping me from taking off. I'm surprised to see a set of stairs right in the middle of the small space, going underground. The eerie voice calls my name again, and as if I'm in a trance, I follow it even though all my instincts are telling me to run away.

I plunge into complete darkness, and there's a solid chance I'll die of a panic attack. My chest hurts. I'm getting dizzier with each step I take. I want to get out of here, to scream, but I've lost my free will. *What's happening to me?*

Finally, I see a little illumination ahead. I walk faster—no, I'm actually running toward it. Maybe this tunnel leads to the catacombs. If so, I can find my way back to above ground. But when I walk around a corner, still propelled by the mysterious force, I find myself in front of the locked chamber again.

"Vivienne," someone calls me from inside the spooky room.

A gasp escapes my lips as a specter emerges from one of the tombs and zaps toward me. I don't have time for anything before it reaches over the metal bars and grabs me by the throat.

LUCCA

My uncle's compulsion wears off as soon as I cross the gates of Bloodstone Institute. It took me a while to get back here, and I've missed sunrise with only a few minutes to spare. Maybe my reluctance to obey accounted for my delay. I don't know. My head always gets fuzzy when he uses his powers on me. He hasn't resorted to that cheap trick a lot during my existence but enough for me to hate him for a few years after. But I don't even have time to be upset about that when another aggravation looms on the horizon. Therese and two of her friends are walking in my direction.

She's smiling smugly, which means she's up to no good. Maybe I wasn't clear enough before.

"Lucca, coming home so late? You almost didn't make it," she says.

"What did I say earlier? Stay away from me. Your presence is nauseating."

Her amused expression morphs into pure hatred. How easily feelings can change.

"I only want to give you a heads-up. I saw your precious regular roaming outside a few minutes ago. I don't think she'll make it back in time."

"What are you talking about?"

"We locked Vivienne out of the building." Her friend snickers, earning a glare from Therese.

Ah shit. They think she's a vampire. If that were true, Therese wouldn't have her head attached to her body right now. It doesn't matter. When Vivienne walks through those doors in one piece, everyone will suspect who she truly is.

That can't happen. I'm not done playing with her yet.

I only have one choice—find her before sunup. Running faster than ever before, I burst out of the institute's front door. A familiar tending to the bushes outside calls out to me, warning me that sunrise is only a few minutes away—like I don't know that. It's something we can sense, even when we're inside a building without windows. It's an ingrained survival instinct.

With ease, I find Vivienne's scent. She headed for the abandoned cemetery in the woods. I remember then that a mausoleum is there.

Good. She must have hidden inside. But when I enter the small space, she's not there. Her scent continues down the stairs, going underground. I'm running as fast as I can now, and I don't even know why. She's not outside, and she was never in danger. I just risked my life over nothing. This can't be only about playing games.

Her scent keeps getting stronger. I'm getting closer to her location, but it suddenly vanishes. I halt, taking deep breaths and catching nothing. That's impossible. Someone's scent doesn't simply evaporate like that. I'm walking in circles now, going out of my mind, when I hear her scream.

"Vivienne!" I call out, trying to pinpoint where the scream came from.

She doesn't scream again, and I don't pick up any other sound either. *What the hell?*

"Vivienne!" I begin to search the walls.

Maybe she's found the secret chamber that Solomon and Isadora were talking about.

I reach a dead end, and I'm about to turn around when she appears out of nowhere, as if she sprang straight from the wall, and collides with me.

She's a mess, trembling and crying. I engulf her into a bear hug, almost crushing her against my chest, despite the hunger that rears its ugly head to torment me.

"What happened? Where were you?"

"It was horrible," she mumbles.

I pull her back, so I can see her face. But my eyes immediately zero in on the red mark around her neck. It looks like someone tried to choke her to death.

"Who did this to you?" I ask through clenched teeth.

She shakes her head while she stares at me with wide eyes. Terror is all I read in them.

"Don't be afraid. Whoever did this to you is not stronger than me."

"It-it was a ghost."

"A ghost?"

She nods. "I heard it calling my name again when I was in the forest. It wanted me to come down here."

"Again? When did it happen before?"

"Can we just get out of here? Please."

Staring at her, so afraid and vulnerable, does something to me. I forget the hunger, the need for revenge. All I want to do is protect her and hunt down whatever hurt her.

I pick her up in my arms and run at breakneck speed, not stopping until we're back in her apartment. Manu is home, but she's retired. When I set Vivienne down in her bedroom, I know she's not over the shock yet. She has stopped crying, but she's still shaking nonstop as she sits on the edge of her bed.

It's been a while since I had to console someone, and I don't know what to do. All I want is to make her forget what happened.

I drop to my knees in front of her and grab her hands. "What can I do to help?"

"I'm not sure you can." She drops her eyes to our joined hands.

"Try me."

She lifts her gaze to mine, and in an instant, I'm trapped. She's reeling me in, and I can't stop it.

"Would you stay with me for a little while?"

"I can do that."

She lies down, getting under the covers, and motions for me

to lie next to her. I pull her closer—into a spooning position, to be exact—and try not to breathe at all. It's not only her blood that's calling me now; it's also her entire being. This is madness.

She falls asleep right away. I can tell by the slowing down of her heartbeat and the evenness of her breathing. I barely dare to shift my position, afraid any sudden movement will snap my self-control.

My uncle's words come back to haunt me. He told me to surrender to the hunger, but what if I end up losing myself if I do?

26

VIVIENNE

I blink my eyes open, but my mind is still foggy as hell. It's only when I notice a strong arm draped around my waist that everything that happened yesterday comes rushing back. Therese's trap, the ghost in the catacombs, and most importantly, Lucca.

Oh my God. He spent the day with me. Does that mean that we did more than sleep?

"You're awake," he says gruffly.

If possible, my spine becomes even more taut. "How did you know?"

"Your pulse quickened, and your body tensed." He pulls his arm away and sits up.

Slowly, I turn to him. "I can't believe you stayed the whole day."

He's staring at the wall opposite the bed with a grim expression. "You asked me to."

He doesn't seem happy about it, which is making me even edgier. I sit up as well, pulling the sheets up to cover my chest. I'm still dressed, but somehow, I need this barrier between us even if it's flimsy.

"Thank you." My voice comes out raspy. I touch my throat, finding it tender.

"Did a ghost really do that to you?" he asks.

"Yes. I know it sounds crazy."

"No, not at all." He looks at me. "Please promise me you will not go back to the catacombs."

His intense gaze renders me speechless. "Why are you being so nice to me?"

He frowns. "Vivienne, I thought we were … *friends*."

"Friends? Oh, you mean friends with benefits." My face goes up in flames, and the only reason I don't glance away is because I don't want to look more pathetic than I do already.

Lucca's face is a blank mask, and his dark eyes reveal nothing as he stares at me. He jumps out of bed suddenly, runs a nervous hand through his hair, and announces, "I have to go."

He's out the door before I can blink.

What did I do? Did I say something wrong? I hug my knees, not knowing why I feel so depressed all of a sudden. *I can't possibly be falling for Lucca, can I?* He's a Blueblood, savage and cold. He'll hate me once he discovers the truth.

I rest my head in my hands. *Shit.* We slept in the same room, and I totally blacked out, missing the best opportunity I'll probably ever have to steal his necklace. I can't believe this.

I reach for my cell phone, checking the time. *Crap.* I have less than twenty minutes to get ready for class. Like a lunatic, I run to the bathroom, yanking off my clothes as I go. The shower bit is an in-and-out situation. It's a pity that I don't have time to relax under the hot jets. Getting ready doesn't take long either. Makeup is a necessity tonight, especially the heavy layer of concealer on my neck. I don't want to explain how I got these nasty marks.

I'm clean and ready—sort of—for another grim evening at the institute, but when I walk out of my room, Manu is in the kitchen, making a mess out of the blood bags. There's literally blood splattered everywhere. *Disgusting.*

"Can you eat without turning the kitchen into a horror-movie scene?" I say before I can help myself.

She turns her deranged eyes in my direction. The gold has flecks of red in them. She's about to go psycho on me, but surprisingly, I'm not afraid. What I am is mad at her. She beguiled Karl into a lifetime of servitude, only to turn her back on him.

"What did you say?"

"You heard me."

She tosses another bag to the side and takes a few menacing steps toward me. But I hold my ground.

"You think that because my brother has taken a sudden interest in you that it gives you the right to defy me?"

"This has nothing to do with Lucca."

"Oh, so who is it all about then? Karl?" she sneers. "What's your end game, Vivienne? Conquer every single male at Bloodstone?"

"I can't believe this. You're jealous of Karl and me?"

She twists her face into a scowl. "You're delusional."

"You tricked him into becoming your familiar, and for what? Was that one of your capricious games?"

"I didn't trick him into anything," she grits out.

"Bullshit. Karl is the most caring, kindhearted person I've ever met. He'd never get involved with a cold bitch like you out of his own free will."

Holy crap. I must have lost my mind. One swipe from Manu's clawed hand, and it's game over for me.

But she doesn't retaliate. She simply stays frozen with a new emotion etched on her marble face—agony.

She whirls around and disappears into her room without uttering another word. I don't move for a few seconds, still processing what just happened. But then my common sense returns, and I head out. That could have been a stroke of sheer luck, and I don't want to be here when Manu decides to act like herself and kill me.

I'm still replaying my argument with Manu when I reach the main area of the institute. Damon finds me on the way to Keepers Etiquette class.

"Hey, Vivi. Have you seen Cassie?"

"Not since yesterday. Why?"

"She was supposed to meet me at the end of the day, but she bailed, and now, she's not answering any of my texts or calls."

"Have you checked with her roommate?"

"Yeah, she told me Cassie didn't spend the day there. Do you think something has happened to her?"

It takes a lot on my part to keep my face worry-free. I don't want to freak out Damon more even if I am freaking out myself.

"Maybe she had to go home. Don't worry. We'll find her."

"Okay."

Damon walks away with slumped shoulders and heavy steps. I glance at the flux of students heading to class and decide that keeping a perfect attendance record for a job I don't want is not my priority. Finding Cassie is.

I call her while I go in search of someone who can help me. Either Karl or Aurora will do. Lucca's name crosses my mind, but I immediately scratch that idea. I don't know what we are to each other anymore. He's no longer my predator, but am I still his prey?

I don't have any hope that Cassie will pick up the phone, so when her scratchy voice rings in my ear, I halt mid-step.

"Cassie. Oh my God. Are you okay?"

"Vivi, can you please come get me?" she whispers, but I manage to catch the fear in her tone.

"Yeah. Where are you?"

"In the east wing."

"I'll be right there."

I pivot and run in the opposite direction. If I'm not mistaken, that part of the building is closed off for renovations.

"Are you okay?" I ask.

"No. Can you please hurry?" she sobs, and then the call goes silent.

Fuck. Did it drop, or did something worse happen?

I call again, but it goes straight to voice mail now. *Damn it.*

When I reach the east wing, I call out Cassie's name. The corridors are darker here and much older. It smells moldy and damp, and in the distance, I can hear the constant noise of water dripping into a puddle.

"Cassie," I say again, and then I hear a muffled sob.

When I turn the corner, I find her at the end of the hallway, hugging her legs and with her head hanging low. Her hair is matted, and it covers her face. I hurry the rest of the way, dropping to my knees when I reach her. At once, I notice her torn-up dress and the purple marks on her arms. There are also angry bite marks on her shoulders. A vampire did that to her.

She looks up, allowing me to see the angry claw marks on her cheeks and her smudged makeup.

"Oh my God, Cassie. What happened?"

She falls into my arms, hugging me tightly as she hides her face in my chest. Being in such close proximity with a vampire would have terrified me a week ago. Now, I hug her back without a second thought.

"I swear I didn't ask for this, Vivi. You have to believe me."

I pat her hair, trying to soothe her. "Of course I believe you, honey. Who did this to you?"

She tenses in my arms, and there's a pause in her crying. I don't believe she's breathing now.

"You can trust me, Cassie."

"It was Boone. He did this to me."

My blood seems to freeze in my veins.

Cassie becomes a blubbering mess again, crying her eyes out. Violent shakes rack her body, and all I can do is rub her back and wait until she calms down. But my mind is spinning, and with each sob from her, my anger grows.

I don't care who he is. He can't keep attacking people and not suffer the consequences. Lucca is forbidden to attack him, thanks to some idiotic truce. But I'm not.

27

LUCCA

—————◆—————

Ronan advances with the katana raised above his head and a war cry. I pivot out of the way, coming at him from behind to deliver a roundhouse kick to his back. He staggers forward, using his weapon to avoid a frontal fall. I break into a run, grabbing the sword I dropped earlier, turning just in time to block his blow.

His eyes are glowing red now. He's pissed that I was able to break through his defensive stance. I'm sure my eyes are shining just the same. My pulse is pounding in my ears, and the fury coursing through my veins is familiar and foreign at the same time. I'm not a stranger to overwhelming emotions, but the reason behind it is what's puzzling me.

In a shitty move, I jam my head against Ronan's nose, and a resounding crack follows.

"Fuck!" He pulls away, covering his face. "Damn it, Lucca. You broke my nose!"

Breathing hard, I don't say a word as I stare at my friend through a crimson haze.

When I don't apologize, he continues, "What has gotten into you?"

I toss the katana aside and head for the bench. It would be easier to list what has *not* gotten into me lately. I woke up after almost a hundred years to a world I don't recognize anymore. I've never felt weaker or more impotent in my entire life. And I'm craving someone I definitely shouldn't.

Dropping onto the bench with my head hanging between my shoulders, I reply, "Everything."

"Is this about your meeting with Solomon?"

I snort. "If only. I'm so fucking angry. I know it's normal to feel disoriented for a few months after awakening, but I feel like I can't control anything in my life anymore."

"You're wrong, Luc. Your uncle had to bend over to Tatiana. So what? *We* don't need to stay here. There's no law that says Bluebloods must attend Bloodstone after hibernation."

"I can't leave." I meet Ronan's gaze.

"Why not?"

Sighing heavily, I say, "I don't know."

"That's bullshit. It's the new regular, isn't it? You've been acting like a mated male around her."

Fuck. Have I? I've never heard of mated vampires developing bloodlust for their partners.

"Mated male," I scoff. "What a load of crap."

"Then explain to me why you can't stay away from Vivienne."

Ronan is not going to drop the subject, and honestly, I'm tired of keeping this secret.

"Vivienne is human."

"What?"

"She's the thief who tried to steal my necklace at Havoc."

Ronan stares at me without blinking for a few seconds before he lets out a string of curses.

"How long have you known?" His hard stare is piercing and annoyed.

"Since her first day here."

"Fuck." He runs a hand through his hair. "Why didn't you say anything?"

"Because I wanted to deal with her on my own. Maybe you would be able not to meddle, but Saxon or Manu?" I shake my head. "Not a chance."

"How has she managed to conceal her true identity?"

"A powerful spell."

Ronan narrows his gaze, and I can almost see the gears in his head at work. "If she's using a spell, then Aurora must have seen through it. And her mother too."

"Probably."

"And you haven't wondered why they haven't said anything about it?"

I've been so obsessed with Vivienne that I didn't even consider that. *Fuck.* "Not until now."

"Hmm." Ronan crosses his arms. "You said you wanted to handle her on your own terms. How is that working out for you?" He raises an eyebrow.

Truth be told, I've been holding back. I could have been ten times worse toward Vivienne than I have. I spent the day in her bed, for crying out loud, even though it pained me in more ways than one.

"Terribly," I say.

The urge to see her again returns with a vengeance. I've been denying my hunger all this time, lying to myself that I just need to torture her more. In the end, I've been torturing us both.

I jump off the bench, filled with renewed energy.

Ronan's brows shoot to the heavens. "Where are you going?"

"I'm putting an end to this."

Faster than lightning, he blocks my path. "Whoa. You're not going to kill her here, are you?"

Here. He said here, and that feels like a punch to my chest. If she were anyone else, that'd be the outcome. I have never been a merciful Blueblood, and I don't think I've changed. I can be a great ally or a terrible enemy. But despite Vivienne's lying and scheming, I can't hurt her.

The problem is, do I only want her blood and her body, or do I want more?

I shove Ronan out of my way. "I'm not going to kill her, dumbass."

Before he can stop me, I zoom out of the gym. The hallways are empty. It seems I worked out for longer than I thought, and classes have ended for the day. I stop in front of Vivienne's apartment just as my sister is about to head in with another human toy in tow.

I slip in between her and the door, bracing my hand against the frame. "Go somewhere else."

She arches her eyebrows. "Excuse me?"

"Just go," I grit out. "You can ask for any favor later. Just don't come back until sundown."

"We can go back to my place," Manu's snack pipes up. "I don't live far from here."

She glances at him like he just said the dumbest thing. "The sun will be up in less than an hour, moron."

"Just take my room," I say.

"Fine!" Manu glares at me, poking me in the chest with her finger. "But you owe me. Big time."

She whirls around, whipping her long white hair. Her human follows her like a lovesick puppy. It's always the same deal with them. They live in hope and die in despair. Vampires very rarely fall in love with their food.

Then why do you want the apartment to Vivienne and yourself, Lucca?

I shove the pesky thought to a dark corner in my mind, but the actual front door I close with a soft click. I don't want to announce my arrival yet. Moving as silently as I can, I head to her room. The door is partially open, allowing me to see Vivienne sitting on her bed, surrounded by old books and scrolls. Her eyebrows are creased together as she peruses the content of a yellowed-out parchment and then tosses it aside, irritated.

My throat begins to burn a little as I watch her while I try my best to ignore the steady sound of her heartbeat. But there's another urge competing with the bloodlust. I want to hold her, protect her, and I don't know why I want all those things. Pure lust I get; it goes hand in hand with feeding. But this isn't about sex.

Unable to stay away any longer, I push the door open all the way and walk in. Vivienne lifts her gaze to mine, gasping in surprise.

"What are you doing here?" She shuts the book in her hand fast, almost as if she wants to hide something.

"I came to see how you were doing." I grab one of the scrolls near the edge of her bed, immediately noticing Vivienne's sharp intake of breath.

When I glance at the scroll, I understand why she's nervous. This is a family tree of Tatiana's bloodline. An old anger unfurls in the pit of my stomach, surging through my body in an instant. I crunch the paper in my hands while trying to contain the dark emotion.

"What are you doing with this?"

"I want to know more about Boone." She keeps staring at me without flinching. And yet I can sense her increased pulse and see the slight trembling of her hands.

"Why?"

Her nostrils flare, and her sweet lips become nothing but a slash on her face. "Because I'm going to kill him."

Not many people are able to surprise me, but that's what Vivienne just did. The shock only lasts a few seconds before I process her words and, most importantly, her motives to want my nemesis dead.

"What did he do to you?" I growl, taking a step closer to her.

She winces as if she's afraid of me. *Damn it.* That's not what I want anymore.

"You can tell me."

"He attacked one of my friends."

A human? The question is on the tip of my tongue, but I hold it at the last second. Now is not the time to tell Vivienne I know who she is.

"Who?" I ask instead.

"Cassie. She's a regular. I think …" She drops her gaze to her lap, releasing a shaky breath. "I think he raped her."

My fangs descend fully, and my nails turn into sharp talons. It was only a matter of time before Boone showed his true colors. He's a monster, and he deserves to die like one, destroyed into pieces. My breathing is ragged, and I'm a moment away from hunting him down.

"You can't go after him." Vivienne is suddenly in front of me.

I was so lost in my rage that I didn't even see her moving.

"He has to pay," I snarl. "This is not the first time he's hurt a female, and it won't be the last until someone stops him."

"I don't think Cassie will be willing to denounce him, and you can't attack Boone unprovoked." She touches my hand, sending an electric shock up my arm.

I reach over, sliding my hand to the back of her head and grabbing a fistful of her hair. "You're crazy if you think I'm going to let you get near that depraved male."

"Let me? I'm not your property."

My arm snakes around her waist, pulling her closer to me. Boone and his punishment get pushed to the background. The reason I kicked Manu out of her own apartment becomes the only thing that matters now. I'm here to stake my claim, to finally let the crave win.

"No, but you're mine."

I crush my lips against hers, hard and demanding. She resists but only because she's mad. It doesn't last though. Vivienne surrenders to me with abandon, matching each stroke of my tongue with the same amount of possessiveness as me. I'm not sure anymore who is claiming whom. She owns me with her body, with her mind, with her soul.

There's no space between our bodies, but I need more contact, more friction. I lift her from the floor as I walk, and as if reading my mind, she wraps her legs around my hips. I only stop moving when her back meets the wall and I'm pressing my erection against her heat.

Her pulse has skyrocketed, which works like a beacon to me. I leave her lips to kiss down her neck, dying to do more than just run my tongue over her skin. If I don't taste her blood, I might die. I graze a sweet spot with my fangs, ready to give in, but when Vivienne's body turns from supple to rigid in an instant, I stop. She's shaking in my arms, and it's not because of desire.

But the hunger wants me to ignore her panic; all that matters is drinking until I'm fully satisfied.

"Lucca, please," she begs, and her plea goes right through my chest.

I regain control for a moment and pull back. She's crying. *Fuck.*

"Did I hurt you?"

"You can't ..." She shakes her head. "Please."

Her image becomes fuzzy, or maybe it's my head that's clouded. She speaks again, but this time, I can't hear it because the sound of her blood pumping in her veins is louder. I'm going to lose it. If I start drinking from her, I won't be able to stop.

With the last bit of self-control that I have, I let go of Vivienne and run to the fridge, hoping there are enough blood bags stocked here. There are a few. I grab them all, not even sure if this will help me control the bloodlust. I savagely puncture the first bag, not caring if blood is spilling out or dripping down my chin.

Vivienne steps out of the room, mincing forward as if she were a frightened animal. If she were smart, she would run far away from me. *Can't she sense how close I am to ripping her throat to shreds?*

"You need to go." I toss the first empty bag in the sink and search for another one.

"Are you in pain?"

"Yes." I take a large gulp, not peeling my eyes off her. I'm gripping the edge of the counter with my free hand so hard that I might break a piece in any second.

"It's my blood, isn't it? You're craving it."

I close my eyes, hoping that if I don't see her, it will be easier to resist. "Yes. I don't want to hurt you."

"I want to help you."

I look at her again, questioning her sanity. "How are you going to help me? I want to drink from you, Vivienne. But if I do, I won't stop."

"You need a distraction." She drops to her knees in front of me and unzips my jeans.

I'd protest more if I were stronger. But when her fingers wrap around my cock, any arguments I might have die. I grab another bag, careful not to rip the plastic too hard and get blood all over her. Our gazes are locked when I inhale more blood, and Vivienne sucks my cock into her mouth.

Shakes run through my body, and now, I'm panting for another reason other than wanting to drink her dry. Feeding and sex go hand in hand for vampires, and somehow, Vivienne thought this would help me. She's not wrong. I can't drink her blood while I fuck her, but this is the next best thing.

28

VIVIENNE

⚔

I'm the stupidest girl alive. I know what's going on with Lucca. He's on the verge of bloodlust, and instead of running away from him, as I should, I offer to help. Maybe I'm caught in his bloodlust as well without the need to drink blood. I just want him.

I blame that incendiary kiss. It had the power to rob me of common sense. He's a predator, ready to devour me, and I'm the prey who can't stay away. It's like his demons are calling me, daring me to exorcise them.

But the way he took care of me yesterday and then his declaration that I was his spoke to a deep-rooted need in me. I've never felt protected before. I've been on my own pretty much my whole life. My brother has had too many issues to ever be the caring figure in our dysfunctional family.

As crazy as it sounds, it feels right for me to be on my knees, at Lucca's mercy. If I'm being honest with myself, it's something I've been dreaming about since I got here. All I can think about now is savoring him and pushing him off the edge while I do it. The fear that hit me a minute ago is gone, and now, I wish his fangs were deep inside my neck. It would be easy to blame vampire compulsion for my insanity, but I know he's not doing it. This is all on me.

He's getting bigger inside my mouth, so I suck harder, using my hands as well. He groans and then takes control. His fingers are in my hair, keeping my head steady as he fucks my mouth. He lets out a savage growl when he comes, moving even faster than before. I take everything that he gives me, and when he's emptied out, I want more.

Sitting on the balls of my feet now, I wipe my face with the back of my hand. I'm a little dazed, and I don't know why.

You've never given a vampire a blow job before, Vivi. Maybe his jizz is special.

Strong hands wrap around my arms and lift me up. The crimson is almost gone from Lucca's brown eyes, and there isn't any blood smeared on his chin anymore. He would look almost back to normal if a new kind of hunger wasn't shining in his gaze now.

"You're a crazy fool," he says gruffly.

"I know."

In a move I don't expect, Lucca picks me up, throwing me over his shoulder.

"What are you doing?" I twist my torso, trying to see where he's taking me.

We're back in my room. Without missing a beat, he yanks my bedspread off, sending all the books and notes that were on my bed to the floor. He then sets me in the middle of the mattress and stares at me.

His fangs are still on full display, and his breathing is coming out in bursts.

Shit. Is he going back to that savage state?

"Are you okay?" I ask in a small voice even though I'm not afraid.

"I'm fine. But you aren't." He grabs the back of his T-shirt, pulling it off to reveal the most amazing set of abs and chest I've ever seen.

Taut skin that's begging to be explored, muscles that are defined but not overly bulky. He's the model of perfect male beauty, and I want to lick every single plane and ridge of his body. I'm too busy ogling him that I only process his comment when he joins me in bed, on his hands and knees, stalking me like he's indeed a predator in the jungle.

I scooch back until there's nowhere else to go. "What do you mean, I'm not fine?"

His lips curl into a mischievous smile, sending a heat wave from the tips of my toes up to the roots of my hair.

He walks his fingers up my leg until they disappear under my skirt. "I want to return the favor."

The room is getting hotter and hotter, and my pussy is already throbbing in anticipation. Not taking his eyes off me, he curls his fingers around the sides of my panties and rolls them down my legs.

"God, you're so aroused; I can't wait to taste you again."

He opens my legs wider, and then he's between them, not holding back. I cry out at the first sweep of his tongue, arching my back. He's not wrong; I'm so horny that I'll probably come in the next minute. Twisting the sheet underneath me with my hands, I try to hold off the release for as long as I can. Then, I feel a pressure at my entrance—his finger—and I lose it completely. The orgasm is so intense that I have to grab a pillow and bite into it to muffle my screams.

Lucca's caresses down below cease when I'm no longer shaking, and a second later, he removes the pillow from my face. He's smiling from ear to ear—an expression I've never seen before on him. My heart expands and overflows with a heady feeling that leaves me breathless and ecstatic at the same time. But then my attention drops to his necklace, dangling just above my nose. The post-orgasm euphoria evaporates, and the cruel reality returns, cutting in like a sharp knife.

He doesn't seem to notice my inner turmoil as he brings my hands up, linking his fingers with mine and letting our joined hands rest on each side of my head. On his knees, he just hovers above me, radiating pure sexual allure.

"You're beautiful," he says just before he leans down and tenderly kisses me.

I melt, and right then and there, I decide that I won't let anything destroy this moment. Screw responsibilities and promises. I want to enjoy every second of this experience, so I can treasure the memory forever once I'm gone. I don't have any illusions. Whatever is going on between Lucca and me has an expiration date. The tightness in my chest is hard to ignore though.

Determined to not drown in the dark feeling competing for space in my heart, I wrap my legs around his hips, hooking them at the ankles and pulling him to me.

Without breaking the kiss, he lowers his body to mine, pressing his erection against my core. There are still too many layers of clothing between us though, but since he's still keeping my hands trapped under his, I can't do much about it.

"Lucca," I murmur between kisses.

"Yeah?" He gyrates his pelvis, rubbing his erection right where I so desperately need it.

"I want you. All of you."

He pulls back and watches me for a moment. "Are you sure, Vivi?"

I nod, unable to form words now. He called me by my nickname, injecting the butterflies in my stomach with pure adrenaline. I can't let hope gain ground in my heart. This will never be anything more between us than a hook-up.

Lucca stands up, getting rid of his pants in vampire super-speed. Then, instead of joining me again, he remains still next to the bed in all his naked glory, watching me with a gaze so intense that it unravels me. The drumming inside of my chest is so strong that it feels like my heart has been replaced by an entire marching band.

His lips curl into that wicked grin that has the power to turn my brain into cotton candy. Not that I'm not already completely undone by him.

"Now it's your turn, sweetheart."

Heat rushes to my face. I've gone further with Lucca than with any other guy before him, and yet I'm nervous about getting out of my clothes with him watching. I sit up, and then, with a deep breath, I close my eyes and tug my shirt up.

Then, Lucca is there, sitting next to me. "Shh. There's no need to be nervous, Vivi. Here, I'll help." He slowly pulls my shirt off, lobbing it to the side. His heated stare lowers to my breasts for just a second before his eyes connect with mine. "Are you okay?"

"Yeah."

I don't want him to think I'm a china doll just because I'm a virgin. I unhook my bra and then slide the straps down my arms. Lucca drops his gaze to my chest as he runs his fingers across my cleavage, leaving a path of goose bumps over my skin.

My eyes close, and a little moan escapes my lips. When Lucca's warm tongue captures one of my nipples, a wave of desire shoots straight down to my core. My clit is throbbing again, ready—no, *begging* for more. When I open my eyes, my room is spinning out of control. I feel dizzy, but it's not a bad thing. Lucca's hand disappears under my skirt, and his fingers find my bundle of nerves, drawing another delirious moan from me.

"That's right, Vivi. Let go of all your inhibitions. Tell me what you want."

I sense the dare in his tone. My face is in flames, but I meet his eyes without fear. My voice is steady when I say, "I want your mouth all over my skin. I want to feel your power between my legs. I want you to consume me."

His eyes flash bright red, and I fear I said too much. With a hard yank, he tears my skirt in two. Then, he gets onto his knees in front of me, pulling my hips off the mattress so my pussy is at the same level as his cock.

"This might hurt a little, darling."

He presses the head of his erection against my entrance. It slides in a little, and it feels glorious. I want more.

"I don't care," I breathe out.

He pushes forward, gently filling me. There's a pinch, and then he's sheathed inside of me fully. I tense, worrying that I might bleed. But Lucca's eyes remain brown.

"Are you okay?" he asks, his voice a little strained.

"No," I tease, but when his gaze becomes filled with guilt, I'm quick to add, "You stopped moving."

Narrowing his eyes in a mischievous way, he digs his fingers into my skin while pulling out almost all the way. "That can be fixed."

He thrusts back in fast, drawing a cry from my lips.

"That's right. Cry out, little minx."

I capture his gaze, making sure he can read the challenge in my eyes. "Harder."

Shaking his head, he chuckles. "Oh, you're in trouble now."

He complies, and I agree with him. I'm very much in trouble. His thrusts become faster and deeper, and each time he fills me, he pushes me closer to the abyss. But as much as this position feels good, I miss the closeness. I want to feel the weight of his body over mine.

I reach over, trying to pull him to me. "Come here."

Lucca's nostrils flare, and his eyes turn a shade darker. "I'm not sure if that's a good idea, darling."

"Is it the bloodlust?"

"Yeah."

Oh no. "Did I bleed?"

"No," he groans. "It's not that. Thank fuck."

"You're not going to give in. I trust you."

The words surprise me. They're the absolute truth. I trust him like I've known him my entire life.

A flash of emotion crosses his eyes. It's different than hunger or lust. His expression softens though, and then he lowers his body to mine. I grab his face between my hands and kiss him like this is the last time. Fury, fear, passion, and guilt are all mixed in it.

Lucca continues to pound away, matching the tempo of his hips with his tongue. I want to believe this moment feels as amazing for him as it does for me even if it's wishful thinking. But even if his heart doesn't surrender, his body does. We're moving in sync now, so much so that I don't know anymore where I end and he begins.

A bubble of pleasure seems to envelop my entire body until it bursts, and I explode into tiny fragments.

"Fuck, Vivienne. I can't …" Lucca's entire frame convulses, and he's gone too.

Boneless. That's the state I'm in. I've lost count on how many times Lucca made me come, and the only reason we didn't fuck all day long was because I'm human and I would have ended up with a broken body for real.

Nightfall is a few hours away still, and now, Lucca is sound asleep next to me. I can't sleep yet, so I just stare unabashedly at him. He looks so much younger now that his face doesn't carry the weight of a centuries-long existence. Despite fearing vampires for most of my life, I've always wondered what it would be like to live forever. *Is their immortality the reason some of them are vile and cruel?*

My eyes drop to his neck and the jewelry around it. This is my chance. I could take Lucca's necklace and be far away before he woke up. My hand is now hovering above it as I think about Rikkon at Larsson's mercy. I've helped him out of trouble more times than

I can count, and anyone, especially my friends, would tell me I'd more than repaid my debt. And yet I can't walk away from him, but I also can't steal from Lucca.

There's no logic that can justify my conflicting emotions. As I stare at Lucca, I get again the sense that I've known him for a long time, which is impossible. *Why is he evoking this deep sense of loyalty in me?*

With a heavy sigh, I drop my hand, and instead of doing what I came to Bloodstone for, I kiss his cheek.

29

VIVIENNE

I did manage to fall asleep, and when I wake up, Lucca's side of the bed is empty but not cold to the touch. He must have just gotten up. I'm disappointed that he left without saying good-bye, but I try to psych myself out of it. It's better this way. I can't fall deeper into this rabbit hole, or I might never crawl out.

My head is still fuzzy, thanks to the lack of rest. It's probably the only explanation as to why I don't hear the shower is on until I walk into a foggy bathroom. Lucca is in there, just about finished with rinsing his hair.

"Good evening, darling. Are you joining me?"

My jaw is on the floor, and my eyes are bulging out of my skull. I must look like a silly cartoon character now. "I thought you'd left."

"Not without saying a proper good-bye." He dumps a good amount of liquid soap on his open palm and then proceeds to lather his body.

I follow the movements of his hands down his abs until he holds his rock-hard erection in his fist. And just like that, my skin is ablaze. Lucca's heated stare scorches my naked body before our eyes meet again. One of his eyebrows rises in a silent challenge.

Damn it. In for a penny, in for a pound. Maintaining eye contact, I walk over, and that's when I see a stack of blood bags next to my shampoo bottle.

"I got hungry," he says sheepishly.

My stomach decides to complain just then, groaning loudly. There's no hoping the sound of the water jets covered that. If I heard it, so did he. I become a little tense. *What if Lucca decides to offer me some of that blood?*

As if hearing my thoughts, he says, "I'd offer you some, but being in your presence is still triggering. I need to drink as much as I can to keep the hunger at bay."

Ignoring for now the fact that something about me is giving Lucca bloodlust, I exhale in relief. "It's okay. I'll eat something later."

"Well, I want to eat something now." He grabs me by the waist and pushes me against the tiled wall.

His body is covering every inch of mine when he plunges his tongue in my mouth at the same time his fingers find my entrance. I'm still sore from yesterday's marathon, but I welcome his invasion with gusto. He's fucking me with three fingers now while his thumb plays with my clit.

"Luc … oh my God," I say when he gives me the chance to speak.

"Sweet Vivienne, I need to be inside of you right this second." His hand is gone, but it's quickly replaced by his shaft.

This won't take long at all.

He lifts one of my legs, allowing him to go deeper at this angle. We're all slick, thanks to the soap, but somehow, that doesn't affect Lucca's ability to fuck me, keep me upright, and drink from one of his blood bags.

The sight of him gulping down all that blood should nauseate me, but how can I be disgusted when he's looking at me like I'm the most desirable woman he has ever seen?

He tosses the empty bag aside, braces his free hand against the wall, and kisses my shoulder. His lips don't return to mine, not even when we climax almost at the same time. Here, there's no pillow to muffle my reaction, and not even the shower can cover my screams of ecstasy.

I'm still on cloud nine when we finally get out of the shower. Since my body is mush, I sit down, wrapped in my towel, and watch Lucca get dressed like he's a movie star and I'm his biggest fan. He buttons his jeans and then turns to me with a knowing smile.

"You're not getting dressed?"

"In a minute."

He grabs his T-shirt and then stops to stare at me with a new glint in his eyes, more serious.

"What?" I sit straighter.

"There are other ways to get what you want."

Alarm bells ring in my head, and fear drops like lead in my

stomach. "I don't know what you mean."

His lips become a thin, flat line.

Shit. Does he know who I am? Did he seduce me as some kind of twisted punishment?

"A better life," he answers finally. "You don't need to become a Keeper to have that."

I let out a shaky breath. "Oh. I'm not so sure that's true. The reality for regulars is very different than that of Bluebloods." I glance at my hands, feeling ashamed even though I shouldn't, not because of my background anyway.

I might be living a lie here, but I feel his statement fully. My reality is a far cry from his. Lucca is royalty, a prince. I'm trailer trash.

"I know. But you don't need to be the product of your environment. It doesn't matter what kind of shitty family you have or where you grew up."

This is beginning to sound too close to my life, making me hella uncomfortable. *And why is Lucca saying all this anyway?* It doesn't make any sense. He can't possibly be interested in someone like me, or at least the pretend me—a regular vampire without connections or pedigree.

The apartment's front door bangs open, announcing Manu's arrival. I frown. The last time we traded words wasn't pretty.

"I'd better get going. I kicked Manu out yesterday, so she's most likely not in the best of moods."

"Oh, that's nice. You piss her off, and now, I have to deal with her wrath." I pucker my lips.

"Don't do that," he says.

"Do what?"

"Pout. It's very … tempting."

"You'd better be on your way out, Lucca boy," Manu shouts from the living room.

Grimacing, he glances at me before he disappears through the door.

Shit. I wish I had gotten dressed, so I could have walked out of the apartment with him. I'm not sure if it's safe for me to be alone with his sister. Too late now.

I grab the first ensemble of clean clothes I can find, and five minutes later, I'm braving the unknown.

Manu is perched on a high stool, checking her long and sharp nails. She doesn't glance up when she speaks to me. "I hope you got your fill, roomie."

"Excuse me?"

She meets my gaze. "Lucca doesn't do repeats. He fucked you, and now, he's going to move on."

Her words are poison, and her eyes shine with cruelty and glee. It's hard not to feel the cut of her remark.

"I don't care if he moves on. I'm not staying long."

30

VIVIENNE

———⟨♦⟩———

I didn't cry. That's good. I'd hate myself if I had let Manu know she'd gotten to me. But I'm so fucking sad about everything. I lost my chance to steal the necklace, and worse, I fell for my target. *How stupid can a person be? And how in the world did I let this happen?* I'm in love with Lucca Della Morte.

Vivienne Gale in love with a vampire. Inconceivable!

My phone pings, announcing an incoming text. My heart skips a beat, as I immediately think it's from Lucca. Then, I remember I never gave him my digits, and also, why would he be texting me now? We just saw each other.

You're also not two teenagers in love, Vivi. Well, maybe you are, but he's definitely not.

The text is from Karl. He wants to talk, and he's offering food as a bribe. I smile despite myself. Eating breakfast would be nice, but I want to speak with Damon first, so I head to Keepers class.

Cassie is not waiting for me at the base of the stairs. She took a leave of absence to recover from her ordeal. I'm not sure what excuse she gave the institute's administration, or her parents, but she certainly didn't rat Boone out, which makes me furious every time I think about it. When I enter Hanson's class, Damon is already there, letting out his frustration against a punching bag. *Did Cassie tell him what had happened?* They're close, and I suspect they're more than friends. Hmm, maybe he doesn't know, or he would have tried something against Boone for sure.

"Hey," I greet him, keeping my distance from his punches.

He grunts in response.

I don't have time to ask him anything because Hanson comes in and demands our attention.

"Today, I have a very important announcement to make. As you know, you're training to one day service a Blueblood family. It can be a difficult transition to some, and maybe you will realize that you're not cut out for that line of work. In order to avoid wasting time and resources, I've come up with an internship program."

A quick glance around the room tells me that my classmates are as surprised as I am. *Good.* For once, I don't feel like a fish out of water.

"A few Bluebloods have volunteered to take one intern each. You will work with them for four weeks for at least three hours a day."

Ah hell. I don't want to intern for anyone. Maybe it's time I say good-bye to Bloodstone for good since it's clear I won't be able to accomplish my goal. Besides, the spell concealing my human identity will expire in three weeks. I will have to come up with another way to buy Rikkon's freedom.

"I don't need to stress this hard enough: you'd better not screw up during your internship. It's not your reputations that are at stake but mine. One step out of line, and you'll find yourself out on the curb." He takes his time to stare at everyone, but he seems to take extra time to glare at me.

Fucker.

The gym door opens, and the Bluebloods who volunteered for the program enter as if their arrival was coordinated precisely to coincide with the end of Hanson's speech. I'm watching the parade of pompous vampires with bored disinterest when I see the monster enter last.

Boone.

My blood runs cold in an instant, almost at the same time that my fury unleashes from the pit of my stomach. I glimpse at the daggers meant for us, which are still on display just outside of the tatami, and calculate the likelihood that I can take one and plunge it deep inside Boone's guts before anyone can stop me. If I were as fast as a vampire, I'd risk it.

Hanson is talking again, but I can barely make out his words. There's a loud buzz in my ears, the sound of my rage pounding away.

"Vivienne!" Hanson is suddenly in front of my face, glowering.

"What?" I shout back.

"If you can't be bothered to pay attention in this class, then you have no business being here."

"Maybe I don't want to be here," I grit out.

Movement behind him catches my attention. Boone is coming over. *Damn it. If I only had a blade on me.*

"It's okay, Hanson. Four weeks of working for me will set her straight."

"Uh, what?" I ask.

"Boone has specifically requested you to be assigned to him," Hanson replies with an air of boredom.

"I'm not working for him," I sneer.

Hanson grabs me by the arm, digging his fingers in hard. "You will not challenge my authority, little nothing. Get out of my sight before I forget corporal punishment is no longer tolerated."

He shoves me in Boone's direction, and he doesn't miss the opportunity to paw me as well. He holds me just as hard as Hanson did, only his nails are sharper and being near him makes me physically ill.

"Come on, Vivienne. I have a list of things for you to do."

I make the mistake of glancing in his eyes, and immediately, my resistance begins to wane. *No. No. No.* Boone is using compulsion on me. Because Lucca or any of the other Bluebloods I've dealt with have never resorted to that, I naively thought they simply didn't have that ability.

My mind is rebelling, but my body willingly goes with Boone. He steers me out of the gym and heads toward the stairs to the catacombs. All my muscles are seizing, and my airway is beginning to close up. Finally, Boone is going to get what he wants. He'll try to destroy me, just like he did with Cassie.

I look left and right, but the hallway is deserted. I'd scream if I could, but it seems he took that ability from me too. We soon plunge into darkness, and I'm shaking from head to toe by the time we reach the underground level.

No sooner do we get there than Boone shoves me against the wall, holding me by the neck, and he brings his ugly face near mine.

The stench emanating from him is awful and permeates everything.

"I've finally got you alone, fresh meat, and this time, Lucca won't be here to save your ass."

A gust of chilly wind kisses my skin, and then I hear the eerie voice that has called to me twice before. *Shit.* The ghost from the secret chamber knows I'm here. I glance to my right, trying to gauge the distance to that hidden room. I'd rather take my chances with the wraith than face Boone. If only he'd let me go for a moment, I'd be able to disappear. Aurora said no one was supposed to find that place. Lucca couldn't.

Boone pinches my chin between his forefinger and thumb, forcing me to look at him. "What are you staring at? No one will come to help—at least, not before I have my fun."

He releases my neck to rip my top down the middle. I can't remember what kind of bra I'm wearing, but Boone is momentarily transfixed by my breasts. This is my chance. I don't have enough room to kick him in the nuts hard enough, but I can stomp on his instep.

He howls, hopping on one foot. I shove him away from me, and thanks to sheer luck, he trips and falls. I bolt toward the secret chamber, hoping I make it there before Boone can catch me.

"You filthy whore! I'm going to make you pay for this." His angry voice echoes behind me, too close already.

But the ghost's voice is getting louder, so I must be getting nearer. Something akin to a boulder collides with my back, sending me careening to the stone floor. The impact is jarring. I hit my elbows and end up biting my tongue, drawing blood. Then, Boone yanks my hair back, eliciting a cry from me.

"That's right; scream, bitch. That only makes me hornier."

I hear a zipper open, and then Boone is tearing my pants. I'm in a situation that would probably send me to a place that I'd never be able to crawl out from. It's déjà vu but also much worse. However, a strange sense of calmness takes over me. I don't know if I'm already losing my mind, but then the specter of a woman materializes in front of me. She's behind the bars that keep the secret chamber separated from us. If I reached with my arm, I could touch them. There's a spell that prevents her from crossing. I sense it now.

"Blood," she says in my head. *"Give me your blood, and I will help you."*

I don't know how I'm going to do that, but then Boone smacks my face against the hard ground. White-hot pain shoots up my forehead, and then something warm pours from my nose. My skull is throbbing in a blinding way, making me unaware of what Boone is doing to my body now. I feel nothing.

"What the hell?" he yells suddenly, getting off me.

A terrible shriek echoes in the tunnel, and then all I hear is Boone's desperate screams.

The compulsion that trapped my body a moment ago vanishes. I push myself off the floor, getting up on shaky legs. My clothes are in tatters, but I'm still wearing underwear. He didn't have time to violate me.

He and the specter have vanished from sight, but I can hear his cries from somewhere nearby. I hope the ghost shreds him to pieces.

31

LUCCA

I'm being grilled by Saxon about where I spent the night when the loud pounding on our front door interrupts his tirade. He and Ronan trade a glance.

"Are we expecting someone?" Saxon asks.

"Not me." Ronan shrugs.

Saxon raises an eyebrow in my direction. "Maybe it's Lucca's favorite regular."

"Fuck off." I throw the closest object within my reach at him, which turns out to be a thick book about social media.

He bends out of the way, and the book ends up knocking one of the TV speakers to the floor.

"Hey, you break it, you replace it," Ronan complains.

The knock comes again. "Lucca, open up."

"Who the hell is that?" Saxon reaches the door first, opening it

Looking past him, I find Damon, a regular vampire who I've seen with Vivienne before. I'm off the barstool in a split second.

"What do you want?" Saxon asks.

"I need to speak with Lucca." The male sounds worried, and he's positively acting like something terrible happened.

"Let him in, Sax," I say.

"Boone has Vivienne." The words blurt out of his mouth without preamble.

"What?" My entire posture changes, and I'm in the male's face, pulling him closer by the lapels of his jacket. "When did this happen?"

"Ten minutes ago. Boone came over to the gym, and he took Vivienne with him. I'm certain he used compulsion."

"Where was Hanson during that?" Ronan asks, but I'm no longer interested.

I shove Damon out of my way and run out of the apartment.

"Luc, wait!" Saxon calls after me.

Ten minutes. Vivienne has been at the hands of that motherfucker for ten minutes. He could have done a number of awful things to her in that amount of time. I'm going to rip his head off this time. *Fuck the Accords. Fuck everything.*

It's not hard to catch Vivienne's scent in the air when I reach the institute's lecture area. I know exactly where Boone took her. To the catacombs. My vision is completely tinged in red. There's nothing in the world that will keep me from tearing Boone apart limb by limb. As fast as I'm moving, I can't stop in time when Vivienne steps into the hallway. We collide, and she ends up hitting her face against my chest straight on. I barely feel the impact, but she becomes dead weight in my arms.

"Vivienne. Wake up." I shake her a little.

There's dried blood coming out of her nose and an angry mark around her neck in the shape of a male hand. Boone did this to her.

I sense when Saxon and Ronan join me in the hallway and also when they take in Vivienne's current state. It's impossible to miss the aggression emanating from them now. I don't dare to inspect her further, afraid of what I might find. Instead, I pick her up in my arms, cradling her tight against my chest.

"Where's Boone?" Ronan asks.

"I don't know."

Manu, Karl, and Aurora come running from the other end of the corridor. When Karl's expression twists in a look of pure horror, I hold Vivienne tighter while shakes of rage run through my body. I'm torn between finding Boone and taking care of her.

"We'll find him," Saxon says as if reading my mind.

He and Ronan run to the catacombs while Aurora steps closer to me. "She needs medical attention."

Manu takes a deep breath, and then she narrows her gaze. "She's human."

So lost in my fury, I didn't even register the scent of Vivienne's blood. It should have sparked the bloodlust, but there's another emotion stronger within me. It's trumping everything else.

"Lucca, come on. We have to get her out of here," Aurora urges.

"Let's go back to my apartment."

I'm pacing in the living room while Aurora is with Vivienne in my bedroom, doing God knows what. She wouldn't allow me to stay close, afraid my bloodlust would be triggered at any moment. So far, I'm okay. Maybe it's the desire to find and kill Boone that's helping me control my hunger.

Manu is sitting on the couch opposite Karl. The guy hasn't said a word since we got here. I'm not a mind reader, but I can tell guilt is consuming him. It's consuming me too. I knew Boone wouldn't give up on Vivienne. I should have protected her—or better yet, sent her away from Bloodstone. I didn't do it for my own selfish reasons, and she paid the ultimate price.

"I can't believe you knew Vivienne was the human thief from Havoc, and you didn't tell us." Manu glares at me.

"My friend was just assaulted by a predator, and you're bitching about not knowing her secret?" Karl snaps. "Seriously, Manu, what is wrong with you?"

She has the decency to show remorse, but Karl is right. Sometimes, her ruthlessness is infuriating. I'm about to add a few angry remarks myself, but then Aurora steps out of my room.

"How is she?" I stop in front of her.

"Besides a few lacerations and bruises, she's fine." She looks straight into my eyes. "He didn't accomplish his goal."

A great weight is removed from my chest, but I'm far from satisfied. He dared to touch Vivienne. He hurt her to punish me, and I won't let it slide. Accords or not, he's dead meat.

"Is she awake?" I ask.

"Yeah."

I step around the witch, but she places a hand on my arm. "Wait, are you sure it's a good idea for you to see her right now?"

"I'm not going to hurt her." My response comes out almost like a growl.

"Your crazy vampire eyes say differently."

Shit. They must be glowing red. "It has nothing to do with bloodlust."

Saxon and Ronan come through the door, their expressions grimmer than ever. I notice when Saxon's eyes zero in on Aurora's hand on my arm and how his posture changes. She steps away from me, and he follows her movements. Whatever is going on between them is not important right now.

"Did you find him?" I ask.

Ronan grimaces. "Yes. You won't have to worry about him for a while now."

"What's that supposed to mean?" Aurora asks. "Please tell me you didn't do something foolish."

"Relax, little witch. We didn't lay a hand on that son of a bitch," Saxon replies. "When we got there, he was cut in so many places that he'd have died in a pool of his own blood if he were human."

My eyes become rounder. "Are you saying that Vivienne did that to him?"

"No. Something much worse got to Boone. He was mumbling words that didn't make any sense, but one he kept repeating constantly was *specter*." Ronan looks at Aurora. "Do you happen to know anything about that?"

I glance at the witch, immediately noticing her ashen face. She doesn't answer right away, but I bet she knows exactly what attacked Boone in the catacombs. It's probably the same thing that got Vivienne the other day.

As much as I want to know what secret Aurora's mother and Solomon are hiding in the bowels of the institute, I have other priorities. I leave my friends behind and veer toward my room. Vivienne is lying in my bed with her eyes closed. I stop near the door, taking a moment to get a grip on my emotions. There's a tightness in my chest now, a new worry that makes me question everything about my long existence.

I never allowed myself to feel anything for any female. I believed that having the love of my family and friends was enough. It wasn't fair to get involved with someone while I had this damn curse hanging over my head.

Then, Vivienne came along and changed everything.

She stirs in her sleep and then slowly opens her eyes. When our gazes meet, an enormous lump forms in my throat.

"Lucca," she whispers.

In the next second, I'm in bed with her and she's in my arms. I hug her tightly, crushing her face against my chest. The annoying hunger decides to rear its ugly head again, but fuck that shit. I'm not going to let it ruin this moment.

"I'm so sorry, darling. I never should have let you out of my sight."

"This wasn't your fault. Boone found a way to get me alone that was completely sanctioned by the institute."

My gums ache as my fangs descend. It's not bloodlust that's making me react like a wild animal; it's the thirst for revenge.

"Hanson arranged this?" I ask with barely contained rage.

"He assigned me to Boone at his personal request." She pulls back. "You're not going to do anything to him, are you?"

"He knew Boone had already attacked you before. He shouldn't have put you in harm's way."

"What about the Accords?"

"The Accords only protect Boone and his followers from me—that is, allegedly. If Boone thinks he's safe, he's sorely mistaken."

Vivienne's eyes widen in fear. "I'm not going to let you get in trouble to avenge me."

I capture her beautiful face between my hands. "You deserve to be avenged, darling. Many times over."

My lips find hers, ending any protests she might have. She's human, and I still crave her blood with a deranged obsession. Despite that, I want her but not only as nourishment or distraction; I want her wholly for as long as she will allow me to be near her.

Pressing her hands against my chest, she pushes me back, ending the kiss too soon. "Lucca, I need to tell you something."

She won't meet my eyes, keeping her gaze fixed on the hollow of my throat.

"What is it, Vivi?"

She releases a shaky breath. "I'm not who you think I am."

I place my index finger under her chin, lifting her face to mine. "I know who you are, darling. I've known since your first day."

Her beautiful eyes turn as round as saucers. "Wait a second. You know that I'm the girl who tried to steal from you at Havoc? You know that I'm human?"

I smirk. "Yeah."

Her expression changes suddenly, twisting into a scowl. She jumps out of bed, wearing nothing but her underwear, and glares at me with her hands on her hips. "You knew I was human, and you made me drink blood? What kind of asshole does that?"

Ah hell. I completely forgot about that. *Shit.*

32

VIVIENNE

I'm beyond pissed. I'm livid. Lucca knew I was human from the get-go, and he let me drink from that poor woman. That's the lowest of the low.

"I'm sorry about that, Vivi. Truly."

"Are you really sorry? Or is that part of your twisted game?"

He jumps out of bed and walks over, hand up in supplication. "This is not part of any game. You need to calm down."

"Don't tell me to calm down!" Angry tears roll down my cheeks.

In the back of my head, I know I shouldn't be yelling at him. I'm in a dangerous situation here, but I don't care. Maybe being attacked by Boone snapped that part of my brain that had any common sense.

"Fine. Don't calm down. Yeah, I forced you in that situation because I wanted to know how far you were willing to keep up with the charade. Why you would risk your life, coming here to steal from me."

I hastily wipe my face, suddenly feeling like a fool for allowing myself to fall for him. This has been nothing but a wicked and drawn-out revenge. "What is my punishment then?"

His eyebrows arch. "Punishment? What are you talking about?"

"You're not going to simply let me go, are you? I lied to you. I'm a thief." The words taste bitter in my mouth.

He breaks the distance between us and holds me by the arms. "I'm not going to punish you, silly girl. Yes, I wanted to in the beginning, but it's been a while since my priorities have changed."

"Why?"

I search his eyes, which are brown with flecks of red in them. *Is he on the verge of succumbing to the bloodlust?* Even with that possibility, I don't have any great survival instinct urging me to run for the hills. I must have a death wish.

"I don't know. I just can't stay away from you—and not only because I crave your blood."

My heart wants to believe him so desperately, but I can't.

"I've been to your neighborhood," he adds.

"What?"

"And I know about your brother. As a matter of fact, I went to Ember Emporium with every intention to get him out of there."

"Wh-what happened?"

Lucca lets go of me, stepping back. "My uncle happened. He forbade me to speak with the dragon-shifter. Compulsion was involved."

I can't believe this. *Lucca tried to help my brother?* My brain is whirling. I don't know what to think anymore.

"Why does Larsson want your necklace?" I ask.

Lucca covers the medallion with his hand. "I don't know. It was my mother's. It's actually the only thing I have left of her." With a hard pull, he breaks the chain off and offers the necklace to me. "Here. If it means your brother's freedom, you can have it."

I stare at the offering without blinking, but I don't move to accept it. My chest feels horribly tight. It doesn't feel right to deprive Lucca of something so personal to satisfy the whim of a criminal.

"I can't take it."

Lucca's brows furrow together. "You went through all this trouble, risked your life, and now, you won't accept my gift?"

"I could have stolen your necklace yesterday. I couldn't do it. It's not right."

He reaches for my hand, forces it open, and drops the necklace onto my palm. "This piece of jewelry won't bring my mother back, Vivi. But it can save your brother."

Tears form in my eyes again, but they're different. I stare at Lucca's necklace, fighting the waterworks. A lump the size of Texas lodges itself in my throat, making it hard for me to breathe.

"Thank you."

"Now, you can leave."

I whip my face up so fast that I pull a muscle in my neck. "You want me to go?"

"No. That's the last thing I want. But you can't stay here. You're not a vampire, familiar, or snack. Bloodstone is not a place for you."

The first fat tear rolls down my cheek. "I used to think so, but now, I'm not so sure."

Lucca pulls me into his arms and kisses the top of my head. "You're not safe here. Boone doesn't know you're human. You can return to your old life. You can leave Salem behind, follow your dreams."

"What do you know about my dreams?" I ask through a choke.

"I know a lot, Vivi."

Unlike me. Everything I thought I knew about Lucca has turned out to be wrong. He's savage and dark, but he's not cruel. He's the vampire I love. But I feel foolish saying that to him out loud, so I don't.

Someone knocks on the door, and without waiting for a reply, Aurora pushes it open and sticks her head in. "Sorry to interrupt, but we have a situation."

"What now?" Lucca grumbles.

"The headmaster has sent for Vivienne. It's about Boone."

My stomach becomes a twisted mess, hurting like a mother. "I need to give him a statement, don't I?"

"Yes, most likely," she replies.

Lucca wraps his arm over my shoulders, pulling me closer. "I'll come with you."

"I don't think that's wise, Lucca. I'll take her to Solomon's office, and if possible, I'll stay with her."

Lucca's body is tense next to mine. "That's not good enough. If this meeting is anything like the one I attended, I won't let her go alone."

"Your presence will only make matters worse," Aurora retorts.

I turn in his arms, so I can capture his gaze. "I'm fine. I can face the headmaster alone."

"You're not fine, and no one expects you to be fine." Lucca stares at me intensely.

I take a deep breath and step away from his cocoon of safety. As much as I would like to wear him as my armor, this is a battle I must face without the added protection. Besides, if I have to relive every detail of my ordeal at the hands of Boone, I'd prefer if Lucca were not privy to it.

I switch my attention to Aurora. "If you can get me something to wear, I'll go see the headmaster now."

Despite Lucca's many protests, in the end, only Aurora and Karl accompany me to the headmaster's office. I'm not feeling particularly chatty, and they both leave me alone. From time to time, Karl steals glances in my direction, but I pretend I don't notice them. I can't deal with any emotion I might find reflected in his eyes.

He knows about my first vampire attack experience and how it left me with permanent scars. He must be expecting me to break at any minute now. Or perhaps I'll find reproach or pity in his gaze.

I'm not sure how I'm holding my torn pieces together. Maybe I'm in shock. Lost in my thoughts, I don't pay attention to my surroundings. I'm letting Aurora lead the way. When she stops in front of a richly decorated door, I turn into a ball of nerves. It seems the numbness is fading, and I can finally feel the full impact of my terror. I bite the inside of my cheek, hoping the pain will distract me from the jitters racking my body.

Aurora knocks once, and then the door opens inward by itself.

The room is austere with dark wood furniture and paneled walls. Bookcases, filled to the brim with old tomes, occupy most of the space, and in the middle, there's a long, solid oak table where an older male sits behind it. His hair is shaggy and white, and his beady eyes are almost too close together and a little hidden by his bushy eyebrows. I've never seen a vampire who looks quite like him.

"So, you're the infamous Vivienne Gale." He clasps his hands together, watching me over his wide nose.

"I don't know about infamous," I say, trying not to show how freaked out I am.

He switches his attention to Aurora and Karl, who are flanking me. "I'd like to speak to Vivienne alone, please."

A bout of panic threatens to take hold of me. I look at Aurora, pleading with my eyes for her to stay.

"Vivienne has been through hell. She needs moral support." Karl speaks before her.

"Oh? Those aren't the reports I've heard from multiple sources."

"What sources are you referring to?" Aurora butts in.

"Hanson, for starters."

She takes a step forward with her hands balled into fists. "He's a snake, and he can't be trusted. He knew Boone had attacked Vivienne before, and he was more than glad to pawn her off to him."

The headmaster narrows his gaze, leaning forward. "Aurora Leal, you seem to be forgetting your place in this institution. You're not a High Witch yet; you're an apprentice."

Tired of hearing them talking about me as if I weren't even in the room, I move closer to his desk. "Boone tried to rape me. Are you saying that because he's a Blueblood, somehow I'm at fault?"

He leans back, widening his eyes. "That is a serious accusation."

"He also attacked one of my friends. Cassandra Alencar," I add.

"What's your relationship with Lucca Della Morte?"

I'm taken aback by his question. It's like he didn't hear a word I said.

"How does Vivienne's relationship with Lucca pertain to what we're discussing here?" Karl chimes in, not hiding his angry tone.

"Mr. Eriksson, you've been living the past five centuries cut off from this world. Don't pretend you know a thing about it."

"It wasn't by choice. And just because I was banished doesn't mean I was out of the loop."

Banished? I didn't know that. *Why was he banished?*

"You should know then that my question is not irrelevant," the headmaster replies.

"Lucca and I are friends," I say, and it's the best answer I can come up with. The status of what we have is still unknown to me.

"You said Boone attacked one of your friends?" The headmaster turns to me.

"Yes."

"That would give you a motive to attack him."

I freeze for a moment, not daring to breathe as I process his words.

"Vivienne didn't attack Boone. You know that, Solomon," Aurora retorts indignantly.

"Is that what he's claiming? That I attacked him?" My voice rises to a shrill. "He attacked *me*."

"He was found in tatters by Hanson in the catacombs."

"Something else got to him," I say. "A ghost."

Solomon's eyes widen, and then he switches his attention to Aurora. I don't have time to question that shared glance before the door to his office opens, and a mean-looking male enters, accompanied by three other Blueblood vampires wearing leather dusters and oozing darkness. Those are the types of vampires that used to give me nightmares.

"What's the meaning of this, Jacques? This is a private meeting." Solomon rises to his feet.

"I'm here because I can't let you handle the situation alone. That lowly vampire dared to attack Tatiana's heir. She must be punished and used as an example that the Accords are to be followed."

My head is spinning, making me dizzy. I can't believe what's happening. I'm the victim, and in a twisted turn of events, I'm now the aggressor?

"Vivienne didn't attack Tatiana's spawn. He's the predator." Aurora steps in front of me, followed by Karl.

"Boone can't even speak coherently after what she did to him. And we all know about her association with Lucca Della Morte."

"I didn't do anything to that vermin!" I yell. "But he deserved what he got."

"See? That's a confession in my book. Guards, seize her."

The three Bluebloods advance, but Aurora does some strange movements with her arms, something akin to tae kwon do, and they freeze. There are now two shields made out of pure energy glowing from her hands. Next to her, Karl growls, a sound that's definitely not human.

"You're not taking Vivienne anywhere," Aurora says.

"Insolent girl. How dare you stand in my way." Jacques moves closer to her, but she doesn't back down.

I hate that I'm this useless human and that I need others to defend me. Even if I had a weapon on me, I wouldn't be a threat to anyone.

Solomon calmly walks around his desk, revealing to be much shorter than I anticipated. No longer resembling a mad scientist, he raises his arms wide and releases a powerful blast that knocks

Jacques and his guards down.

"I won't have my authority questioned in my own domain." Solomon speaks in a voice that feels ancient and powerful, almost familiar. "Vivienne hasn't been charged with anything, and you won't be taking her anywhere. You're advised to leave the premises or deal with the consequences."

Stunned, Jacques and his minions slowly stagger to their feet. "You've just made a huge mistake, Solomon. With the Nightingales gone, you're nothing but a glorified pet."

Five males clad in leather uniforms storm the room. They're huge, built like warriors, and also emotionless. They each carry a short sword that gleams when it catches the moonlight pouring through the window. A flash of red in their vest catches my attention. A stylized red rose is embroidered on the left side above their chests.

Without a word, the newcomers detain Jacques and his guards and then escort them out. The tallest of the group, the one who seems to be the leader, looks over in Solomon's direction and nods. Before he turns to leave, his deep blue eyes crash with mine, giving me chills. *That's one scary dude.*

When they're gone, Karl faces the headmaster. "This is not over. Jacques will try to get Vivienne, no matter what you decide."

I begin to tremble like a leaf in the wind. That's exactly what I need, a psycho Blueblood on my tail.

"I can't stay here a minute longer," I say.

Solomon shakes his head. "You must stay. Bloodstone is now the safest place for you."

I glance at Aurora, hoping she can say something to get me out of this situation.

"Don't fret about your disguise, child. The spell can be

extended," Solomon continues.

My eyes bug out of my skull. "You know I'm human?"

He smiles. "Of course. From the very beginning."

33

LUCCA

Hating that I was forbidden to accompany Vivienne to Solomon's office, I go in search of the weasel responsible for putting her in harm's way—Hanson. Ronan and Saxon follow me, but there's nothing either can say or do that will stop me from giving Hanson what he deserves.

I find him in the gym. He's practicing with a couple of blades, moving fast enough that he'd be a blur to human eyes. Not to me though.

He misses a step when he sees my approach. His eyes widen, and I can see he's ready to launch into a bunch of BS. But my hook finds his jaw first. He goes down on the tatami like a sack of trash. I could do so much more than simply punch the male, but if I rough him up more than that, it will give him too much leverage over me.

Leaning on his elbow, he touches his busted lip. "What the hell is wrong with you?"

"That was just a little warning. The next time you try to hurt Vivienne to get to me, you will end up strapped to a tree outside, waiting to greet the sun."

"You can't threaten me. I'm a faculty member and a Blueblood!"

"I don't care how many accolades or titles you have. You're nothing but a rat to me. You've been warned."

I turn around and walk away, but a prickle in the back of my neck warns me of a new danger. Then comes the whistle of a blade cutting through air. I pivot fast enough to catch the dagger meant for my back. *The fucking asshole.*

I'd retaliate, but Saxon and Ronan are already on it. In the blink of an eye, Hanson is pinned to the floor in a spread-eagle position by four blades, one for each appendage.

He yells, glancing at his hands, which have been pierced through by his own daggers, "Motherfuckers! You've just earned your death sentences."

"I don't think so," Ronan replies calmly. "You attacked a member of the royal family when he had his back turned. That's treason in my book." He glances at Saxon.

"Mine too," he replies with a smirk.

With a chilling smile on my lips, I walk over to Hanson. This is not even close to what this bastard deserves, but I can't deny it's satisfying.

I spin his dagger between my fingers, and then I let it fly. It strikes an inch away from his right ear.

"You shouldn't have crossed me, Hanson. I'm not called the Dark Prince for nothing."

This time, I do walk out. It won't take long for him to get free, but I don't foresee any new sneak attacks from him tonight. He will try again though, probably another stab in the back. It's what vampires without honor do.

"You should have ended him, Luc," Saxon says.

"I know. But even having a solid reason to do so, if I kill him, I won't know what he's planning."

"Nothing good. I wouldn't be surprised if he finally picked Tatiana's side."

"One more reason to let him live … for now."

There are people milling about in the hallway, including Therese and her posse. This is the first time we've crossed paths since she tried to kill Vivienne. She's another Blueblood deserving of punishment, but since her deadly prank is the reason that I was finally able to let go of my revenge plan and accepted my feelings for Vivi, I'll give the bitch a free pass.

She changes her posture when she sees me. Her spine becomes tense, and she won't hold my gaze. A moment later, she steers her friends in the opposite direction. I begin to relax, but then I catch Vivienne's scent. She's coming back from her meeting with Solomon, sandwiched between Aurora and Karl.

I don't miss the side-glance Therese throws in her direction though. Vivienne doesn't acknowledge the female but keeps her stare straight ahead. I know Therese too well; she won't leave Vivienne alone. Her pride is bigger than her fear of me. I'm surrounded by fucking assholes.

I'm moving toward Vivienne before I know it, meeting her halfway. She stops abruptly, almost as if she's afraid of what I'm going to do. Not giving a damn that we have an audience, I invade her space, trapping her face between my hands, and kiss her without reservation. My heart is soaring, beating so fast that I'd have a heart attack if I were human.

The hunger is there, ever present, but I push it to the back of my mind and savor Vivienne's sweetness despite my irrational craving for her blood. When I pull back, her eyes are at half-mast, and her cheeks are flushed. That's a reaction that's mostly human, so I pull her into my arms, trying to hide her red face from all those prying eyes.

"I guess it's official then," Aurora murmurs.

"What is?" I ask.

"You're a couple."

I sense Vivienne tense in my arms. Maybe she has zero interest in that. I can't blame her if she doesn't. We're different species; she's the prey, and I'm the predator. And worst of all, she's mortal, and I'm not. Without the ability to turn her into a vampire if she wanted to, I'm fated to watch her die. The thought is gut-wrenching. I don't want to lose her.

"Let's get out of here. There's much to discuss."

"I'm not leaving," she says, and I'm equal measures ecstatic and concerned.

"As much as I want you to stay, it's too dangerous for you here."

"Not really," Aurora pipes up. "Jacques wants Vivienne's head now. He doesn't know she's human, but that secret can be easily discovered. Who is going to protect her outside the walls of Bloodstone?"

226

I glower at the witch. "What does that bastard want with Vivienne?"

"He's claiming she attacked Boone, not the other way around," Karl replies from across the room.

I can't help the roar that comes from deep in my belly. Vivienne winces, stepping away from me. It helps get my rage in check.

"I'm sorry, darling. I didn't mean to frighten you."

"God, will you quit with the sugary nicknames, brother? It's nauseating." Manu wrinkles her nose in disgust.

"Shut your piehole, brat," I retort.

In true Manu fashion, she takes a step forward, aggression levels through the roof. "Make me."

"Shut up! Both of you." Aurora gets in between us, arms raised.

Shit. I must be losing my mind for real when an apprentice witch has to run interference.

"Damn, I love a woman who takes charge." Saxon laughs, giving Aurora an appreciative once-over.

She twists her face in annoyance. "Not even in your dreams, jackass."

Saxon sticks a blood lollipop in his mouth and smiles. "You can't stop me from dreaming, sugar."

"Can everyone stop acting like an ass and focus for a second?" Karl interrupts. "Vivi staying here is only a temporary solution. She can't pretend to be a vampire forever."

"There's only one option then," I say. "Boone must die."

Manu snorts. "Good idea, Luc. Just kill Boone and start the damn V wars again."

"It's better than living in this fake peaceful time," Ronan rebuffs. "If we're putting it to a vote, I stand with Lucca."

"Me too," Saxon adds.

Soon, another argument breaks out, but I'm no longer invested in it. Vivienne is standing quietly in a corner, withdrawn and paler than before. I whisk her into my arms and take her to my room, locking the door for good measure.

"Are you okay?" I set her on my bed.

"No. I'm scared."

Sitting next to her, I tuck a loose strand of hair behind her ear. "You don't need to be afraid, darling. I won't let anyone hurt you again."

"I'm not afraid for me. It's you I'm worried about."

My chest expands and then overflows with joy. This is foolish, and it will only lead to heartbreak. But I'm cursed anyway. One day, I'm going to sleep and never wake up.

My uncle's last words come to the forefront of my mind. He told me to surrender to the hunger. *Could he be talking about the curse?*

My mind begins to whirl at the speed of light. I jump out of bed and start to pace.

"Did I say something wrong?" she asks.

"I've craved your blood with a feral hunger since the first time I met you."

She pinches her lips together, hugging herself. "That's not normal, is it?"

"No."

I remember the photograph I took from her trailer. I never showed it to Aurora. I've been carrying it with me since I stole it, so I pull the folded picture from my pocket and hand it over to Vivienne.

"What is it?" She watches me curiously.

"The night I went to your trailer, I found that photo."

"You broke into my house?" Her voice rises in indignation.

Damn it. I did awful things to her. I'd better get back there and fix the mess I left behind.

"I'm sorry. I had to know who I was dealing with. You were pretending to be a vampire, and you did try to steal from me."

Her face becomes beet red. She lowers her gaze to the picture in her hands. "Why did you take this particular photo?"

"I assume that's your brother. But who is the woman?"

"My mother."

"You and your brother are wearing similar bracelets with charms on them. Do you remember who gave them to you and what those symbols mean?"

She scrunches her brows together, looking at the photo closer. "I forgot about those bracelets. Rikkon bought them and made me wear mine throughout the entire month of October. I couldn't take it off, even to sleep."

"Did he say why?"

She meets my eyes. "No. Do you think the bracelets were magical?"

I'm beginning to suspect as much, but I can't tell her I think she's a Nightingale descendant, and thanks to the curse, I'll be compelled to drink her dry. It's the only explanation to why her blood keeps giving me bloodlust.

"Maybe. I wanted to show them to Aurora. Maybe she could tell me what they mean."

Vivienne traces the picture, getting lost in it. "I do remember when this picture was taken. It was a good day. My mother was sober for once, and none of her shady friends were around."

"I'm sorry she wasn't the mother you deserved."

Vivienne pulls my necklace from her pocket. "I wish you still had yours. What happened to her?"

My chest feels tight, and for a moment, I can't speak. My mother's demise is directly linked to the curse. I can't tell Vivi what happened to her without saying too much.

She puts the necklace and the picture on my nightstand and walks over, stopping right in front of me. "You don't need to tell me if it's too painful. I understand."

"Thank you."

I rub her bee-stung lips with my thumb, dying to kiss her senseless again, but I hold back. She just survived a sexual assault. I can't possibly try anything now even though my very bones are on fire, yearning for her.

She sucks my thumb into her mouth, making me hiss.

"Vivi, what are you doing?"

Without breaking eye contact, she lets my thumb go with a loud pop. "I can't stay away from you. Even if it's not safe."

"It isn't safe." My voice is strained, low.

She walks into my space, grabbing my hands and placing my arms around her waist. "You want to drink my blood, and you've been denying yourself all this time." She tilts her head to the side, offering me her neck.

My gums ache as my fangs extend fully. My nails turn into claws. I'm becoming a monster right in front of her, and I can't stop it. The entire room disappears. All I can see is her vein pumping blood; all I can hear is her pulse.

"No!" I shove her roughly, sending her to the floor.

She looks at me, startled, and I can't stand that I did that to her. Ashamed, I do the only thing I'm still able to do. I run.

34

LUCCA

———❦———

As much as I'd prefer to run to my destination, sunrise is only an hour away, and I can't risk it. I took the SUV, even though I haven't mastered driving it yet. I'm not even sure if I'll be able to find my uncle. He has a secret estate in Salem, but he spends a lot of time in Boston too.

He'd better be in Salem because there's no way I can get to the big metropolis before sunup. The tinted windows in the car won't prevent me from turning into ashes.

The farther away I get from Bloodstone, the clearer the picture becomes. Vivienne's blood has been calling to me since I took my first whiff of it. And with all the not-so-subtle hints my uncle gave me, I was an idiot for not piecing it all together. I never asked her where she got the powerful concealment spell, but I'd bet a limb that Uncle Dearest helped.

I take the car through a dirt path in the woods, not bothering to slow down. There isn't supposed to be anything in this area besides dense forest. The path leads to a dead end, blocked by a large tree. I gun the engine, heading straight for it. A split second before the collision, the tree vanishes, and the rough path gives way to a paved road. After another minute, King Raphael's mansion appears in the horizon, surrounded by tall stone walls and a thick wrought iron gate. The construction style is similar to my own house but much larger in scale. Nothing less for the king of vampires. Gothic and dark, it belongs in an old horror movie. It's exactly the kind of place where you'd expect a creature of the night to live.

The gate opens as soon as my car approaches. The moment I crossed the magical barrier keeping his mansion hidden, his familiar was alerted of my imminent arrival.

When I get out of the car, the sky is already lighter. I most definitely won't be making it back to the institute today. My heart immediately fights the idea. I don't want to leave Vivi alone for that long, but considering I have a primal desire to kill her, maybe it's best if I stay away.

Mauricio Libell, my uncle's familiar and butler, opens the great mahogany door and greets me with a scowl. "For heaven's sake, Lucca, what are you doing here at this hour?"

"I have an urgent matter to discuss with my uncle. Is he here?"

He moves out of the way, letting me pass, but keeps his glowering strong.

"I'm here," my uncle replies from the top of the grand staircase. "You can leave now, Mauricio. Thank you."

With a shake of his head, the towering male walks away. A bear in his animal form, he retained his large frame when he became a familiar. He's also stubborn like a bear, and when I lived with my uncle, he was a pain in my ass.

"Why are you here this late, Luc? Did something happen?" my uncle asks, already at the bottom of the stairs.

I cut straight to the chase. "Is Vivienne the Nightingale descendant you hinted about?"

Nothing changes in my uncle's expression. He maintains his calm, emotionless mask. "Yes."

Yanking my hair back, I snarl, "No! I can't believe this. You set me up."

"Luc, I had to intervene. You weren't even looking for her. It's like you don't want to break the curse."

"The curse can't be broken! Maewe made sure of it." I shake my head, laughing without humor. "And now, I'm in love with the woman I'm fated to kill."

"You can't let Maewe get in your head. The fact that you love Vivienne increases the chances of your salvation."

I glare at him. "Are you mad? I'm not going to risk her life. I'll never feed from her."

"The longer you remain close to her, the harder it will become to resist."

"Then I'll move away."

"Stop with this nonsense. I've had enough of your whining. You *will* go through with it and break this damn curse."

"And if I don't, are you going to compel me to do it?"

He flinches, a rare reaction from him. I must have hit a nerve.

"You've already tried, haven't you?"

He sighs loudly. "Yes. But I'm not proud of it."

I could scream or punch him in the face, but what good would that do? He's the king; he can do whatever he pleases.

"Save it. I'm tired of your half-baked excuses. First, I wake up to find out you bent over to Tatiana, and now, this. I feel like I don't know you anymore."

He avoids my gaze, walking over to the fireplace. His shoulders are slumped forward; he looks defeated. *Damn it.* That's definitely not the male who braved wars, who inspired thousands of soldiers, who conquered whatever he wanted.

"You're right; I haven't been truthful with you. I didn't want to add another worry to your plate."

I walk over, stopping next to him. "You can tell me. I can handle it."

He looks at me, finally letting go of the mask. His eyebrows are pinched together, and his eyes are turbulent, conflicted. "A strange malady has hit the first-generation. They're losing their grip with reality, imagining things that aren't there, forgetting others. I suspect it has to do with the Nightingales' departure from this world."

"So, besides the rest of us needing to hibernate periodically, you're going crazy?"

"It seems so. It started a few centuries back. Five first-generation vampires turned completely insane. We thought it was an isolated case, especially when we didn't hear any new reports. Until seventy years ago, when another first-generation vampire showed signs of mental deterioration."

Fuck. Please don't say it is you, Uncle.

"Who?"

"Tatiana."

I take a step back, not hiding the surprise on my face. "But what about the truce?"

"It's a sham to hide what's going on with her from her followers.

Not even her son, Boone, knows."

Rubbing my face, I begin to burn a hole through the Persian rug. "Why are you protecting her? That female tried time and time again to end your life."

"I'm not protecting her. I'm protecting our way of life. What do you think will happen if the news spreads that first-generation vampires are going crazy? Do you think only Tatiana is thirsty for power? We can't let others find out."

I freeze on the spot for a second and then turn to him slowly. "You're afraid your mind is going to desert you too."

He nods solemnly. "Yes. That's why you have to be free of the curse. If I go, you need to take my place."

I shut my eyes for a second, having a terrible time dealing with the news. My uncle is the only parent I have left. He's the solid foundation in my crumbling life. I can't lose him too.

"Where is Tatiana now?" I ask.

"Locked in her mansion. Isadora cast a spell around her property, so she can't leave, but thanks to her illness, she doesn't know she's living in a prison."

"And no one knows about that? What about Jacques?"

"Tatiana has been compelled to deny visitors."

Son of a bitch. No wonder the male is going out of his way to impose his dominance.

"Why go through all that trouble? Why not just kill the bitch?"

"If she's gone, we'll have a civil war on our hands. Her highest-ranking officers will fight for leadership. The Council of Elders decided unanimously to keep her alive until we find a cure."

"If this disease is linked to the Nightingales' departure, how do you propose to find it?"

"One more reason to bring them back."

"For centuries, we have looked into it. They're gone for good."

My uncle clenches his jaw hard and then looks away first. "I can't lose hope. I won't give up." After a moment, he glances at me again. "And you can't give up either."

35

VIVIENNE

———⊰════✦════⊱———

Aurora is the first to come into Lucca's room after he took off. Karl follows right after her. I'm still sprawled on the floor, dealing with the mortification that I offered my neck to Lucca like a cheap blood whore and he refused.

"What happened?" Aurora asks.

"Did Lucca hurt you?" Karl follows.

I get back on my feet, making sure I don't lock gazes with either of them. "No."

"He looked like the devil was after him," Aurora adds.

Well, I think in this scenario, I'm the devil. I don't voice that thought out loud.

The picture he took from my trailer catches my attention. Now, I want to know as well if the bracelet Rikkon gave me had a purpose.

I take the photo and give it to Aurora. "Do you see the bracelet

Aurora raises both eyebrows. "Yeah. What about it?"

"Look closely. There are strange symbols carved on the charms. Do they mean anything to you?"

"Shit. They're so small." She squints, bringing the picture closer to her face. "I think they're ancient Druid runes."

"Can I see them?" Karl asks.

He spends maybe ten seconds scrutinizing the image before he looks at me with troubled eyes. "I think those charms are used to erase someone's memories."

"That doesn't make any sense. Why would Rikkon give me such a charm and also wear a similar one himself?"

Aurora is staring at me in a different manner now, almost as if she were trying to X-ray me with her vision.

"Shit," she blurts out.

"What?"

Shaking her head, she walks around me. "I have to go."

"Hell to the no." I run after her. "You're not going to leave me hanging like that."

I'm surprised when I find the living room empty. Maybe Manu and Lucca's friends went after him.

I grab Aurora's arm, turning her around. "You can't leave without giving me an explanation."

She glances at Karl, who is now sporting an extremely grim expression.

"Cut the crap. You two are freaking me out," I say.

"You'd better tell Vivi what you suspect, Aurora. Enough with the cloak-and-dagger attitude."

She takes a deep breath. "Fine. I'm probably going to regret this." Looking into my eyes, she says, "I don't think you're human,

Vivi."

I let go of her at once, stepping back. "Nonsense. Of course I'm human."

"You know the secret chamber you stumbled upon, the one with the five coffins?"

"Yeah?"

"It's protected by powerful wards. Only the headmaster, my mother, and I are able to break through. No one is even supposed to know that corridor is there, but you found it the first time you went to the catacombs."

"And that automatically makes you think I'm not human?"

"Not until you showed me that picture."

"What kind of creature do you think Vivi is if not human?" Karl asks.

"I don't know. Have you ever smelled her blood?"

I grimace, and Karl does the same.

"Yeah."

"But did you actually take a good whiff, like dissected every single note of her scent?"

"No. Why would I do that? I'm not a vampire." He crosses his arms.

Aurora whirls around and walks over to the kitchen. When she faces us again, she's holding a knife in her hand.

"What do you think you're doing with that?" I widen my eyes, concerned about the witch's state of mind now. She looks positively deranged.

"I want Karl to smell your blood."

I shake my head. "Nope, absolutely not. You're not cutting me."

"I agree with Vivi. That's unnecessary."

"Oh, come on. Don't be such a baby. You can't be afraid to bleed a little. Your boyfriend is a vampire. Eventually, he's going to bite."

Fat chance of that happening. He ran for the hills when I offered.

"That's a futile experiment. If I could tell Vivi wasn't human by the scent of her blood, I would have done that already."

Aurora sighs in resignation, dropping the knife on the kitchen counter. "You guys are no fun." She turns toward the front door and then stops halfway. "Oops, I almost forgot my bag. Do you mind? It's right behind you."

The leather bag with colorful flowers embroidered on the front is heavy as hell. "What do you have in here? A collection of rocks?" Before I turn around to give her the bag, a sharp pain comes from my forearm. "Ouch!" I immediately drop the accessory to see what happened.

"What the fuck, Aurora!" Karl exclaims.

She's holding a small Swiss knife in her hand, which is gleaming with my blood now.

I cover the small gash on my arm and glower at her. "You cut me! I can't believe this."

"It's just a scratch." She turns to Karl. "Here, take a deep breath of this."

He grabs the knife from her hand with a brusque movement. I bet that if Aurora weren't a girl, Karl would kick her ass. But he brings the blade under his nose and takes several deep breaths.

"And?" she asks eagerly.

"Will you give me a minute?" he snaps.

"God, I thought you were a wolf. Shouldn't you have better

senses?"

He flips her off, reminding me of the Karl I used to know, the one who I thought was human.

I'm still mad at Aurora, but I'm also on pins and needles. Me not being human could explain why Lucca is obsessed with my blood. It wouldn't solve anything though.

"So?" I ask after a while.

"Give me a second. I think there's something different about your blood after all." He takes another whiff. "It's almost like something was done to it to conceal ... well, something."

I hug my middle, afraid now that I might be an awful creature. Why else would Rikkon want to make me forget who I am—if that's what he did? We don't know for sure.

"Oh, for fuck's sake. Can you tell what's different about Vivienne's blood or not?" Aurora asks without any patience left.

"It's familiar. It's—" He lowers the blade while his eyes go wider. His skin looks paler too.

"It's what?" I ask.

"I think you have Nightingale blood."

I blink fast, trying to process his words. *What the fuck?*

"That would explain why the wards didn't work on you," Aurora murmurs.

"They're the immortals who created the vampires. But what happened to them? I've never heard about the Nightingales until I came here."

"They left this world many centuries ago, but it's possible they left behind descendants, half-bloods. Rumor has it that they liked to mingle with humans," Aurora replies.

"So, you think I'm the lost great-great-great-granddaughter of one of those beings?"

"Yeah." I read regret in his eyes, which seems out of place.

"If the Nightingales were so powerful that they could create several species, then how come I don't have an ounce of their magic?"

Aurora shrugs. "Maybe your lineage got too diluted. Who knows?"

"It doesn't matter if you don't have powers. You can't let anyone know about your connection to the Nightingales," Karl says in a serious tone.

"Why not?"

"Because diluted or not, your blood has power even if you don't possess abilities. And I know many Bluebloods who would kill to get their hands on it."

Not only their hands on my blood. Rikkon's too. Everyone is telling me that I have to stay in Bloodstone, but what about my brother, who's in the hands of that awful dragon kingpin? I can't hide here and forget about him. I have to get Rikkon out of there.

36

VIVIENNE

I wait until it's high morning and everyone who should be tucked in is sleeping away the day. The familiars and humans staying at the institute have adapted to the vampires' nocturnal schedule, so I shouldn't bump into anyone. But that doesn't mean I can simply walk out of the institute's front door.

Manu didn't spend the night in her room. Where she went, I don't know. I hope she's with Lucca. The way he ran out of my room yesterday left me reeling. I'm still worried about him, but getting to Rikkon is now my top priority. I don't know what's going to happen once he's free or if I will ever come back here. But I can't allow my mind to dwell on those questions, or I will never leave.

To be safe, I wear a hoodie, keeping my head low when I head out of my apartment. Lucca's necklace is safe deep in my jeans pocket, and in my hand is my other lifeline—my phone. When I reach the main building where all classes are held, I want to run

But if there's anyone around, the sound of my hard steps on the floor would draw too much attention.

I speed-walk, wishing I could do it as fast as vampires do. It seems to take forever to reach the stairs leading to the catacombs. The scariest experiences I've had at Bloodstone happened in the bowels of the institute, and here I am, heading back down there less than twenty-four hours after Boone's attack. But that's the only secret way out of here that I know of. All other exits are locked to avoid any accidents—aka attempted murders or suicide by sun.

My heart feels like it's on the verge of smashing straight out of my chest. I'm shaking all over, remembering the nasty encounter with the ghost from the secret chamber. I haven't forgotten how it tried to choke the life out of me or the terrifying screams it brought from Boone. What if it's still here, waiting for its next victim? *Shit.* I should have thought about that before venturing in its domain.

I use the Flashlight app on my phone, hoping I can remember which of these tunnels lead to the mausoleum. I'm not even a minute in this dark maze when I hear a soft moaning behind me, followed by a cold breeze. Fighting the terror that's trying to get a grip on my mind, I increase my pace.

"Vivienne, you can't run away from me," the disembodied voice of the ghost I freed says from behind me.

Fuck. I break into a run without direction. The ghost cackles nearby, but now, I don't know anymore where the noise is coming from.

"Leave me alone!" I scream.

"Release us," she hisses.

A cold, clawed hand grazes my shoulder, making me yelp.

"Give us your blood," the ghost whispers close to my ear.

Like an idiot, I whirl around and flash the light at it. Then, I really scream. The ghost is more gruesome than I remembered. Decaying skin, dark holes instead of eyes, and the longest, sharpest fangs I've ever seen. She's a fucking vampire ghost. I should have known.

She reaches over with her talon-like hands, too fast for me to stop her. She's going to shred me to pieces just like she did with Boone. A split second before she touches me, a bright blue light illuminates the entire tunnel. The ghost backs off, shrieking, and then it vanishes.

A solid, warm hand touches my arm, making me jump.

"Relax, it's me," Aurora says. "Come on. Let's get out of here. She'll be back."

"I-I don't know the way out anymore."

"The stairs back to the institute are straight ahead."

"I'm not going back there."

"Are you running away?" Her tone is incredulous.

"I'm going to get my brother back."

Aurora lets out a string of curses under her breath. "Fine. I'll come with you. I need a break from all these bloodsuckers anyway."

"We have to get to the old cemetery. There's a tunnel here that leads to the mausoleum." The air becomes cooler even though there's no breeze now. I hug myself while keeping the beam of light pointing forward. "These tunnels all look the same."

"Shh. Quiet. I'm gonna try something." Aurora closes her eyes, and a couple of beats later, a glowing symbol appears on her forehead. It's a crescent moon. When she opens them again, her eyes are also glowing a pure white light.

Freaky.

246

After a moment, the light fades from her eyes. "I got it. Let's go."

I follow the witch girl, hoping she knows where she's going. We turn several times, and it seems to me we're getting more and more lost. The time on my phone tells me we've been walking for almost ten minutes. I don't remember taking that long to reach the secret chamber when I came in through the mausoleum entrance.

"Vivienne," the ghost calls out again.

"Did you hear that?" I look behind me.

"Yeah, I did. We're almost there."

"Vivienne!"

I point my phone toward it, seeing the ghost zipping down the tunnel toward us.

"She's coming!"

Aurora pulls my arm and shoves me ahead of her. "Keep going. The stairs to the mausoleum are at the end of this tunnel."

My muscles lock tight, and for a second, I can't move.

"Go! Run and don't look back," Aurora shouts in my face before whirling around to deal with the deadly wraith.

Propelled by her command, I snap out of my paralysis and take off down the tunnel, pushing my muscles to the limit. There's another shriek and then a yell that sounds like it came from Aurora. *Damn it.* I should turn around, but I'm useless. I have no power or weapon to fight a ghost. I finally see the stairs. With a last push, I jump the steps three at a time, zooming upward until I reach the dark mausoleum. The door is closed, keeping the dusty room in shadows. But thankfully, it's not locked.

Shoving the door open, I stagger forward and collapse onto a patch of overgrown grass and weeds while I gasp for air. My heart is climbing so high in my throat that I think I might throw up. When another body falls next to mine, I don't have the energy to turn my head.

"Damn it. That specter is strong," Aurora says, also sounding a little out of breath.

"I heard your scream."

Aurora sits up, rolling up the sleeve of her jacket to reveal a nasty gash on her forearm. "She managed to get a swipe in."

I force my body into a sitting position, but the nausea hasn't passed. "I'm sorry."

"It's not your fault." She pulls a glass vial from her leather bag and pours the contents over the wound. Her face twists into a grimace, but that's the only sign she's in pain. She doesn't make a sound.

"What's that?"

"Just a generic purifying potion. I have no idea if that specter's talons have poison in them. One can't be too careful."

"She looked like a vampire zombie ghost. Scary as hell."

"That's a way to describe it." She puts the empty glass back in her bag and turns to me. "So, what's the plan?"

I push myself off the ground and then offer my hand to Aurora. "Now, we meet our ride. They should be waiting for us at the end of the road."

"They?" She raises an eyebrow.

"My bandmates, Cheryl and Vaughn."

"Of course. You played in a band, right?"

"Yeah, Nocturnal."

Aurora chuckles. "How appropriate."

"So, about that ghost, aren't you worried it's going to come after us?"

"No. I believe your blood freed that spectral bitch from her prison, but she's bound to her other companions, who are still locked in the chamber. So, she's trapped in the catacombs until all of them are free."

"And my blood is the key." I snort in derision. "Great."

"Yeah, it sucks to be you."

"But what are those ghosts anyway?"

"Honestly, I don't know. My mother and the headmaster are super enigmatic about that. I think I'll only earn the right to that secret when my mother dies and I become the High Witch."

"Oh my God. That's awful."

"Yep. My life is on hold until my only parent dies. It's peachy to be me."

It seems no one's life is easy—at least, no one's life that has been touched by the supernatural.

"Aren't we a pair?" I laugh.

"Tell me about it."

"Can I ask you a question?"

"Sure."

"Why didn't you rat me out when you discovered I was a human pretending to be a vampire?"

"You've met the headmaster. I knew there was no way he'd allow you to cross the gates of Bloodstone, pretending to be something you're not, without a motive. So, I wasn't about to blabber without more information."

"Do you know why he wants me there?"

Aurora stops suddenly, placing a hand on my arm. "When you were with Manu or Lucca, did the subject of his curse ever come up?"

My eyebrows arch. "Curse? What curse?"

"I guess that's a no." She looks straight ahead with her brows furrowed. "All the pieces are starting to come together."

"What pieces? You're beginning to scare me."

"Many centuries ago, Lucca killed a Nightingale priestess by drinking her dry. That was the most serious crime a vampire could commit."

I gasp, not because I'm appalled by the story, but because it sounds familiar. But that's impossible. *Where would I have heard it?*

"It wasn't his fault," I say with conviction, and I don't know why.

Aurora narrows her eyes. "How do you know that?"

"A hunch?"

She shakes her head, dismissing my outburst. "Well, good one because it wasn't really his fault. The history books say he was wounded terribly after a great battle, and he had lost a lot of blood. His mother, desperate to save her son, tricked the Nightingale priestess to feed Lucca. But because he was on the verge of dying, he entered bloodlust and couldn't stop feeding until the poor female was dead."

My heart begins to beat slow and hard. That's what's going to happen if he feeds from me. No wonder he acted the way he did last night.

"What's the curse?"

"To die slowly and painfully. Lucca's life force is waning. He needs to sleep longer than most vampires, and when he's awake, his strength deteriorates fast. He seems powerful now, but it won't be so in a year."

I can't imagine Lucca not being the godlike Blueblood that he is now.

"Is there a way to break the curse?"

"Yes. Lucca has to drink from a Nightingale again and not kill them. But here's the caveat: Nightingale blood will always give him bloodlust. He's fated to drink them dry. If that happens, he'll condemn his soul to eternal damnation. In my opinion, that's a worse fate than dying slowly."

"What if he can control his bloodlust and not kill?"

"Then the curse will be broken."

Now, everything is beginning to make sense. I'm the Nightingale who has the power to save him or destroy him completely, and there's not a damn thing I can do about it.

"I'm sorry," Aurora says.

"Yeah, I know. Me too."

37

VIVIENNE

———❖———

The band's van is already parked at the side of the road when Aurora and I reach the meeting spot. Cheryl and Vaughn get out, one more awake than the other. Vaughn covers his mouth, trying to hide the yawn. It's past eleven in the morning, but I'm betting he didn't get to bed until the sun was up. Vaughn is a night owl. He'd make a perfect vampire.

Cheryl gets to me first, hugging me tight. "Damn it, Vivi. I can't believe you've survived this long at that school of horrors."

"It's not that bad, and I've had help."

She pulls back, studying my face with her intense green eyes. Now that I know she's a shifter, I can see the wolfishness in them.

"Karl," she guesses.

"Among others."

"Who is your friend?" Vaughn glances over my shoulder.

"I'm Aurora, one of Vivi's *other* friends." She smirks at me.

"You're the High Witch's daughter," Cheryl adds.

"Yep." She shrugs.

Suddenly very much awake, Vaughn saunters toward her. "What happened to your arm?"

"Oh, it's just a scratch."

"We had an encounter with a very nasty ghost while we were trying to sneak out," I say.

Vaughn's eyes widen. "There are ghosts, too, in that place?"

"Don't tell me you're afraid of them." Aurora raises an eyebrow.

He tries to recover, but he can't hide the sudden drain of blood from his face. "Me? Afraid? Of course not."

Cheryl switches her attention to me again. "How did you manage to steal the necklace from Lucca?"

I don't remember ever telling her the details of my deal with Larsson. "How did you know that was my task?"

Her lips become nothing but a slash on her face, and her eyes are hella guilty now. "Please don't be mad at me."

"What did you do?"

"I caught Lucca sneaking out of your trailer not too long ago. I told him that Larsson had your brother. When he went after the dragon-shifter, I made some calls and ended up learning about your deal."

"So, it was you who blabbered to Lucca. I thought Karl was the culprit."

"Lucca wanted to know why you were at Bloodstone. I thought if I told him you had a compelling reason, he wouldn't hurt you."

No, he didn't hurt me. He did much worse. He's conquered my heart.

"I guess you've also known him for a while, huh?" I say, trying to hide the nature of my thoughts.

Cheryl cuts a glance in Vaughn's direction, but he's busy chatting up Aurora. *Oh shit.* Vaughn doesn't know Cheryl and Karl are wolf-shifters.

"We should get going," I add.

Suddenly, I'm wary of heading to Ember Emporium. It's not meeting Larsson again that's giving me anxiety; it's confronting my brother. I have so many questions pertaining to our heritage. What I want to know the most is why he tried to keep our lineage a secret.

During the ride, Vaughn monopolizes most of the conversation. He's fascinated with Aurora, but that doesn't surprise me. He has a soft spot for pretty girls. Aurora doesn't seem to mind the attention though. She sounds like a different person, much friendlier and more approachable. Maybe everyone who attends Bloodstone must wear a mask to survive.

Fifteen minutes later, Cheryl parks the van right in front of Ember Emporium, next to all the bikes that weren't there the last time I was here.

"The bar can't possibly be open at this hour," Cheryl says.

"Maybe they're having a gang meeting." Aurora looks out the window. "I've never been to a dragon hangout before."

"Oh, goody," Vaughn replies.

With my hand on the door handle, I say, "Let's go. The sooner we go in, the sooner we can get the hell out of here."

I'm totally faking my bravado. There's a knot of worry sitting at the pit of my stomach, like a bad junk-food decision that won't go away.

"Shouldn't you call Larsson first to let him know you're coming?" Vaughn asks. "I mean, so we don't become dragon chow by accident."

"Okay."

I call Rikkon's phone since I don't have a direct line to the kingpin. It goes straight to voice mail. "The battery of Rikkon's phone must have died."

"There's nothing for it then but to go in." Cheryl is out of the car before anyone can say anything.

I join her outside and wait for Vaughn and Aurora. We spend a moment staring at the building's facade. Somewhere inside, Larsson is keeping my brother. I hope he's over getting all the drugs out of his system. If not, that could be a problem.

"Ready or not, here we go." I push the door open, bracing for what we're going to find inside.

I don't take more than a couple of steps forward before I stop, unsure of what to do. It seems Aurora was right. They must be having some kind of meeting because I've never seen so many bodybuilder types in one location.

Most are wearing biker clothing. Leather vests and chaps along with a mean-looking attitude. Obviously, they all turn to look at us.

"Does anyone feel like maybe we shouldn't have barged in?" Vaughn asks, moving closer to me.

"What's the matter, kids? Are you lost?" an older male with a bald head and long gray beard asks. He has a dragon tattoo taking up most of his right arm that almost looks like it's alive.

I clear my throat, so I don't sound like a small, fearful child. "I'm looking for Larsson."

"Jesus." The male turns around and addresses the room. "I didn't know the boss was sniffing around in the kindergarten."

Some of the shifters laugh; others simply grunt. I almost puke in my mouth.

"He's in his office, kid. It's in the back," the bartender says as he polishes a glass behind the counter. He's another competing for the title of Mr. Universe with his Alpine-like biceps and towering height.

"Oh, he's cute," Cheryl whispers near my ear.

She's not wrong; he does have a *Tudors* Henry Cavill look to him, but this isn't really the time to be ogling anyone, especially a dragon.

"Seriously?" Aurora retorts.

"What? I'm not blind."

Ignoring both of them, I stride toward the back of the bar, purposely avoiding all the stares aimed my way. There's a door that says *Staff,* and when no one comes to block my way, I open it and continue on down the corridor. The sound of an angry male's voice leads me to what I can only assume is Larsson's office. I stop right in front of it and then look over my shoulder.

"Hey, where's Cheryl?"

"She got thirsty," Aurora replies with a hint of reproach.

Shaking my head, I decide to not worry about Cheryl. She's a wolf who has been around for a long time. She can take care of herself.

I let out a long breath to steady myself, and then I knock.

"Who is it?" Larsson asks.

"It's Vivienne, Rikkon's sister."

Not a second later, the door opens wide, and the great dragon kingpin fills the frame. He's not wearing a jacket today but a white button-down shirt that stretches to the max against his wide chest. I don't want to be like Cheryl, ogling every piece of hot ass I come across, but it's really hard not to notice the dragon's physique.

I try not to flinch under his scrutinizing stare, but when he looks over my head, I let out the breath I definitely knew I was holding.

"You brought company," he says.

"I got the necklace." I get straight to the point before he decides to kick my companions out.

He squints for a second and then moves out of the way. "Come in."

I have to hold my jaw shut as I take in Larsson's office—if one could call the ginormous room spread before us that. It's a two-floor space with an atrium in the middle—a mix of mall arcade and a sports bar. It has everything—games, several flat screens, pool table, foosball table, a few leather couches, and lots and lots of color.

"Wow!" Vaughn stares at it all with the awed expression of a kid in Candy Land.

"Damn. Talk about sensory overload." Aurora rubs her forehead. "I'm getting a headache already."

Larsson walks around a massive black desk, taking a seat on a comfortable-looking leather chair. He leans back, resting his linked hands on his flat stomach. "So, the necklace. Where is it?"

"I want to see my brother first."

"Show me the necklace." His expression remains neutral, but I don't mistake the command in his voice.

Since I'm in no position to piss him off, I fish the necklace from my pocket and dangle it in front of me. Immediately, Larsson's posture changes. He sits straighter in his chair, and his eyes are wide and alert.

Without a word, he raises his right hand and signals to someone who, until now, I didn't even know was in the room. Then, I see that at least four of Larsson's associates are here, all semi-hidden in the shadows.

Jeez, paranoid much? What does he think two humans and a witch can do against his kind?

A moment later, the associate who walked away returns, holding a scrawny figure by the arm.

"Rikkon!" I run to him, still clutching Lucca's necklace in my hand.

He looks up, revealing a gaunt face with pale skin and dark circles under his eyes. "Vivi," he murmurs.

I hug him even though Larsson's associate is still holding Rikkon in his grasp.

His free arm sneaks around my back while he rests his cheek against my shoulder. "I knew you would come."

As happy as I am that I was able to save Rikkon's ass this time, I'm also mad that he once again put me in this situation.

A throat clearing brings my attention back to the here and now. I ease off the embrace and turn around.

"Here's your payment." I toss the necklace in Larsson's direction.

It disappears in his large hand, and a pang pierces my chest. There goes the last link Lucca had to his mother.

"Do you know what the necklace means to its former owner?" I ask, not hiding the contempt in my tone.

Larsson pierces me with an intense glare, but I've had my share of similar threatening looks during my stay at Bloodstone. I'm immune to those now.

"I guarantee you, Vivienne, this necklace has more value to me than it does to Lucca Della Morte."

"I doubt it."

"All right," Vaughn interrupts, "Rikkon is free, and the dragon has his payment. We should really get going."

"Yes, please. Let's go," Rikkon says.

"A word of caution, punk," Larsson speaks up. "If I catch you selling in my domain again, I won't be as merciful as I was this time."

Rikkon's face becomes even paler. He swallows hard, his Adam's apple bobbing up and down. "I'm done with that shit."

"Yeah, right. Get out of here already. I'm sick of looking at your pathetic face."

Aurora and Vaughn are already out the door when Larsson calls my name. I motion for Rikkon to keep walking while I face the dragon kingpin.

"What?" I ask.

"Tell Lucca his heirloom is in good hands."

I stare at the dragon for a couple of beats, surprised to see something akin to sorrow in his gaze.

"Come on, Vivi. Let's go," Rikkon urges from the door.

I follow him out, but I'm still thinking about Larsson's parting comment, even when we reach the main area of Ember Emporium. Aurora and Vaughn have stopped and seem to be searching for something. I turn to the bar, noticing there's a different male tending to it.

"Where's Cheryl?" I ask.

Damn it. She had to go and stay behind to flirt. I don't think she was taken against her will, but she's our driver.

I call her, and it rings and rings until finally she answers, "Hello?"

"Where the hell are you?"

"Oh, you're done?" she asks, a little out of breath.

There's a distinct grunting in the background and hard breathing. *Oh my God.*

I cover my mouth with my hand and whisper, "Are you screwing the bartender?"

Her reply is a loud moan. Cringing and with my face now in flames, I tell her to hurry up, and then I end the call.

Aurora, Vaughn, and Rikkon are all now staring at me.

"Let me guess," Aurora says. "She asked the bartender to show her around?"

"Something like that," I mumble.

A minute later, Cheryl comes back, sashaying her way to us while she finger-combs her hair. The bartender follows her, tucking his shirt in his pants.

Shit. Could they be more obvious?

"Were you waiting long?" she asks with an air of innocence.

Aurora shakes her head. "Shifters, ugh."

"Let's go. I don't want to overstay our welcome." I glance nervously at the rough crowd who is still eyeing us with suspicion.

"Oh, we're fine." Cheryl waves her hands in a dismissive way.

"Don't trust anything that comes out of Cheryl's post-O-town mouth," Vaughn rebuffs.

"I'm beginning to think you can't trust her *ever*," Aurora replies.

The normal Cheryl would take offense to that. Post-coital-bliss Cheryl simply shrugs with a smile.

I grab the keys from her purse. "I think Vaughn should drive."

We have to steer her to the exit because she seems to have lost her ability to walk on her own. She does wave like a silly girl at the bartender, making me wonder if the male is more than a dragon. An incubus comes to mind.

Once we're all inside the van, Vaughn asks, "Where to?"

I want to say back to Bloodstone, but now that I have Rikkon back, there isn't really a reason for me to return. Well, there's the fact that Jacques wants my head, but he doesn't know I'm not a vampire. But my heart doesn't need a motive. I want to see Lucca again even if it's to say good-bye.

"Home, of course," Rikkon answers.

"Yeah, let's go home," I say, keeping my gaze down.

Cheryl is riding shotgun while Rikkon, Aurora, and I are in the back. A pregnant silence descends upon us, so thick that we could make sushi with it. I have so many questions for Rikkon, but I'm suddenly tongue-tied. During the ride, I sense Aurora burning a hole through my face with her intense stare.

It's not until we're out of dragon territory and closer to the trailer park—and by default, Bloodstone—that she decides to speak up. "We have time before nightfall. I think you should have a talk with your brother and then make a decision."

"What's going on? Make a decision about what?" Rikkon asks.

I turn my attention to the front of the van. I don't want anyone else to know about my Nightingale blood, not even Cheryl and most definitely not Vaughn. It could be dangerous for them to know.

Aurora follows my line of vision, and perhaps guessing my thoughts, she raises her hand and recites a spell in a foreign language. A ball of energy whooshes from her palm, creating a glowing wall between us and the front that vanishes after a second.

"You can speak freely now. They won't hear a word."

"Cool trick," Rikkon says. "But what's up with all the secrecy?"

"I know about our heritage," I say, getting straight to the point.

Rikkon's eyebrows furrow, matching the confused glint in his eyes. "What's to know?"

"Cut the crap, Rik. We're descendants from the Nightingales, and you used a spell to make me forget. Just confess it already."

He opens and shuts his mouth like a fish out of water. Then, he says, "Who in the world are the Nightingales? Vivi, you're not making any sense."

"Oh crap," Aurora says.

"What?"

"Remember the photo you showed me? Rikkon was also wearing the same bracelet with the enchanted charms. I don't think he knows anything."

I wriggle my fingers together, feeling stupid for not coming to that conclusion. "Isn't there a spell that can bring our memories back?"

"Maybe. But I have to ask—"

The van stops suddenly, sending us forward hard. I hit my head against the panel behind Cheryl's seat.

"What the hell!" Aurora leans forward, sticking her head between Vaughn and Cheryl. The magical barrier glows, and then it dissolves with a ripple. "Why did we stop?"

"Uh, do you see that?" Vaughn replies.

I have to push Aurora to the side a little to peer out of the car since the back of the van doesn't have windows. A massive wall of gray fog is blocking the road. "Shit, where did that come from?"

"Out of nowhere. It's not even that cold today. Is that fog normal?"

A dark shape emerges from the fog. I can't tell if it's a man or woman, for the stranger is wearing a dark, hooded robe, which is keeping their features concealed.

"Who is that?" I ask.

"Shit! A mercenary mage," Aurora replies. "Vaughn, get us out of here now!"

Vaughn puts the car in reverse, but when he presses the gas pedal, the van won't move. "Fuck! Fuck! Fuck!"

"It sounds like the wheels are spinning over mud," Rikkon pipes up.

"There was no mud before," Cheryl replies.

The mage disappears, but the fog continues to creep forward. It's almost upon us. It will swallow the van in the next minute.

"Everyone, out of the car!" Aurora jumps to the side to open the sliding door. But when she does, gray mist enters the vehicle, drifting in too fast.

My head becomes fuzzy, and my body seems to be moving at a sluggish pace.

"What's happening?" I ask, seeing double of everything.

"Magical fog." Aurora coughs. "Trap." She collapses out of view.

The fog has taken over the inside of the van completely.

"Rikkon!"

"I'm here." He hugs me. "It's going to be okay. It's going to—"

His hold slackens, and then he's leaning against me, dead weight. I fight the effects of the fog for as long as I can, but my eyelids are too heavy. I close my eyes, and then nothing.

38

VIVIENNE

———◦⊱✦⊰◦———

I feel like I'm swimming in a void when rough shaking wakes me up.

"Vivienne, get up!" someone urges me.

Blinking, I try to get rid of the fogginess in my sight. It's hard to see in the dimness. Finally, Aurora's frantic face sharpens in front of me.

I sit up, rubbing my eyes. "What happened?"

"We were drugged."

Next to me, Rikkon groans and then sits up. "Why is it so dark?"

"Because it's nightfall already." Aurora begins to take items out of her bag, fighting through the trembling of her hands.

Cheryl turns on her seat to glance at us. "How is everyone?"

"Groggy but okay," I say.

"Vaughn, get the engine running. We need to go back to Bloodstone at once," Aurora commands.

"Why? Let's just go home," Rikkon argues.

There's a distinct clicking noise when Vaughn turns the key, but the van won't start.

"Shit!" he curses. "I think the battery is kaput."

Oh, man, this is bad.

"Can't we call someone?" I pull my phone out but feel an invisible punch to my chest when a black screen greets me. I press the On button, getting nothing. "My phone is dead."

"Mine too," Cheryl says.

"And mine," Vaughn adds.

"Okay, guys, it's clear we're not getting any help. Let's think fast," Aurora pipes up.

"Why would anyone want to strand us here?" Rikkon asks.

I grab his hand in mine, squeezing it tight. "I've made some powerful enemies, Rik. Nasty Bluebloods, and they're coming for me."

His eyes widen, but then he surprises me when he turns to Aurora. "Do you have any weapons in your purse that I can borrow?"

She hands him a small dagger. "Here. Do you know how to use this?"

"Stick them with the pointy end?" He smirks.

"Shh!" Cheryl commands. "Something is coming."

Aurora and I trade a glance.

My chest constricts. "Jacques?"

"Or Boone. Either one, we're in a bad spot," she replies. "I don't have another blade for you, but here, take this." She gives me a glass vial. "It's vampire's bane. If a bloodsucker gets close enough to you, shove it down their throat."

I take her offering, trying to ignore how my stomach is spiraling out of control or how my throat muscles are getting tighter and tighter. I feel the familiar cloak of panic drape over my shoulders, attempting to bury me under its weight. But allowing the emotion to overwhelm me can be deadly tonight.

"I count at least five vampires approaching, but some might be staying out of my reach," Cheryl says, and then she adds, "We're not far from Bloodstone. Aurora and I can hold them off while Vivi, Vaughn, and Rikkon make a break for the institute."

"I'm not going to run away," Rikkon protests. "I can help you hold them off while Vivi and Vaughn escape."

Cheryl arches her eyebrows. "I think—"

"No!" I cut her off. "Rikkon has to come with me."

I lock gazes with Aurora, hoping she understands my decision. If my blood has power that vampires can use for nefarious reasons, so does my brother's.

"I agree with Vivi. You need to stay with your sister and protect her," she tells Rikkon.

"Okay. Better if I don't have to babysit anyone," Cheryl adds. "You need to go now before they surround us. Ready?"

Aurora turns to me. "You can do this. Run as fast as you can and don't look back."

My eyes burn, but I refuse to cry. "Are you going to be okay?"

"Yes. I'm a witch, remember? I have a few tricks up my sleeve."

"Thanks for worrying about me too," Cheryl complains.

"Shut up. I *am* worried."

"Fuck! I have visual. Go! Go!" She gets out of the car, and a second later, I hear a distinct wolf snarl.

The side door is already open, so Rikkon and I jump out and meet Vaughn at the back of the car. I make the mistake of looking toward the forest, and when I see the red glow of a few vampires' eyes, my muscles freeze.

"Come on!" Rikkon grabs my hand and pulls me in the opposite direction.

We run as fast as we can, but we're still close enough to hear when the fight commences. My friends are risking their lives to give us a chance to escape, and I feel unworthy of their sacrifice. I should have given myself up and saved them instead. *What kind of selfish person am I?*

"We need to stay on the main road," Rikkon warns Vaughn.

Chill licks the back of my neck. We're being pursued. *Does that mean my friends are gone?* Tears are turning my vision blurry, and a sob gets lodged in my throat. The sudden glare of headlights illuminates the road. The car is coming around the curve too fast.

"Vaughn! Watch out."

Tires screech, and the sound of burned rubber fills my nose. Then comes the impact, and Vaughn flies to the side.

"Fuck!" Rikkon screams.

The driver gets out of the car. "I didn't see him. He came out of nowhere."

We ignore him, going straight to check on Vaughn. He's trying to get up, but there's a big gash on his thigh now.

"Come on. We have to go," Rikkon urges.

"He needs medical attention," the man says. "I'm not going to jail—"

A yell. Then the gurgling sound of someone drowning in their own blood.

A vampire took the stranger down, ripping his throat open. Another one is coming from the right. The white-blond hair, the fiery red in his demented eyes. Boone. A cold numbness rushes over my body. That's it. He's going to kill me.

Rikkon jumps in front of me, pushing me back. "Go, Vivi. Go!"

Vaughn is hopping on one foot; he can't run anymore. "Get help," he says.

Blindly, I whirl around and enter the forest hugging the road. It's the shortest way to the institute, but I have zero hope that I can make it there before Boone catches up with me. My only chance is to make it to the mausoleum's entrance and pray the vampire zombie ghost is willing to help again.

My pulse is drumming away in my ears, muffling all other sounds. But I know I'm being hunted by Boone, and he's getting close. I uncap the vial in my hand, turning just in time as he leaps on me with his mouth wide open and fangs ready to tear me to pieces.

LUCCA

I head back to Bloodstone as soon as the sun sets, and it's no surprise that I don't go to my apartment. Instead, I veer straight to Vivienne's because spending a day away from her was harder than I'd thought it would be. Not because of the hunger. I miss having her in my arms, the smell of her hair, the curve of her body pressed against mine.

In my long, immortal life, I've met countless females—humans and vampires alike—fucked plenty of them, but none ever stirred in me the passion, the desire to spend the rest of my life by their side. It's the cruelest joke that I'd fall in love with a Nightingale descendant, the woman I'm cursed to kill.

It's early in the evening, but I find the apartment empty. I know Manu, Ronan, and Saxon spent the day in our mansion when they realized I went to see my uncle. None of them wanted to be near me during my long-overdue confrontation. But Vivienne should be here.

On a hunch, I look for my necklace in her room. It's nowhere to be found, and her phone is also missing. *Son of a bitch.* She must have gone to Ember Emporium during the day. If she finally got her brother back, there's no reason for her to come back here. Even with the threat of Boone and Jacques going after her, she'd be smart to leave Salem and never return.

That would be the best outcome, and I should be happy that she's gone. But my chest feels hollow, almost as if she took my heart with her. Dejected, I sit on her bed and pull her pillow to my face, taking a deep whiff of her scent that's still fresh on the fabric. I never want to forget how she smells.

My phone rings. I glance at the screen, and when I see Manu's name pop up, I ignore it. They'll be here soon enough, grilling me. A second later, the ringtone resumes. I'm tempted to simply turn it off when I see it's coming from an unfamiliar number. *What if it's Vivienne calling me?*

"Lucca speaking."

"Good evening, sir. Sorry to bother you. We caught a female trying to sneak in, and she claims she's your friend."

I stand, immediately on edge. "Who is it?"

"Cheryl Eriksson."

Fear twists my stomach into impossible knots. She'd never

come here without a solid reason.

"I know her. You can let her in."

There's a pause, and then the security guard replies, "She's frantic, sir. I think she's been attacked, and she's not making any—hey!"

There's a scuffle in the background, and then Cheryl's voice pours through the phone. "Lucca, Vivi is in trouble."

The heart I thought was missing from my chest strikes hard against my rib cage. I'm on overdrive, flying out of the apartment while keeping the phone glued to my ear.

"We were ambushed by Boone and his minions," she continues. "I'm not sure if Vivi made it to somewhere safe or not. Aurora held the line while I came here for help."

I end the call when I reach the front of the gates. Cheryl's clothes are in tatters, and she has multiple scratches and bite marks on her body. She's been through hell, but I don't hesitate to grab her by the shoulders and shake her roughly.

"Where is she?"

"We were on Arlington Road, just before Widow's Peak Bend. Vivi, her brother, and Vaughn were supposed to come here."

And they never made it.

VIVIENNE

I shove the vampire's bane vial down Boone's mouth, cutting my hand on his sharp teeth. We fall together with him pinning me down, but he's now choking on the poison. Propelled by adrenaline, I roll him off me, but I'm shaking so terribly that getting back on my feet fast enough seems impossible. On my hands and knees, I crawl until I find a tree to use as leverage. Boone is writhing on the ground, and when he rolls on his side, I see the hilt of a sword sticking out from the harness. I consider stealing that weapon for a hot second, but in the end, getting as far away as I can from Boone wins.

I run and don't look back. I break through the canopy of trees into the clearing of the old cemetery. The mausoleum is nothing but a dark shape in the gloom. *Do I dare take the tunnel through the catacombs again?* Without Boone on my heels, that doesn't seem like the best choice. That ghost has nothing but bad intentions for me.

From the frying pan into the fire. Fuck!

A twig snaps nearby. My heart shoots upward, slamming at the base of my throat. I whirl around, trembling so terribly that I might be having a seizure. When a dark shape emerges from a cluster of trees with eyes glowing red, my legs threaten to give out from beneath me. The vampire's bane is gone. I have no blade, nothing to use as a weapon.

The shape turns into a blur, and then I'm being crushed against a familiar chest—Lucca's.

"You're okay; you're okay," he mumbles against the top of my head.

"I can't believe you're here."

He eases back, looking into my eyes. "I'd move mountains, shake the very fabric of the universe to get to you."

I lift my hand to touch his face, but I've forgotten the cut.

Lucca's nostrils flare, and his body goes rigid in an instant.

Oh no. The curse. The bloodlust.

I'm still stuck on that realization when Lucca sends me flying backward and turns to meet Boone, who came out of nowhere.

There's a grunt of pain, and Lucca is bending over.

Then, Boone leans in to whisper in his ear, "I still have the vampire's bane–forged sword, bitch."

"No!" The scream comes from the pit of my stomach.

Boone pulls his weapon-yielding arm back, revealing the blade covered in blood. Lucca falls to his knees with his head hanging low while Boone grabs the sword with both hands and lifts it over his head, ready to deliver the final blow.

I'm too far, and I'll never reach Boone in time before he strikes. He glances in my direction with a cruel smile slashed across his face.

"Don't you dare look away. I want you to see when I remove your boyfriend's head. Then, I'll take my time breaking every single bone in your body."

With a cry, Lucca leaps from the ground. He punches Boone's chest, but instead of striking the vampire down, he keeps him trapped with one hand while he reaches over and takes the sword away. Boone is not moving, and I don't understand why until Lucca pulls his arm back and Boone falls to the ground. Something dark and oily is in Lucca's hand now—Boone's heart.

I don't have time to rejoice in the asshole's defeat. Lucca collapses in the next second, letting the bloody heart roll off his hand.

"Lucca!" I run to him on shaky legs, almost throwing myself at him when I'm near.

Even through the blurriness of my vision, I can see that Lucca's life force is waning. His eyes are open, back to brown and glazed.

I pull him into my lap, clutching his shoulders. "Lucca, please don't leave me."

He looks at me and tries to reach my face, but he can only raise his arm halfway before it drops again. "I don't want to leave you, darling. But if someone has to die tonight, it has to be me."

"No! You can't die. I won't let you."

"I'm sorry for everything I've done to you, Vivi. I love you. More than you will ever know."

His eyelids begin to close. His body is shutting down, going into hibernation, which means I will never see him again.

The curse. I have to break it.

I rub my bleeding hand over his lips, hoping to ignite the bloodlust again. Lucca's eyes fly open, glowing red now. He grabs my wrist in a tight hold and bites. I don't cry out even though it hurts. If there's a chance that my blood can save him, I will give him everything. He takes one hard pull before he pushes me back, pinning me down to the ground. His fangs are now on my neck. There's no soft kiss, no caress. He pierces my skin with a savage strength, and then he drinks until my world dims into darkness.

39

VIVIENNE

─────◆─────

I *was told not to get near the battlefield, that I shouldn't assist in a war that had been fought for many generations. But I'm the heir to the House of Gael, and it's my duty to help the Bluebloods who sacrificed their lives to save ours. I have my mother's powers running through my veins, ready to be unleashed.*

The smell of spilled blood reaches my nose. I'm getting close to the thinnest part of the veil separating our worlds, so I conceal myself as I cross the invisible barrier.

I come up on a hill, and in the valley below, I see the troops of the two opposing Blueblood royal houses. Raphael's and Tatiana's forces. I don't know why the war between them started, but it's only getting bloodier and more destructive. My mother and the royals from other Nightingale realms are mostly displeased with how their creation is behaving. They won't let it go on for much longer, and when they make a decision, it will be devastating.

Squinting my eyes, I search the battlefield, looking for the person who, despite not knowing me, gave me the courage to disobey my mother's orders. Lucca Della Morte, King Raphael's nephew. I have never been brave enough to reveal myself to him. But knowing that the Nightingale Royal Council is about to punish all vampires finally gave me the push I needed.

There can never be anything between us. The Nightingale Royal Council was clear when they created the first vampires. We're forbidden to them. But they never said I couldn't warn Lucca of what's to come.

When I finally find him, my stomach drops through the earth. He's on his back, and there are several arrows sticking out of his chest. I don't see any of his friends nearby, but the enemy is coming for him. I become nothing but air and zoom across the distance, materializing in front of Lucca in the next second. The vampire soldier who was running toward him slows down when he sees me there. He's not a Blueblood, but he knows what I am.

I raise my hands, and the ground beneath his feet vanishes. He disappears through the hole, and then I close the gap, burying him alive. When I turn around, Lucca is no longer lying still. He's back on his feet, swinging his sword left and right, hacking at the enemy.

A rough hand clutches my arm, pivoting me around. "What the hell are you doing here, Vryenn?"

I pull my arm free from Rikkon's grasp. "I came to warn King Raphael of what Mother is planning to do."

"Liar. You came because you're in love with the vampire prince." My brother pierces me with his unyielding stare.

I clamp my jaw shut. There's no point in denying it. Rikkon knows me too well.

"We have to go before Mother finds out you crossed the veil," he continues.

"There are other Nightingales on this side. Why can't I stay?"

"Because you're Queen Maewe's daughter. Your place is in Ellnesari."

Rikkon's image becomes distorted, and then I'm in a different place without him. I'm lying on my back, staring at a pitch-black sky. Lucca is with me. He's drinking from me, but I don't have any strength to say a word. I feel my life force ebb away. Darkness begins to pull me in again. Not much longer now.

"You will not defy me again, Vryenn! You're a daughter of the House of Gael."

"Mother, I beg you. Don't do this. Not all vampires are bad. King Raphael and his followers are still trying to do the right thing. It's Tatiana who has gone mad."

"Silence! The decision has been made. We will seal the veil to the mortal lands and take our magic with it."

"Then I'm not staying in Ellnesari."

Thunder echoes not far from us. It's the sound of my mother's rage.

Her eyes are sparkling with fury as she walks closer to me. "Are you willing to turn your back on your own people to stay with those beasts?"

"If they're beasts, you made them so," I spit back.

She moves her arm brusquely, sending me flying across the throne room. I hit a crystal panel, shattering it to pieces. Little fragments puncture my skin, but they don't draw blood. Shaking my head, I get back on my feet, keeping the glower aimed at her.

"Mother, please. Let's all calm down." Rikkon gets in between us.

"I'm calm and clearheaded. The one who is confused is your sister."

"I'm not confused." I raise my chin. "If you seal all the portals, I'm staying in the mortal lands."

My mother's face twists into an ugly mask of hatred. For the first time in my long existence, I'm taking a stand against her.

"If you stay behind, you will have nothing, no family name and no powers. You will live forever as a miserable human who can't die."

There's a sudden dagger slowly piercing my chest. The pain is sharp and excruciating.

"You can't take away her powers. She'll go mad," Rikkon interjects.

"It's her choice."

My stomach feels like lead, and the invisible dagger is now deep in my chest. Queen Maewe thinks I'm going to bend to her will, but I guess she's underestimated me.

"I'd rather live for all eternity, powerless, than spend another minute in your presence."

"Vryenn, no. Don't do it," Rikkon begs me.

"Silence! It's obvious she has made her decision. Vryenn is hereby banished from Ellnesari. Forever."

Rikkon's cerulean-blue eyes become brighter as the tears gather in them. He glances at the queen—I refuse to call her my mother now—and then, in a surprising move, he stands next to me.

"If you banish Vryenn, then you have to banish me too."

LUCCA

Blood has memory, and I see it all. Vivienne is not only a Nightingale, she's also Maewe's heir. I live through her memories, shocked to discover she had been in my life before and I didn't know.

I watch her struggle in the first decades of her banishment, having to move from town to town in order to hide the fact that she didn't age. And Rikkon, the brother who is now a shell of the male he used to be, sticking by her side through it all. He, too, had been stripped of his powers, and slowly, he lost his mind.

If I thought the punishment the Nightingales bestowed upon my kind was harsh, it doesn't compare to what Maewe did to her own children. Only a heartless creature would do that. They suffered when their mortal friends grew old and died. They spent years living as beggars.

Why didn't they come to us? My uncle wouldn't have turned his back on them.

In the end, Rikkon was the one who procured the charms. He convinced Vivi that it would be easier if they forgot who they were. He even changed their family name from Gael to Gale. It didn't work. It only made it worse. It not only took away their memories of who they were, it also gave them messed up new ones.

I catch a glimpse of Vivienne's first vampire attack. She wasn't younger, as she believes, and it wasn't her mother who sold her. The woman was a human trafficker. If Rikkon hadn't gone berserk and killed the vampire, the worst would have happened.

And now, I'm killing her, thanks again to Maewe's cruel games. My head is screaming at me to stop. My heart is bleeding, dying with each gulp of Vivienne's blood I swallow. Her heartbeat is slowing down. She will die because, Nightingale or not, she can't survive if I drink her dry.

I'm pulled again into one of her memories. She came to see me soon after I was cursed. I was mourning my mother's death. I was beside myself. I called her kind the most atrocious things. I had so much hate in my heart. Now, I know why she never came to us for help.

She defied her mother; she left her entire world behind because she loved me. *And this is how I'm repaying her? By letting her mother win again?*

No! Maewe will not take Vivi from me too.

"No!" I scream from the top of my lungs, and it echoes in the dark forest.

I stop feeding.

My breathing is coming out in bursts, and my head is fuzzy, but one thing is glaring. The hunger is gone.

My heart stops beating for a second, and then it accelerates to a hundred.

Vivi.

Her eyes are closed, and her face is terribly pale. I pull her into my arms, pressing my ear against her chest, searching for a heartbeat. At first, there's nothing.

She's dead. I killed her.

Then how come I'm still here and not being dragged through the pits of hell? No. This is a far worse punishment.

I curl my hands around her jacket, hugging her limp body tighter.

A thump. Then another one. I don't dare to breathe. Her heart is beating softly, but it's there.

"Vivi, my love." I touch her cheek. "Wake up."

Her eyelids twitch, and then she blinks her eyes open. "Lucca?"

I don't know if I should laugh or cry. "It's me, darling."

"You're alive," she says in awe.

"Yeah. I am now."

I crush my lips to hers, pouring every emotion swirling in my chest into that kiss. I give my all, and Vivienne does the same.

"Please don't ever leave me again," I breathe out.

"Are you crazy? I've been in love with you for centuries. Now that I have you, I'm not ever letting you go."

"You remember then?"

"I think breaking your curse also broke the memory spell."

I trace her face with the tips of my fingers, almost not daring to believe she's real. "I love you."

She closes her eyes, letting out a loud exhale. Two fat tears roll down her cheeks. "I've been waiting a long time to hear you say that."

"You'd better get used to it because I won't get tired of repeating it for all eternity."

The sound of running feet breaks our tender moment. I jump to my feet, pulling Vivienne with me. I'm ready to dispatch any new threat to hell with fangs bared and claws out. But then I catch their scents.

Manu and Ronan appear in the clearing, reminding us that breaking the curse isn't our only problem.

"Oh my God. You're okay." Manu reaches us first, stepping right over Boone's corpse.

"You need to come with us right now," Ronan says.

"What happened? Is it Rikkon?" Vivi asks.

"It's your friend Vaughn," Manu says with a hint of regret in her eyes. "He doesn't have much time."

40

VIVIENNE

❧ ⊰═══⊱ ❧

Lucca needs to carry me all the way to where Vaughn is since I'm a powerless immortal and too slow. If Mom Dearest hadn't taken away my powers, I could have turned into the wind and flown at the speed of light myself. But I don't have time to dwell on bitterness now when my friend is lying in a pool of his own blood, dying before my eyes.

Aurora is crouched next to him, and a quick once-over doesn't show any serious visible wounds on her, only a few scratches. Rikkon is leaning against a tree, clutching his arm, which has a makeshift bandage stained with blood. Other than that, I don't see any other obvious injuries. It seems he and Aurora got lucky, not poor Vaughn though.

I drop next to him, taking his hand in mine, and try not to stare at the open gash on his abdomen or the guts spilling out of it.

"Vaughn, how are you holding up?" I ask.

"He's not in pain anymore," Aurora says. "At least that much I could do for him."

He turns to me and smiles despite his cracked lips. "Vivi. You're all right."

"I'm fine, hon. And you will be too. The ambulance will be here at any minute."

Two more people join us, Karl and Cheryl, running here as wolves and shifting just before they walk the final distance to us. Karl pushes his hair back, staring at Vaughn with a look of pure anguish that quickly morphs into anger.

"Oh my God." Cheryl covers her mouth with her hands, tears already spilling down her cheeks.

I was trying to keep my own tears at bay, but I'm not that strong.

"Hey, why are you all crying? I'm gonna be fi—" He coughs up blood, and I can't look anymore.

I stare at the bloodied ground, choking on a sob.

"One of you bloodsuckers, do something!" Cheryl yells.

"What do you want us to do, Cheryl?" Ronan asks, frustrated.

"Turn him."

I glance at Lucca, knowing very well they don't have that power anymore. Guilt flashes in his eyes even though he shouldn't feel that way. It's not his fault they lost the ability. It's my mother's.

"You have to try!" Cheryl insists.

"You don't even know if Vaughn wants to be turned," Rikkon interjects, openly glowering at her.

"Am I dying?" Vaughn asks.

"Yes," Aurora replies. "I'm sorry."

He closes his eyes for a second. "I'm not ready to go. I can't leave my mom and my sisters behind. They need me."

"I'll do it." Lucca steps forward.

"Luc." Manu's tone is reproaching. "You know that's not possible anymore."

"If anyone here has a chance of succeeding, it's me," he argues.

Aurora scooches out of the way, and Lucca takes her place. He bites his own wrist, slashing a vein open. Dark blood quickly pours out of the gash, dripping on Vaughn's torn-up shirt.

"You need to drink this." He places his wrist over Vaughn's lips. "Take as much as you can."

Vaughn can barely pull anything at first, but as Lucca's blood enters his system, he begins to gain strength. He sucks harder and harder to the point that Lucca twists his face into a grimace. Vaughn's appearance gradually begins to lose the gaunt mask of death, and the open wound in his abdomen begins to heal.

"Oh my God. I can't believe this." Manu's jaw drops.

When Vaughn's green eyes turn crimson, Lucca pulls away, pressing his arm against his chest. The silence is absolute. Even the forest seems to grow quieter. Everyone is staring at Vaughn. He sits up slowly, checking his abs and arms in complete awe. But suddenly, his body becomes tense. He peels his lips back, displaying his new set of fangs.

Lucca moves in a blur, pulling me away from Vaughn, while Ronan, Saxon, and Manu jump on him just as he is about to attack Aurora.

"What's going on?" I ask.

"Bloodlust. All new vampires suffer through it."

Vaughn hisses and thrashes on the ground, trying to break free. Aurora jumps to her feet. She's clutching a stone in her hand now, and her eyes are doing the strange glowing thing.

"On the count of three, stay clear of Vaughn," she warns.

"Are you crazy? We can't let him go. He'll attack you," Saxon retorts.

"Let him go. I know what I'm doing. Ready? One, two, three. Now!"

At once, Saxon, Manu, and Ronan jump off Vaughn. He leaps onto his feet like a deranged animal, snarling and ready to make a meal out of someone. Aurora hits him square on his chest with a shining energy ball, sending him back onto the ground.

"Shit! What did you do to him?" Cheryl runs to check on our friend. "He's out cold."

"I had to get him out of commission. I might not have seen a recently turned vampire before, but I've read about them. They're at their strongest during the first hours."

"We could have held him," Saxon complains.

"For how long? Besides, he needs to get blood into his system pronto and not from a live being. Do you see any blood bags lying around?" She opens her arms in a grand gesture.

Now that Vaughn has been subdued, the coin finally drops.

I turn in Lucca's arms, capturing his gaze in mine. "You did it. You made a new vampire. What do you think that means?"

41

LUCCA

No good deed goes unpunished. I broke the curse, saved Vivienne's and her friend Vaughn's lives, and all the fucking Bloodstone Council is concerned about is the repercussion of me killing Boone in self-defense. I've been standing under their scrutiny for over an hour, first recounting the events repeatedly until they were sure there were no holes in my story. And now, I have to endure them arguing about what to do with Vaughn. It's already daytime, and I'm about to collapse from exhaustion.

Plus, Vivienne is waiting for me, and I'd much rather spend the day with her than with those three stooges in front of me. I suppose I should be grateful that Jacques is no longer allowed on the premises.

"Fine. We all agree we won't disclose that Vaughn is a newly turned vampire for now," Solomon says.

"That's the wisest choice. We don't want to give false hopes that vampires suddenly have the power to turn humans again and end up with a killing spree on our hands," Morgan adds.

I have no arguments against that decision. Humans can only be turned if they're on the brink of death. We haven't been able to turn humans in so long, I'm sure there would be a surge in attempts.

Isadora meets my gaze. "You'd better not try to turn any other human, Lucca. It's possible your ability was a one-time occurrence."

"Trust me, I have no intention of making new vampires. Can I go now?"

There's a three-way glance among Solomon, Morgan, and Isadora.

Then, Solomon replies, "Yes, you may return to your apartment, but don't go anywhere outside of Bloodstone grounds. We all know Boone's death was deserved and warranted, but Jacques won't let it go without trying something."

"I didn't break the Accords. He can't go after my uncle's crown."

"That doesn't matter to Jacques," Isadora replies.

"If he wants to restart a war, I'm more than ready for it."

Morgan shakes her head. "You might be willing to return to the age of blood and ruin, but most of our kind is not. Remember that."

I clamp my jaw shut, swallowing the angry retort on the tip of my tongue. I don't want to waste another hour engaging in a pointless argument. There will be plenty of time for that in the future.

The institute is deserted at this hour. Every single vampire in residence is in their dorms or apartments. I head straight to Vivi's, hoping Manu is not there or is at least in her bedroom. My wish is granted when I find the living room deserted. My heart begins to thump faster in giddy anticipation when I smell Vivienne's unique scent and don't go crazy with hunger. The curse is truly broken.

Once again, I find her in her bed with books sprawled all around her.

Leaning against the doorframe, I fold my arms in front of my chest and cross my legs at the ankles. "I never pegged you to be a nerd, but you can't deny it anymore."

A delicious shade of pink spreads across her cheeks, igniting a raging fire in the pit of my stomach. My mouth waters, but it's not her blood that I crave now.

"How did the meeting go?" She stands up, drawing my attention to her long, toned legs.

I walk over as slowly as I can, which is an exercise in self-control. Since I met her, it seems I've been running at full speed. Without the shadow of the curse hanging over my head, I want to take my time to appreciate every single bit of her.

"Dreadful, but let's not talk about it now." I grab her by the waist, pulling her flush against me.

Her smooth, warm body fits perfectly with mine. Something clicks in my chest; the piece that was missing from my heart finally falls into place.

She tilts her head, piercing me with her enigmatic eyes. There's a slight crease on her forehead, which I want to smooth out.

"You're frowning. That's not allowed anymore."

"How are we going to make this work, Luc? No one can know Rikkon and I are Nightingales."

"Where is he now?"

"He's with Cheryl and Karl." Her eyes fill with sorrow.

I caress her cheek, hoping she knows she can count on me for anything. "I don't want to see you sad."

She lets out a shaky breath. "I can't help it. Rikkon is a junkie now because of me. My mother warned us we would lose our minds if we decided to stay here. But he did anyway, so I wouldn't be alone." She drops her gaze to the hollow of my throat. "It's my fault he's like that."

I place my finger under her chin and bring her face up to mine. "No, it isn't. He made a choice, knowing full well about the consequences. Don't you dare feel guilty about it."

"He still doesn't remember a thing. If the spell gave me awful new memories, it must have done the same to him."

"We'll find a way to break it. Now, enough doom and gloom. There will be time to think about our problems tomorrow."

"What about me? I can't keep pretending to be a vampire, and you can't be dating a human."

"Says who?"

"You're the prince."

"And you're the princess. We're a perfect match."

"I'm not a princess anymore. I'm trailer trash."

Now, it's my turn to frown. "Don't say that. You're not trash. You're the most precious being I've ever met. You're my soul, the sun to my midnight heart."

Her blue eyes become brighter. "I never knew you were so poetic."

My lips curl into a smile. "You bring out the best in me."

She rises on her tiptoes and kisses my chin. "I think I want to bring out the worst in you now."

My fangs are on full display, an automatic reaction to my arousal. Vivienne doesn't flinch or tense; she grabs my face between her hands and kisses me without reservation. When my fangs graze her tongue, she lets out a moan that sends pure libido down my cock, making it harder and bigger, if that's even possible.

With a possessive groan, I fly us to her bed, falling with her in my arms on top of all her damn books. One hardcover pokes me on my side, but I'm already too lost in Vivienne to care. I don't want her to be in any discomfort though, so reluctantly, I break the kiss to clear the mattress of everything.

"You know, some of those books are almost as old as we are," she says.

The corners of my lips tug upward while my hand sneaks under her shirt. "You're older than me, aren't you? So, what does that make you? A cougar?"

Her pretty eyes widen. "Hey! I'm not a cou—" She gasps when I pinch one of her nipples.

"You were saying?"

"Oh, do you want to play games?" She unbuttons my jeans and reaches for my shaft.

I hiss when her fingers curl around me, and her thumb rubs my cock's head. "No games. I just want to fuck you into oblivion."

Grabbing her wrist, I pull her hand out of my pants.

"Hey!" she protests, but I cut her off with my tongue.

I don't hold back, giving her a clear idea what I plan to do with her. Impatient to get her out of her clothes, I abandon her lips to leave a trail of open kisses down her body. She arches her back, threading her fingers through my hair. Needing both hands now, I peel off her sweatpants, burying my face between her legs before the pants are completely off. I'm dying for another taste of her, but I want to do every naughty idea in my head all at once because, damn it, she's so fucking delicious. I reach for her breast with one hand and plunge my fingers inside of her while licking and sucking her clit.

"Lucca, you're killing me."

"Never," I groan.

She yells, spewing dirty words that only make me want her more.

"Fuck." I get out of bed for one second, long enough to rip my own pants off, and then I'm back between her legs, plunging my cock deep into her heat.

I should slow down, savor this moment longer, but Vivienne is doing everything she can to spur me on. Her knees are up, her legs are trapping me, and her nails are scratching my back. It's like my savagery has rubbed off on her, and I love it.

"Luc," she breathes out.

"Yes, darling?"

"I want you to do something for me." Her eyes are at half-mast, and her cheeks are flushed.

I hope she doesn't ask me to slow down because that'd be pretty hard.

My balls are tight, and I'm on the verge of release, so all I can muster in response is a groan.

"I don't want you to be gentle," she says.

"I didn't realize I was." I pull almost out, slamming back in hard the next second, drawing a delicious sound from her lips.

She kisses the corner of my lips and then whispers in my ear, "I want you to bite me."

I stop moving at once, something I didn't think was possible. "Vivi, I don't know if—"

She covers my lips with her finger. "Shh. You broke the curse. You can drink from me without fear. Nightingales are cruel but not tricksters."

My mouth is salivating, but even so, I hesitate. Vivienne still has the mark of my vicious attack on her neck.

Maybe guessing my thoughts or reading the conflict in my eyes, she offers me her wrist. "I want to know what a vampire love bite feels like. Please?"

Damn it. I can't really say no when she's looking at me like that, like a sex goddess who has the sole mission to tempt me.

I take her offer, licking her wrist first without taking my eyes off her. When I move my hips again, like a piston in and out of her, she lets out a throaty moan that shoots my libido to the sky.

This is it—the final test that will confirm if the worst five hundred years of my life are finally over. I bite her soft flesh, and the purest nectar fills my mouth. I couldn't appreciate the taste of her blood while I was consumed by bloodlust, but now, it's like I died and went to heaven.

Desire curls around the base of my spine, and then the inevitable happens. The orgasm that hits me feels like a fucking tsunami. It crashes against my body, breaking me into pieces. It sends me tumbling to the bottom of the ocean in a deafening rumble. A moment passes before I realize the noise is my pulse beating away in my ears.

Vivienne cries out, a sound that I want to memorize forever. Her body is shaking, and she's holding on to me so tightly that she might actually leave bruises behind. I stop drinking from her when the wave of her release recedes and her body relaxes under mine. I lick her wrist again, sealing the wound shut, and then I collapse next to her, spent but never more alive.

42

VIVIENNE

Three Days Later

I'm staying at Bloodstone Institute for a while, until things calm down. Now that Lucca has killed Boone, tensions are high once more, and it's possible the Accords and the truce won't mean a thing for much longer. That means I have to continue pretending to be a vampire, which is not the ideal situation, but at least now, it will be easier. I can store real food in the apartment and have the backup of Lucca's inner circle. But continuing the training to become a Keeper is definitely out. Ronan, in his mysterious way, says he has something else in mind for me.

Manu is still my roommate. I can't say we've suddenly become besties, but our relationship has definitely improved since I saved Lucca's life. I'm not sure I'll ever warm up to her completely. She's still the vampire who broke my best friend's heart.

Rikkon is staying with Cheryl at the moment, but he's coming to Bloodstone in a day or two. It was hard to convince him to take up residency at the institute, but he's not safe living on his own when Jacques wants me dead. Plus, Rikkon is still without his memories and susceptible to his old vices. There's no denying we're related, and we can't hide that we're siblings, so that means posing as a vamp is mandatory for him too. We have to drink the magical potion every three weeks to keep up with the charade.

And there's Vaughn, a brand-new vampire who has no clue about how to live as one. If anyone needs a crash course on vampirism, it's him. He's still under King Raphael's care, and that's who Lucca and I are going to see now.

I was apprehensive when Lucca told me his uncle, the powerful king of vampires, wanted to meet me. But as we approach his hidden estate, my stomach is a tight ball made out of a thousand knots. My body is shaking, and not even curling my hands into fists or biting the inside of my cheek is helping.

Lucca reaches over and grabs my hand. "Relax, darling. This is just a casual meeting."

"You don't understand. My mother cursed you, and with the other Nightingale royals, she damned your race to wither and die. How can I face your uncle?"

"You're not responsible for your mother's actions. No one is blaming you for your mother's sins, much less my uncle."

Even so, I can't help feeling the full weight of guilt. Lucca is wrong; I *am* partially responsible for my mother's decision to shut the portals. She's spiteful, and I'm sure my choice to stay in the mortal lands motivated her even more to punish the vampires.

A tall male opens the door for us. Lucca warned me about King

Raphael's familiar, but it's hard to not let my jaw drop. He's not only freakishly tall, he's also built like a mountain. He only spares Lucca one fleeting glance before giving me a scrutinizing once-over.

"So, you're the Nightingale who saved Lucca's whiny ass."

I didn't expect that comment to come out of the male's mouth. I quickly glance at Lucca, and his response is a roll of his eyes. *Okay then.*

"Yes, I'm the one," I reply, tilting my head up so I can look the familiar straight in the eye.

I'm not afraid of him, bear or not. Only meeting his boss is giving me the shivers.

In another surprising gesture, the male captures me in a bear hug—no pun intended. His arms translate as tree trunks, and I disappear under them.

"Thank you. From the bottom of my heart," he says.

Lucca clears his throat, prompting the familiar to release me. He fixes his jacket and composure and then steps aside to let us in.

"King Raphael is waiting in his office," he says.

"Thanks, Mauricio."

Steering me to the right of the grand staircase, Lucca moves fast, not letting me linger anywhere long enough to inspect the king's lair. The decor is dark and gothic though. It seems he never got out of the Dark Ages.

My heart has leapfrogged up to my throat, and the loud buzz in my ears is competing with the sounds of our footsteps echoing along the wide hallway.

When Lucca finally stops in front of a thick wooden door, he looks at me. "Ready?"

"No."

He chuckles. I'd hit him upside the head if he didn't look so adorable doing that. Now, I'm nervous about meeting his uncle and a little horny.

He leans closer and whispers in my ear, "After we're done here, I'll show you my old room. The bed there is wicked good."

Desire licks my spine, which is mortifying since I bet vampires can notice arousal with their enhanced senses.

"You're the worst," I reply.

With a mischievous smirk on his lips, he winks. "I know."

"Quit your lovebird nonsense and get in here already," a gruff male voice commands from inside the room.

Shit. Of course King Raphael could hear us.

My face is in flames when we finally enter the king's office. It's a large room but not as pompous as I expected it to be. It's also not quite as dark either. The walls are covered in a light-gray wallpaper, and the thick curtains are off-white. The furniture is all dark wood though and sturdy.

The king is standing in front of one of the windows, gazing outside. He's a little taller than Lucca and with broader shoulders. I remember him from before my banishment. He had the same coloring as Lucca, but the male with his back to us is gray-haired and familiar.

Son of a bitch.

He's the vampire who approached me outside of Havoc and gave me the spell. When King Raphael finally turns, my suspicions are confirmed. It was him.

"Hello, Vivienne," he says.

At once, my nervousness evaporates, and it's replaced by pure aggravation. "I can't believe this. You set me up."

He smiles. "I take it you have gotten over your fear of our kind."

No, I'm screwing your nephew while I'm still gripped by terror because that's how I roll. That's what I want to say, but common sense prevails.

"Obviously," I reply. "You knew all along I was Queen Maewe's daughter, didn't you?"

He steps away from the window, walking closer to us. "I didn't know you were her daughter. I knew you were a Nightingale though."

I turn to Lucca. "Did you know this?"

"I only found out right before Boone tried to kill us both."

"I purposely kept Lucca in the dark. He would have never tried to feed from you if he knew you were a Nightingale."

"But how did you know?" I ask.

"Since Maewe cursed him, I've been searching high and low for someone with Nightingale blood. I was hoping to find a descendant. I had no idea you and your brother had been banished. The rogue mage who sold Rikkon the memory spell led me to you."

"Did you pay Larsson to kidnap my brother, only to force me to get close to Lucca?"

King Raphael's attention switches to Lucca for a brief moment. There's a flash of guilt in his eyes.

"No. I didn't pay Larsson to kidnap your brother. I offered him a deal to keep your brother alive."

"Was my mother's necklace part of your arrangement?" Lucca asks in a low tone.

"Yes."

The tightness in my chest returns, but it's worse than before, because now, I remember her and how she died at the hands of my own mother.

"Why? What does that barbarian want with my mother's necklace?"

King Raphael looks away and walks around his desk. "There are some parts of history that are better left forgotten."

Lucca lets out a snarl. "Don't you dare give me one of those enigmatic answers again."

He whips his face toward Lucca with eyes glowing red and long fangs on full display. "Watch your tone, boy. I am still your king."

Holy shit. Things escalated fast.

A knock on the door breaks the tense moment. The king's eyes return to brown before he tells whoever is outside his office to come in.

The king's familiar enters. "The High Witch is here."

"Why is Isadora here?" Lucca asks.

"She's here because I asked her to come. There's another issue that needs to be addressed as soon as possible."

"Is this about Jacques going after your crown?"

"No. Something more pressing than that."

At once, the memories of my attack by the vampire zombie ghost return. What could be more pressing than a coup besides a vengeful wraith in the bowels of the institute?

"This is about the secret chamber and the ghost I freed from it, isn't it?" I ask.

"Yes, my dear. But you don't need to worry about that now. I assume you want to see your friend?"

I know he's manipulating me, but I do want to see Vaughn. Besides, I doubt he will answer my questions if I press. Not even Lucca can make the guy talk.

"Yeah, I want to see Vaughn. Is it safe now?"

He nods. "He's over the hump. As a matter of fact, he can return to Bloodstone with you tonight."

LUCCA

The meeting with my uncle was more frustrating than I'd thought it would be. But it doesn't compare to the painful trip back to the institute with Vaughn in the car, firing questions nonstop. I rub my forehead. I haven't had a headache in centuries, but I think the male's incessant chatter will definitely give me one.

When I see the grand building looming in the horizon, I let out a relieved sigh. "Thank heavens."

Vivienne laughs next to me.

I peel my eyes off the road for a second. "What's so funny?"

"Nothing."

"Wow, this is awesome." Vaughn sticks his nose against the window. "I feel like I'm Harry Potter when he arrived at Hogwarts."

"Who?" I ask. I know the name sounds familiar.

"Wait, you don't know who Harry Potter is?" Vaughn asks.

I glance at Vivi again. "Should I?"

"Dude, there isn't a person on this planet who doesn't know who he is," Vaughn pipes up.

Grinning, Vivienne shakes her head. "Don't worry. I'll introduce you to him."

Okay, now I'm annoyed. It seems my lack of modern knowledge

has made me the butt of a joke.

I park my car in the back, not surprised to see Solomon waiting for us in front of the secondary entrance.

When we're out of the car, Vaughn moves closer to Vivi and asks in a low tone, "Who is that funny-looking dude? Is he a vampire too?"

"He's the headmaster, and shh. He can hear you even if you whisper," she replies.

It's gratifying to see the look of consternation on the male's face. Without an ounce of guilt, I wrap my arm over Vivienne's shoulders and head inside, leaving Mr. Chatterbox alone with Solomon.

"Maybe we should have waited for Vaughn," she says when we're inside.

"Fuck no. I've suffered the male enough for one evening."

I take the alternative route to her apartment, avoiding going through the main area of the institute. I want to keep Vivienne all to myself before we have to return to our charade. We haven't really left her room much in three days, but our time is up. Tomorrow evening, we must return to the regular schedule.

Manu is home, but taking into consideration her outfit, I can guess she's on her way out somewhere.

"Oh, back so soon?" she asks.

"Yeah. King Raphael is not one to hold long meetings."

"He also doesn't like to talk much," Vivienne adds.

"Unlike your friend," I groan.

"Well, I'm going to Havoc," Manu announces. "Fancy joining me?"

That's an easy question to answer. "Nope. I have everything I need right here." I pull Vivi closer and kiss her on the cheek.

Manu makes a gagging sound. "Ugh. I think you should get your own apartment. I can't deal with all that sugary stuff."

That's not a bad idea.

"Maybe we will," I say.

"Whatever. I'm out of here. Have fun, kiddos."

She walks out the door with a bounce to her step. I haven't seen her in a good mood in, like, forever.

I turn Vivienne in my arms. "Alone at last."

"Did you really mean it?"

"Did I really mean what?" I kiss her neck, loving how her pulse quickens in response.

"Living together."

I pull back, so I can look in her eyes. "Yeah, I mean it. I can't stand the thought of not sleeping and waking up with you by my side every night." Her eyebrows furrow, which is definitely not a reaction I was expecting. "What's wrong?"

"I've been in love with you for generations, but you've just met me. What if this is only a phase for you? What if—"

"Shh." I cover her lips with my finger. "This is not a phase, Vivi. I love you, and this feeling won't go away."

"How can you be so sure?"

"You reanimated my dead heart. That's how I know. Life had no meaning to me, even before the curse. But you've changed that. I loved you even when I thought I hated you. Even before I knew who you were and what you had sacrificed for me."

Her eyes become brighter, and when one rogue tear rolls down her cheek, I wipe it off with my thumb.

"There's no need to cry, darling."

"These are happy tears." She laughs.

"So, does that mean you're on board with me moving in?"

Her eyebrows arch slowly. "What about Manu?"

I shrug. "I'm her older brother. It's my birthright to piss her off. She can find another apartment. Maybe Vaughn can be her new roommate." I reward her with a wolfish grin.

Vivienne laughs, and it makes my heart sing.

"You're the worst. Poor Vaughn."

Wrapping my arms around her small waist, I pull her flush against me. "Enough about them. We're moving in together. That calls for a celebration."

"What kind of celebration?"

I lean down to whisper in her ear, "The kind where our clothes are off and any surface or room is fair game."

Her eyes shine with mischief, sending a zing of pleasure down my cock. "You're on, my prince."

43

AURORA

My mother told me to stay away from the catacombs, and what she says must be obeyed without question. Once upon a time, she used to be kinder, but that was before my father passed away. Then, I think the demands of her job stripped away any softness from her. And since I'm her oldest child and destined to take her place as the High Witch, I get her worst.

But I've never been one to follow orders, and tonight, I'm sticking to my rebellious side. I want to know what the hell she and Solomon are hiding under the institute. I overheard the conversation between them after she came back from a meeting with King Raphael. They're going to attempt to trap the deadly ghost again during the day, and I'm not going to miss it.

That wraith was a vampire once, and my guess is she was a Blueblood, maybe even first-generation. She felt powerful but also malicious, evil. More so than Boone, and that's saying a lot.

But I can't simply follow my mother at a distance and hope she won't notice me. I'm taking precautions—and by precautions, I mean I'm using a concealment spell strong enough to fool even the High Witch. She would never approve of it. I acquired the potion from a member of the rogue mage guild after all.

It would have been impossible for me to find them if the idiot who had created the poisonous fog on the day of Boone's attack hadn't left behind a piece of his clothing. It was easy to cast a tracking spell with it. A bit harder to convince the guild to assist the daughter of the High Witch. Rogue mages can be hired, and some of them are powerful, but they're all cowards. I had to resort to blackmailing to get what I needed. They'd had no idea their fog job would assist in Lucca's murder attempt by Boone. I promised them I wouldn't rat them out to King Raphael if they cooperated.

Maybe it was stupid of me to waste such a trump card to get a concealment spell, but I'm desperate to know my mother's secret. I'm prone to making impulsive decisions. I hope this one doesn't come back to bite me in the ass like my previous one. I do have the guild by the balls, but I can't keep blackmailing them. It's amoral and also dangerous.

I drink the bitter potion and then head for the catacombs. Everything is eerily quiet, and the small hairs on the back of my neck stand on end. *Shit. Could the ghost have overpowered my mother and Solomon?* I stick my hand inside my bag and pull out an enchanted crystal. It's used to ward off vengeful ghosts, but it will only keep a vampire ghost at bay for a limited amount of time.

My heart is thumping hard and slow against my rib cage. It's impossible not to feel the weight of fear when I know what's on the loose down here. The silence is broken suddenly by a terrifying shriek that sends my heart spiraling up to my throat. *Fuck.* That's the ghost. I freeze for a second, but then I hear my mother's voice. She's reciting a spell.

I walk faster, still mindful of being stealthy. Just before I reach the spot where my mother is, I flatten my back against the wall and stick my head out. My mother and Solomon have the vampire wraith trapped in an orb of green light. She's as freaky as I remember. I never knew vampires could turn into ghosts.

"You can't keep us trapped forever," the ghost wails. "The Nightingales have returned. We will get our revenge."

Shit. The ghost is talking about Vivienne.

"You *will* return to your prison, Madeleine."

"Madeleine?" The ghost laughs. "Madeleine has ceased to exist. Lost in her madness, she made a deal with me. I control her body and her soul."

Solomon trades a glance with my mother. She nods, and together, they send the ghost back to the secret chamber. Her prison.

That's it?

I'm pissed. Not only didn't I get any intel, but I also wasted my leverage with the rogue mage guild in the process.

I quickly retrace my steps before my mother finds me. That would be the cherry on top.

When I get back to my apartment, I make sure all the lights are on. I hate that I can't open the shutters and let sunlight in. They close automatically and won't roll up again until nightfall. I sit on a high stool, leaning my elbows on the counter.

I'm not sure what I was hoping to achieve by spying on my mother. To gain a sense of control maybe, something that's clearly absent in my life. If I had a choice, I wouldn't be at Bloodstone,

I wouldn't be studying to take my mother's place, and most importantly, I wouldn't be promised to a douche canoe from an important magical family.

Running my hands through my hair, I yank it back at the strands. "Fuck."

The sudden knock on my door makes me jerk on my seat. *What now?*

"Who is it?"

"Aurora, it's me, Saxon."

A string of curses runs through my head. I don't want to deal with him, but at the same time, I could use a punching bag.

I cross the room with long strides and then open the door with a brusque movement. "What do you want?"

His hand is braced against the wall, and he looks positively ill. With a grimace, he replies, "The potion you gave me didn't work."

"Impossible. That should have worked."

"Well, it didn't." He stands straighter, imposing, feral. "You're still my damn mate, and if you don't fix this, you're going to be a widow before you exchange vows with your betrothed."

To be continued …

ALSO BY
MICHELLE HERCULES

Wicked Gods (Gifted Academy #1)

Ruthless Idols (Gifted Academy #2)

Hateful Heroes (Gifted Academy #3)

Broken Knights (Gifted Academy #4)

Reckless Times (Paragon Society #1)

Savage Games (Paragon Society #2)

Red's Alphas (Wolves of Crimson Hollow #1)

Wolf's Calling (Wolves of Crimson Hollow #2)

Pack's Queen (Wolves of Crimson Hollow #3)

Mother of Wolves (Wolves of Crimson Hollow #4)

Lost Horizon (Oz in Space #1)

Magic Void (Oz in Space #2)

ABOUT
MICHELLE HERCULES

USA Today Bestselling Author Michelle Hercules always knew creative arts were her calling but not in a million years did she think she would become an author. With a background in fashion design she thought she would follow that path. But one day, out of the blue, she had an idea for a book. One page turned into ten pages, ten pages turned into a hundred, and before she knew, her first novel, The Prophecy of Arcadia, was born.

Michelle Hercules resides in The Netherlands with her husband and daughter. She is currently working on the *Blueblood Vampires* series and the *Oz in Space* series.

Join Michelle Hercules' Readers' Group:
https://www.facebook.com/groups/mhsoars

Sign-up for Michelle Hercules' Newsletter:
https://mhsoars.activehosted.com/f/11

Follow Michelle Hercules on Instagram:
@michelleherculesauthor

Printed in Great Britain
by Amazon